While she cleaned the tunic,
Alex scooped up some water, washing off
his skin. Rivulets of water spilled over his
hard muscles, and Laren found herself
staring at her husband.

He stretched and shivered from the freezing water. Her
eyes followed the water that pooled over his skin, trailing
downward.

He saw her staring, and met her with his own frank gaze.
Dark eyes moved down her face, past her breasts, to her hips.
Unable to help herself, she reached out and touched his cool
skin, wiping away a droplet of water with her fingertips.

Alex didn't move, but he caught her wrist and held it to his
skin. "After the girls are asleep, meet me here again tonight."

He pressed her fingers over his ribs, guiding her hand around
his waist. Though his skin was icy cold from the water, she
leaned in to warm him. His hand cupped her face.

Though he hadn't done anything at all, Laren's breath was
shaky, her body seeking his nearness.

His fingers stroked the side of her face, and she lifted her
mouth to his, claiming the kiss that he hadn't given.

When he pulled back, he let ̶ ̶ ̶ ̶ ̶ ̶ ̶ again around her
waist. "Tonight," he repeated

She nodded and he release

Seduced by Her Highland W̶ ̶ ̶
Harlequin® Historical #1054—August 2011

MICHELLE WILLINGHAM

Seduced by Her Highland Warrior

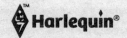

TORONTO NEW YORK LONDON
AMSTERDAM PARIS SYDNEY HAMBURG
STOCKHOLM ATHENS TOKYO MILAN MADRID
PRAGUE WARSAW BUDAPEST AUCKLAND

Recycling programs
for this product may
not exist in your area.

ISBN-13: 978-0-373-29654-5

SEDUCED BY HER HIGHLAND WARRIOR

Author Note

Whenever I've visited a medieval cathedral, my eyes were always drawn to the stained-glass windows. The stunning details and the intricate glass made it hard to believe that I was staring at something that was over seven hundred years old. I was fascinated by the artists who made the glass and those who pieced it together to form sacred art.

I decided to create a heroine with the talent of making her own glass, a craft she learned from a mentor priest. But for Laren MacKinloch, glassmaking provided the solace she needed after losing her newborn son. Grief fractured her marriage with the clan leader Alex MacKinloch, and I wanted to explore how two people could rebuild a stronger relationship after a tragedy.

One resource which I found extremely helpful was *On Divers Arts* by the monk Theophilis. He documented a treatise on blowing glass that explained the techniques used in the medieval era. In addition, this past fall, I was privileged to watch the glass artists at Art of Fire take me through the process of blowing glass. You can view pictures and videos of the process at my Facebook fan page: www.facebook.com/michellewillinghamfans.

You're welcome to visit my website at www.michellewillingham.com for excerpts and behind-the-scenes details about my books. I love to hear from readers and you may email me at michelle@michellewillingham.com or via mail at P.O. Box 2242 Poquoson, VA 23662 USA.

Chapter One

❧❧❧

Glen Arrin, Scotland—1305

Soldiers gripped spears in their palms and charged forwards, their weapons aimed at his wife and daughters.

Blood dripped from a wound on his forearm, but Alex MacKinloch wouldn't stop running. A primal roar resounded from his mouth as he lifted his sword and hacked his way toward the women. His lungs burned as he fought, the battle haze clouding his awareness of reality. In the distance, he saw his wife Laren's gleaming red hair as she struggled through a water-filled ditch. Her skirts weighed her down and she held their younger daughter in her arms. She didn't see the dozens of soldiers approaching as she tried to evacuate the fortress.

I have to reach them. Or they'll die.

It was a reality he didn't want to face, and the thought of his Laren falling beneath a soldier's blade was a horror he couldn't grasp. His arm ached with a vicious pain, but he fought a path towards them. The soldiers blocked his line of vision until all he could see was a swift storm of arrows.

A pulse thundered in his ears until he realised the arrows were coming from their younger brother Callum, who was guarding the women and children. Flames erupted from the wooden keep that stood high above them, like a dying sentry.

The fortress was going to fall. He ran as hard as he could and heard his kinsman Ross breathe, 'Mary, Mother of God.'

As Alex rushed forwards, he heard the cracking of wood.

'Callum, dive!' shouted a man's voice from behind her.

Laren MacKinloch struggled through the forest, her skirts sodden with water as the keep surrendered to the flames and collapsed. She stared through the trees, in shock at the sight of her home.

Gone now.

And what of Alex, her husband? 'Take Mairin and Adaira,' she begged Vanora, handing over her daughters. 'I'll join you in a few moments.'

'You can't go back,' the older matron warned. 'This isn't over yet.'

'I won't leave the trees,' Laren promised. *I just need to see him. I need to know if he's safe.*

She didn't wait for Vanora's reply, but moved back to the forest's edge, holding on to a slender birch tree for balance. Her breath frosted in the evening air as the cold settled around the glen.

When English soldiers surrounded the men from both sides, she felt her heart branching into silent pieces of terror. *Dear God, no.*

She couldn't hear what was happening, but the look of grim finality on Alex's face meant that the worst was near. As she stared from her hiding place, the years seemed to fall back. No longer was he a powerful chief but instead, the man she'd once loved. The fist of heartbreak caught her and tears dampened her cheeks. They'd grown so far apart over the past two years, and now she didn't know if she would see him alive again.

If she had one last moment with him, there were too many words to speak. Too many things she'd locked away in her heart for far too long.

Her palm pressed against the tree bark. Though Alex couldn't see her, she kept her gaze fixed upon him, as if she could memorise his face and hold it for ever.

A fiery pain blasted through her right side. Laren's knees buckled beneath her and she gasped in shock at the arrow embedded within her skin.

The searing agony stunned her and she could barely keep her senses about her. Though it was a shallow wound, piercing the soft skin sideways, near her ribs, she'd not realised how close she was to the battle.

She forced herself to snap off the feathered end, sliding the arrow free of the wound. Blood poured from her side and she pressed her dark cloak against the flow, fighting the dizziness.

You have to go back to your girls, her mind warned. She couldn't stay, no matter how much she feared for Alex's life. One of them had to live, to take care of their daughters.

It wrenched her apart, having to choose between her husband and her children, but she forced herself to continue. If the English gained the victory, they would come looking for the survivors. Her daughters needed her and she had to protect them.

She struggled up to the top of the ridge. Each step sent another wave of pain raging through her side, but she ignored the wound, hiding it beneath her dark cloak. There would be time to tend it later.

When she reached the girls, her elder daughter threw her arms around her waist, weeping. At the ages of four and not quite two, Mairin and Adaira weren't old enough to understand what was happening. Laren caught her breath, keeping Mairin's hands away from the injury while she spoke soft, reassuring words.

'Where is Da?' her daughter demanded. 'Is he safe?'

'I don't know.' Laren's throat tightened with fear, her eyes burning. 'But we have to wait here for him, away from the soldiers.'

'I'm afraid,' her daughter sobbed.

Laren brushed a kiss against Mairin's forehead. *So am I.*

The earth trembled as dozens of horsemen surrounded their army on both sides. Robert Fitzroy, the Baron of Harkirk, watched in fury as more of the Scots poured in, reinforced by the French. His hand tightened upon the hilt of his sword and he wanted nothing more than to bathe his weapon in their blood.

The MacKinlochs were supposed to die this day. Hadn't he burned their fortress to the ground, slaughtering their kinsmen? He'd already planned to set up an outpost here, to secure more land for King Edward Plantagenet, but he could see his victory fading away like smoke.

'Pull back!' he ordered and his soldiers obeyed. Though it splintered his pride, he hadn't survived half-a-dozen battles by making foolish decisions that would endanger his neck.

As they retreated into the hills, Harkirk cast a backwards glance. This wasn't over. Not by half.

He vowed that the next time he looked upon the face of a MacKinloch, it would be mounted upon a pike outside his gates.

It took a quarter of an hour to reach the ridge and Alex helped his brother up to the top of the hill. Nairna looked worried, for although they had survived with only minor injuries, traces of battle madness lurked within her husband's face. But Alex felt certain that once they brought Bram home, his brother would make a full recovery.

When they reached the clearing, the first glimpse of Laren sent a roaring breath of relief back through Alex's lungs. The instinct pulled at him, to go to her. He needed to hold his wife and breathe in the scent of her skin, touching her soft red hair.

Laren started to take a step towards him, but she abruptly stopped, her face ashen. Her hand pressed to her side and then she turned her attention to their girls. Their clansmen were watching, and at their sudden attention she shrank back.

He couldn't understand why. Aye, they'd grown apart over the past two years, but was it so much to ask that she show him a grain of affection? That she could welcome him back into her arms? The pain in her eyes bothered him, for he didn't understand it. Wasn't she glad to see him alive?

Though Mairin and Adaira called out, Laren bent and spoke quietly, as if to prevent them from running to him. Adaira clutched Laren's leg, burying her face in her mother's skirts.

A thousand moments passed by in a single second. Pride

froze out the aching emotions, and Alex stared back at his wife, wishing she would meet him halfway. But she merely gave him a nod and moved away with the girls, unable to face him.

Something was wrong. She'd closed herself off from him and he didn't know why. His hand tightened on the door frame and he forced himself to look after Bram. 'Will you be all right with him?' Alex asked Nairna, who had helped her husband to sit upon their bed.

'Aye.' She poured water into a basin and retrieved a cloth to tend Bram's wounds. When she had wrung out the cloth, she sent Alex a pointed look. 'Go to Laren. She needs you.'

He left them alone, watching the way Nairna cared for her husband. The deep love in her eyes and the answering look in her husband's face brought a surge of envy. He wanted to be with Laren right now, to shatter the invisible wall between them.

The thought became a thorn, digging deeper into his pride. She was the woman he'd pledged to protect. Years ago, she would have thrown herself into his arms, not caring what anyone else thought. She'd have clung to him, whispering words of how she'd worried.

But now she kept her distance from him, almost as if they were strangers.

His frustration strung tighter as he walked among the survivors, asking about their welfare. During that time, not once had Laren moved towards him. Her face was white, as though she were too timid to move.

Damn it all, he didn't care if she no longer wanted him. They'd survived their brush with death; right now he wanted to hold her. He needed her in his arms, whether or not she was too shy to answer the embrace.

He crossed through the people, moving directly towards her. Without voicing a single word, he pulled her into his arms, holding her tightly. She let out a slight gasp, but her hands moved up to his shoulders, resting there. He didn't speak, didn't reveal any of the thoughts coursing through his mind. Adaira and Mairin each grabbed his legs, but right now, he needed Laren.

Dimly, he was aware that she wasn't quite holding him in return. Her hands were there, but there was no warmth, no answering embrace. His heart numbed when he pulled back to look at her, his hands resting at her waist.

He'd mistakenly believed that if he made the first move she would welcome him back, that the past two years of distance wouldn't matter any more, because they were alive. But she didn't look at him, as if she were too shy to speak.

He let his hands fall away, saying nothing. The girls were chattering, asking him questions about when they could go home, where they would sleep, and he couldn't give them an answer.

His kinsman Ross came near, and asked, 'Do you want to bring your family to our home for the night?' Since Ross's home was on the opposite side of the fortress, it had escaped the fires.

Alex never took his eyes from Laren, but agreed. 'Aye, if it's no trouble to you.'

'Not at all. Vanora will want to fuss over the wee ones, as she likes to do.' His gaze grew sombre, staring at the smoke that rose from the valley below. 'And you'll be needing a place to stay until you can rebuild the keep.'

'I'll take the girls there now,' Laren said quietly, 'if you think it's safe to return.' Her voice was shaky, but at his nod she guided their daughters away from the crowds. As they disappeared into the forest, Ross was saying something else to him, but Alex didn't hear a word of it.

His wife was behaving strangely and he didn't know why. Then his gaze drifted down to his hands. Blood stained his palms from where he'd held his wife.

It was Laren's blood.

Laren held Adaira's hand as Mairin skipped forwards. She kept her head held high, even though the tears flowed freely down her face. She kept her hand firmly upon the bleeding wound at her side, trying not to take deep breaths. When Alex had held her, his hands had pressed against it and she'd nearly passed out from the pain. The injury felt like an aching fire, but she refused to pity herself.

She'd said nothing of it to the girls. They were frightened after the battle and the last thing she needed was for her daughters to start crying again. Right now it took her full concentration to keep from breaking down in front of them. She'd never known that a minor wound could hurt this badly.

Now that the enemy soldiers were gone, she could return to Glen Arrin for a little privacy to tend it. The wetness against her hand told her that the bleeding had started up again and stars swam in front of her eyes.

You should have told Alex, an inner voice chided. The very thought of her husband sent a quiet ache of regret through her. When he'd taken her in his arms, the urge to cling to him and sob out her miseries had been so tempting. But the last thing he'd needed was a hysterical wife bleeding all over him in front of everyone. He had to be strong in front of the clan, to be the leader they needed in this time of crisis. There was time to speak of it later, when they were alone.

Laren took a deep breath, wiping the tears away. For now, she had to bring the girls to Ross's home for shelter.

'Why are you crying, Mama?' Mairin asked, coming to her side. 'Are you sad?'

'I'm just tired,' she lied. She had to hold herself together right now. Alex would be busy sorting out places for the rest of the clan to live; likely he wouldn't join them until later tonight.

'Da!' Mairin shouted, breaking free of her. Laren turned and saw Alex striding towards them. Her heart sank, for he looked furious. Instinctively, her hand went back to her wound, pressing against the flow of blood.

'Why didn't you tell me?' he demanded, raising up his hands. Upon them, she saw her own blood.

'It's nothing,' she said. 'I'll be all right.' To the girls she said, 'Mairin, I want to talk to your father for a moment. Take Adaira down to the bottom of the hill and wait for us.'

Her daughter paled at the sight of Alex's face and didn't argue, retreating with her sister.

'What happened?' he demanded.

'It was just an arrow. It pierced the skin here...' she pointed to her bleeding side '...but it's only a small wound. I'll have Vanora help me with it.'

'Were you trying to hide it from me?' In his voice, she heard traces of fear, mingled with his anger.

'You had too much on your mind and I didn't want to be a bother, not when it's something so minor.'

'You were *shot* with an arrow, Laren. Why in the name of God would you think I wouldn't want to bother with that?'

The fury on his face was like nothing she'd ever seen before. She kept her face averted, not knowing how to soften it. 'The girls have lost enough this day, without having to be afraid for me.'

'And what about you?' he demanded, his voice falling into a harsh whisper. He reached to cup her face and Laren instinctively drew back. If he touched her right now, the control over her feelings was going to shatter. She could steel herself against his anger, but not his kindness.

'I'll be all right,' she managed. She started to walk away, but when she glanced back at him, there was disbelief mingled with his frustration. He followed her and when they reached the girls at the bottom of the hill, he bent down to lift Mairin into his arms. He gave her a tight hug as he examined her; then he turned to Adaira, lifting her into his other arm.

He loved their girls. There was no doubt in her mind that he'd lay down his life for them. With Mairin and Adaira, he softened, letting them see a father who cared about more than their welfare. And, in return, they adored him.

'Are you well?' he asked the girls. 'You're not hurt, are you?' He inspected them and then his gaze moved to her, as if in accusation.

Laren met his eyes and pronounced, 'They're all right.' But although her husband had muted his anger in front of the girls, she sensed it simmering beneath the surface.

Adaira started to fuss, reaching towards her. When Laren stretched to take her, Alex held their daughter tight. 'Stay with me, sweet.'

She was grateful for it, for she didn't think she could bear the weight of Adaira, not with the wound.

'Have you eaten?' Alex asked, reaching into his pouch for some dried meat. The girls each took a piece and started gnawing on the venison. Though he offered her a piece, Laren refused it. The very thought of food made her ill.

He set Mairin down, keeping her hand in his as they moved to the far side of the fortress.

At the sight of Glen Arrin, Laren's face turned grim. The keep was a burned mass of wood and hot coals, the dark smoke rising from the damaged structure. Every possession she had, save the clothes on her back, had been in the keep. The tapestries she'd woven, the girls' gowns. The bed that Alex had made for them when they were first married. The tears broke free again, despite Laren's efforts to stop them.

'What will we do?' she asked her husband, knowing that his pain was as deep as her own.

His emotions remained tight, his jaw clenched at the sight of the ruins. 'Bury the dead. And start again.'

Alex led them to Ross's house and ensured that it was safe before he allowed the girls to enter the small thatched dwelling. He remained outside and Laren couldn't read the emotions in his stare. Without asking, he pulled back her dark cloak. The blood had soaked through the woolen gown she wore and he ordered her, 'Don't move. Vanora!' he called out, hurrying toward the matron who was approaching from the hillside. 'Laren was hurt. We need your help.'

The older woman hastened to reach her side and when Alex pulled back the cloak again, Laren's cheeks flushed. Though she'd planned to ask Vanora for her help anyway, Alex was behaving as if the injury were life-threatening.

'Oh, my dear, what happened to you?' Vanora clucked and fussed over her, and Alex stepped back to let her examine the wound.

'It's not as bad as it looks,' Laren said quietly when the woman went to fetch her needle and linen to bind the wound.

The blistering look in Alex's eyes told her that he didn't believe a word she was saying. He was making her nervous with the way he hovered over her. 'You should go and look after the others,' she suggested. 'The clan will need you to guide them now.'

He ignored her, his gaze fixated upon her blood. 'I'm not leaving you when you're hurt.'

'Please, Alex,' she whispered again, 'it's truly nothing to worry about.' She was holding back her pain by a thread and she didn't want to show weakness in front of him. Swallowing hard, she added, 'The clan needs you now.'

'And you don't?'

There was a bitterness behind his words that she didn't understand. When she tried to take a step towards him, he stiffened. 'If you want me to leave, then so be it.'

Between them, the cool distance seemed to magnify. Vanora waited in the doorway, but Laren didn't want to go inside just yet. She wanted to ease his mood, to make him understand that she wasn't trying to push him away.

Though he'd already left, she struggled to catch up with him. 'I'm sorry about what happened to Glen Arrin.' The words were inadequate and they didn't begin to touch the way she was feeling now.

He spun, advancing upon her. 'I couldn't give a damn about Glen Arrin right now. You were shot and tried to hide it from me.'

Laren took a step back, not at all sure of how to respond. Alex caught her shoulders before she could retreat, drawing her to face him. She didn't want to bear the brunt of his anger, not when she was hurting so badly. But when she finally risked a look in his eyes, she saw the raw fear.

'You could have died today,' he said. 'And you think I'm worried about a pile of burned wood and ashes?' He raked a hand through his hair, struggling to push away his temper.

She didn't move, couldn't speak. Beneath his choked anger was a man who cared about her. The realisation seemed to cut off the air in her lungs, for she hadn't known it. Over the past few years, their marriage had deteriorated until now she rarely saw him during the day or even at night. Being together had become a habit instead of a necessity.

'I'm all right,' she whispered.

'Are you?' His stare was harsh, disbelieving.

Her cheeks were wet and she didn't know what to say or do. It was then that she noticed a reddish stain seeping from her husband's sleeve. From the hardened look on his face, it had to be hurting him, yet he'd said nothing at all. Neither of them was willing to admit to injury, she thought, with irony.

'What about you?' she ventured. 'Do you want me to look at your arm?'

'No. See to the girls and their needs.'

Not mine. She heard his unspoken words and they cut her heart a little deeper. Once, he'd have let her touch him, and though she wasn't the most experienced healer, he'd have submitted to her ministrations. No longer, it seemed.

Laren moved closer. She wanted to tell him that she would stand by him through this catastrophe. She wanted to reach out, to let him know that she still cared.

He looked back at her and in his eyes she saw the magnitude of his loss. She knew that he wouldn't come home until late at night, after she was already asleep. Though she wanted to hold him, to rest her head against his chest, he had other, more important duties as the chief.

A hard lump gathered in her throat, but he lowered his head and turned away from her.

The selfish part of her heart wished he'd chosen to stay.

Alex walked across the fortress, his mind caught in a fog of helplessness. The scent of smoke permeated the air, choking his lungs. But even as he approached his brothers, he couldn't stop thinking of Laren.

Confusion and anger collided inside him, along with a heavy fear. The arrow could have pierced a vital organ, spilling her life blood. The thought shook him deeply, for although he'd grown distant from his wife, he didn't want to lose her.

It felt as though he'd been clubbed in the stomach. She hadn't wanted him to stay or to help her. But why?

'Are you all right?' came his brother Dougal's voice. 'I thought you might want help.' Only ten and four, Dougal had never witnessed a battle like this before—only cattle raids and clan skirmishes. There was a new maturity in his brother's eyes, along with a sadness that mirrored his own.

Alex nodded, grateful for the distraction. 'We should bury the dead.'

Within minutes, they were joined by their other brother Callum, who had recently been freed as a prisoner of war. Callum hadn't spoken a single word, not since his release.

Alex bent down and picked up one of the bodies. His brothers helped and they began the gruesome task of gathering up the fallen. The faces of friends and kinsmen haunted him; he wished he could have done something more to protect his clan. But he revealed none of his grief to his brothers, keeping his expression guarded.

He seized a torch and a shovel, taking them outside

the fortress. He chose a spot where the ground was soft and balanced the torch within a pile of heavy stones. He adjusted the makeshift bandage on his arm, so it wouldn't bleed while he worked. Though it had grown dark, the three of them began digging a burial pit. The backbreaking work was what he needed right now to distract him from the sense of overwhelming loss.

He was the chief of the MacKinlochs. They would look to him to make the decisions, to know what should be done next.

You were never meant to be leader, an inner voice taunted him. His father Tavin had chosen Bram to be his successor. As the second-born, Alex had listened on the outskirts, drinking in all the knowledge, never dreaming that he would have to use it.

He'd made a thousand mistakes in the early years. But he'd learned from them, and never once had he revealed his frustrations…not to his kinsmen, and not to Laren. It was easier to pretend that all was well, for they needed a leader of strength. The men had come to trust him, knowing that they could bring their troubles and he would find the answers they needed.

He swore he'd find a way to rebuild what had been lost. Somehow.

Over the next hour, he worked with Callum and Dougal at his side. Having his brothers with him brought him a slight reassurance. Even if their lives had fallen apart, their keep lying in ashes, at least they were together.

Once the pit was finished, they buried the men and spoke a prayer for their souls. 'Do you have a place to sleep tonight?' Alex asked his brothers.

Callum nodded and pointed to one of the other houses

that had been untouched by fire. Dougal joined with his brother and added, 'Bram offered, but he and Nairna—' His words broke off, his ears turning crimson. Alex could guess that the two young men had no desire to dwell with a husband and wife who were trying to start a family.

'Walter has no wife and he offered to let us stay in his home,' Dougal finished.

Since everyone had a place for shelter, Alex picked up the torch. 'Get some sleep while you can. We'll start again in the morning.'

They walked back to the fortress and Alex glanced up at the clear skies. Stars gleamed against the midnight blackness and there were a few hours before dawn. The faint scent of peat mingled with the night air, a familiar aroma that welcomed him towards Ross's home. When he opened the door, he saw his friend and Vanora sleeping on the opposite end. Laren rested upon a pallet, the two girls in her arms. A bandage was wrapped across her side and he couldn't see her face.

Alex stretched out on his side behind her, studying his wife as she slept. Her red hair hung over her shoulder and she slept in the gown she'd worn all day. She'd removed her cloak and spread it over the girls as a blanket. Even in sleep, she guarded and protected their daughters. She'd always been a good mother to them.

He reached for a strand of her hair, curling the silken lock over his hand. Laren stirred in her sleep, moving restlessly.

'It's just me,' he murmured. He released her hair, his hand clenching into a fist.

She finally did roll on to her back. In the dim moonlight he spied the gleam of tears on her cheeks. From the tension in her posture, he saw that she was trying to brave her way through the pain.

'How are you feeling?'

'I'm all right.' She kept her voice low, so as not to wake the children. But when she turned back to her left side, it occurred to him that their polite, quiet marriage had shifted on to unstable ground.

The arrow might well have pierced his own flesh, awakening him to the reality that his wife didn't confide in him any more. If she felt unable to reveal a wound, what other secrets had she kept?

Laren disappeared each day for hours on end, never telling him where she was going or what she was doing. A tightness clenched his throat, for he'd never asked her. He'd been so busy worrying about the keep and its occupants, he'd forgotten about his wife. At the time, he'd believed he was merely giving her the freedom to come and go as she pleased, not wanting to make demands of her.

Perhaps at a deeper level, he hadn't wanted to know why she was leaving, for fear that she wanted to avoid being with him.

He stared up at the ceiling of Ross's home, knowing he wouldn't find sleep this night. It had taken a single arrow to crack his illusions apart. They didn't have a true marriage any more, only the barest shadow.

In the darkness, he rolled over to watch his wife trying to sleep. He couldn't imagine a life without her in it.

He just didn't know what he had to do to get her back.

Chapter Two

In the early morning Laren opened her eyes and saw Alex watching her. His eyes were heavy, as though he hadn't slept at all. 'How are you this morn?' he asked.

'Tired,' she admitted, gingerly easing to a seated position so as not to tear the stitches. The wound was a dull ache now, the pain worse than yesterday.

'I want to see your wound.' Though his words were spoken quietly so as not to awaken their daughters, she detected an edge to his voice.

Laren pulled apart the dress seam they'd cut last night, removing the bloodstained linen she'd slept with. Alex stared at the wound, his hand moving forwards, but he stopped shy of touching her.

'You're staying inside with the girls today. I don't want you anywhere near the ruins, not when you're hurt.'

'It wasn't a mortal wound, Alex,' she reminded him, feeling like a petulant child daring to argue with her parent. She bound up the wound again, adding, 'There's much to do and the girls and I will help where we can.'

Vanora came forward with Ross, and Alex turned to her. 'See to it that Laren rests and doesn't tear the stitches.'

He was talking about her as though she weren't sitting in front of him. Frustration and resentment brewed inside her, but Laren held silent. The wound had torn her flesh in two places, but the stitches held it together and it wasn't too deep. Yet there was no sense in arguing with him, not when he was in no mood to listen.

Soon enough, Alex left the house, not even bothering to break his fast. It was clear that his mind was focused on all of the work to be done. Ross joined him, the two men going off to survey the damage.

Vanora approached her, after the men were gone. 'I've made you a poultice,' she offered. 'We'll wrap it against your wound and it should be healed in a few more days.'

'I'm not staying inside when there's so much to do.' The members of their clan would spend the entire day repairing what damage they could. She didn't want them to resent her by remaining absent.

'I agree with you,' Vanora said. 'There's no point in sitting inside with all there is to do.' She unwrapped Laren's wound, packing the herbs against her raw flesh.

'Mama, does it hurt?' Mairin asked, her face worried when she saw the bandage.

'Not really,' Laren said, pressing a kiss onto her daughter's forehead. 'Vanora has some oat cakes for you if you're hungry.' With the distraction of food, her daughter scrambled away.

'She reminds me of my daughter Nessa when she was younger,' Vanora sighed. 'I do miss her, now that she's gone back to Locharr.' With a glance to Laren, she added,

'But I'm glad she wasn't here when we were attacked.' She reached out and gave the baby a warm hug.

Adaira toddled towards Laren, her baby lips puckered. 'Kiss, Mama.' Though she was not quite two years old, she alternated between wanting to cling to Laren's legs or demanding that she do everything by herself.

Laren leaned down and pressed her mouth against the baby's, feeling the sweetness of innocent affection. 'Go with your sister, sweeting.' To Mairin, she directed, 'Get Adaira a cake to eat.'

'You shouldn't let Alex speak to you that way,' Vanora said, dropping her voice. 'Chief or no, you should stand up for yourself.'

Laren supposed it might seem that way to an outsider. 'It would do no good,' she admitted. 'Once he's made up his mind, he won't listen to any arguments.'

'Nothing wrong with a fight now and then,' Vanora said, sending her a wicked look. 'Sometimes strong words can lead to making up.'

Laren coloured, knowing exactly what the matron was implying. But she didn't enjoy verbal sparring, and it was doubtful that it would lead to anything more. Alex hadn't touched her in a long time. Over the past few months, he'd started coming to bed late at night. He fell asleep almost immediately and rose at dawn. The days when he'd reached for her in the morning, stealing a kiss or making love to her, were long gone.

She didn't blame him for it. It was part of being chief of the clan, and she understood the obligations he faced. But sometimes…she was lonely.

If Alex had shown the slightest desire to be with her, to talk with her the way he'd used to, she might have told him the secret she'd kept for nearly three years—the one that had kept her from burying herself in grief when she'd lost their baby.

When her husband could offer no solace, she'd gone to the priest, Father Nolan. The older man had taught her the art of glassmaking as a means of occupying her time. With fire and breath she'd found redemption and beauty. There was nothing more miraculous than the blending of sand, minerals and heat to form colourful panes of glass. The craft had given her hope and helped her survive those nightmarish months when she'd barely slept or eaten from the heart-wrenching loss.

Within a year, she had become the priest's apprentice and in the craft she'd found the part of herself that she'd lost. Now, she could no more give it up than she could give up breathing. But she'd done it in secret for so long, she was afraid to tell anyone. Only her apprentice Ramsay, Nairna and Lady Marguerite knew of it. She didn't know what Alex would think, for she was afraid he wouldn't see the value in it.

You need to put aside your fear and try to sell your pieces, she told herself. If she could find a buyer, the silver coins would allow them to replenish the food and supplies they'd lost during the battle. It was her best hope of helping the people.

But the last time she'd tried, it had resulted in disaster. She and Nairna had given Dougal the glass, not telling him where it was from, and he'd been cheated by a merchant. The weeks of hard work were lost for ever, and she still felt the disappointment of it.

Vanora cooked more oat cakes for the girls while Laren went to warm her hands near the fire. The beechwood was dying down into coals, with plentiful ashes from the night before. She poked at the wood, stoking the flames.

Though she forced herself to eat with the girls, she wasn't particularly hungry.

As she stared at the heated coals, she thought of the immense heat necessary for making glass. Her mind started to drift, and she imagined spending the day with her sand and minerals. She needed more ashes and—

Ashes. There were plenty of those now, weren't there? If she gathered them up, the raw materials would allow her to make larger quantities of glass. *Alex won't like it,* her mind warned. *He ordered you to stay out of the way.*

She dismissed the thought. Likely he wouldn't even notice she was there. The girls would enjoy helping her fill buckets of ash, especially if she challenged them to bring as many as possible to the cavern.

'Girls, are you finished eating?' she asked. Mairin nodded, taking Adaira's hand. 'Good.'

Laren made sure the girls were dressed warmly enough, pulling a hood over Adaira's hair. 'We're going to go and help your father. I want you to find wooden buckets and you'll help us to clean up.'

'And what will you say to your husband when he finds you've disobeyed him?' Vanora prompted.

She sent the matron a slight shrug and a smile. 'What were you saying about a good fight, now and then?'

Vanora beamed and led the way outside. Laren reached for a wooden bucket and asked, 'May I take this and bring it back to you later?'

The matron nodded. 'I'll come along with you.'

They walked towards the burned remains of the keep. Further ahead, Laren heard the sounds of boys fighting. She motioned for Vanora to keep the girls back while she went to investigate.

'Thief! Did you think you'd get away with stealing?'

The adolescent boy pounded at a crouched figure who was bleeding in the dirt. Another boy stood on the opposite side, kicking the victim.

'Get away from him!' Laren reached in and grasped the older one by the back of his tunic, trying to pull him off the boy she couldn't see.

When she revealed the victim's face, she suppressed her cry of dismay. It was Ramsay, her apprentice. The tow-headed boy was eleven years old, and he had a bloody nose from the fight. But there were also older bruises, likely from his father's fists. In his grimy hand, he held a crust of bread.

'What happened?' she demanded. 'Why would you fight over bread?'

'Our grain stores burned,' the first boy said. 'We caught him stealing from our da.'

'Do you think your chief would let a family go hungry? Would he deny you food?'

'Ramsay should've gone elsewhere to beg.'

Laren shook her head, sending the boy a look of disgust. 'Go back to your homes. Leave him alone.'

When they'd gone, she knelt down beside her apprentice and used her hand to wipe away the blood. 'Can you sit up?'

Pain wrinkled his mouth, but Ramsay managed to nod. His fingers were still clenched around the crust of bread.

'Did you steal that?' Laren asked quietly. His face coloured with shame and his silence was answer enough.

'You could have come to me,' she said gently.

He kept his head lowered and she knew he hadn't asked her for food out of pride. 'Go to the cavern and start the furnaces,' she ordered. 'I'll bring food to you when I come.'

The command seemed to break through his dark mood and stony grey eyes stared into hers. For the past year, Ramsay had been her apprentice, helping her to keep the furnaces running. It gave him a means of escaping his father's fists and she couldn't make her glass without him.

'Do you want me to start a melt after the furnaces are hot enough?' he asked, in a low voice.

'Not yet. I'll join you later and select the melts that I need.' With any luck, she'd have the ashes she wanted by that time.

She helped Ramsay stand, noting that he'd need warmer clothes before long. The last garments she'd given him had disappeared. Likely his father had taken them away or traded them.

As he shuffled towards the cavern on the far side of the loch, she saw the shadow of herself as a girl. She knew what it was to be cold and hungry, too proud to accept handouts from others.

Never again, she swore. She'd not let any of her loved ones go without food or clothing. Not her own children, and not boys like Ramsay, who had no one else to care for them.

Her apprentice had shown promise in the skill of glass-making and his unyielding desire for accuracy had served him well. He drank in the knowledge as fast as she could give it.

When she returned to where she'd left Vanora and the girls, she saw that the matron had brought them among the crowd of people. Several younger men had axes and were walking towards the forest to begin cutting wood. Others were busy hauling away the burned wood in carts.

Laren remained on the outskirts, where she saw Bram's wife Nairna organising people into groups. The woman was like a commander, giving out orders with a natural sense of leadership. She moved with such confidence, as if she knew exactly what to do. She wasn't at all afraid of the crowds or telling people what tasks to accomplish.

'You should be up there,' Vanora said, when Laren reached her side. 'Not Nairna. You're the chief's wife.'

Laren's cheeks flushed at the admonition. But what could she do? Standing in front of large crowds terrified her. She felt every flaw was magnified in their eyes.

'They don't respect you,' Vanora continued. 'You hide away from them without even trying.' The matron took her hand, leading her forwards. 'I don't mean to hurt your feelings, *a charaid*, but if you're wanting to help, you need to stop being so shy and take the role that belongs to you.'

Laren knew Vanora was right, but she couldn't change her fears any more than she could change her nervous heartbeat from racing inside her chest. Her skin grew cold, goose bumps rising up as nerves rippled within her stomach. She wished she could be like Nairna, instead of tongue-tied and not knowing what to say.

As the crowd dispersed, Laren watched Alex and his brothers. She saw the bandage wrapped around her husband's forearm, but he continued to lift away the fallen timbers, with little care for his injury.

His muscles strained as he worked and Laren remembered what it was like to touch his bare skin, the hardened flesh merging into soft. She knew his body well, the contrast between the ridges of his stomach and muscular back.

A shadow fell across her mood, for it had been such a long time since they had touched one another intimately. Last night, when he'd learned of her injury, he'd been so angry. Her feelings were bruised, for not once had he said that he was glad she was all right. His fury was palpable, and though she knew he was angry that she'd been hurt, it almost felt as if he were blaming her for the injury. Then this morn, he'd demanded that she stay inside, as though she were incapable of doing anything to help.

But I can do something, she thought. She would start making more glass today and eventually try to sell it. Somehow.

'Mama, aren't we going to help Da?' Mairin asked, her face impatient.

'Aye. But stay here.' She couldn't simply go up to the ruined keep and begin shovelling ash. Alex would see them and get angry. For this, she needed Nairna's help.

She asked Vanora, 'Will you watch over the girls for a moment?' The matron agreed and Laren kept to the outskirts of the crowd, avoiding Alex as she drew closer to Nairna. Bram's wife would know how to get the ash without making anyone suspicious.

'I need your help,' she confessed, when she reached Nairna's side. 'I want the ash that's left over, if you can spare it.' She met her sister-in-law's gaze with an unspoken reminder about the glass. 'I need the beechwood ashes in particular,' Laren continued. 'It's necessary for…the work that I do. My girls can help to gather it.'

Nairna's green eyes turned shrewd. 'You'll need more help than that. I'll send Dougal, and he'll get the other men to help shovel it into a cart. The men need the space cleared for the new keep anyhow. Leave it to me.'

Laren voiced her thanks and started to walk back to the girls. She'd nearly reached the gate when a hand caught her arm.

'What are you doing here?' Alex demanded. He couldn't believe that Laren was here, not when she'd been wounded.

Her face was pale and he pulled her over to a small pile of stones, forcing her to sit. 'You need to rest.'

Although he'd thrown himself into the physical labor of rebuilding, ever since he'd left Laren's side he'd replayed the vision of the arrow piercing her skin. Even now her face held the pain, and guilt plagued him that he hadn't been able to shield her from it.

'I wanted to help,' she said, rising to her feet.

Arguments rose to his lips, but he forced himself to gentle his words. 'I don't want you to be hurt. There are parts of the keep still standing and we need to tear them down. Just keep the children away.'

'Nairna is helping you,' she pointed out. 'And so are Vanora and the other women.'

'They weren't wounded.' He needed her to be away from the unstable structure, and, more than that, he needed her to rest and heal. 'Do as I ask, Laren. There's nothing you can do here anyway.'

Laren stared at him, a brittle expression on her face as she strode away. He hadn't meant to be that harsh, but it was evident that he'd offended her. He returned to the ruined keep and started tearing down the boards. Splinters pierced his hands, but he ignored them. As he ripped apart the burned wood, an inner voice taunted him.

She didn't tell you about the wound because she doesn't trust you.

Alex grasped another plank and heaved his body weight against the wood, letting the anger and physical labour push away the unwanted thoughts. For nearly three years he'd worked endless hours, ensuring that each person in the clan was fed and had a place to sleep. He'd told himself at the time that it was necessary. It was his obligation as their chief.

Laren understood it, just as he did. His hands stilled upon the wood and a trickle of blood ran down between his fingers.

She was happier before you were chief, the voice continued. *She never wanted this life. You forced it upon her.*

He'd always expected that she would change, once she saw the responsibilities. It would take time, but he'd believed Laren would be a good Lady of Glen Arrin.

Instead, she'd retreated…both from this life and from him.

There's nothing you can do.

The words stabbed at her mood as Laren stalked away. Alex viewed her as a nuisance, someone who needed to stay out of the way while he worked with the men to rebuild. She supposed he was merely trying to keep her safe, but did he really believe she could sit inside, staring at the walls, while everyone else was working? She couldn't.

When she found Vanora back at her dwelling, Laren stopped to collect her daughters, along with some food for an afternoon meal. She walked along the shoreline with Mairin and Adaira, her elder daughter running ahead to stamp upon the ice fragments on the edge of the loch.

Her cave was hidden on the far side of the water's edge, formed on the side of a large hill. There were enough crevices in the ceiling of the cave for ventilation and it was far enough away from the keep that no one ever came close. The proximity to the shoreline also gave her access to the vast quantities of sand that she needed.

Father Nolan had built his furnaces inside the cavern and it kept the atmosphere warm and dry, perfect for making glass. Laren was grateful that he'd constructed all of the large ovens, for she'd never have been able to build them herself.

As she neared the familiar entrance, she saw Ramsay had begun the fires as she'd asked. A deep warmth suffused the air, but it would be several hours more before it would be hot enough for glassmaking.

She fed the girls a small meal of dried apples and meat. Afterwards, she spread out her cloak and laid Adaira down, rubbing the child's shoulders until she went down for a nap. It wasn't long before Mairin yawned and stretched out beside her sister. The warmth of the fires made it easy for them to fall asleep just at the entrance, on the soft sand.

Laren kept the children in full view, casting glances at them while she took note of her supplies. Although Father Nolan had left her with his tools and his stores of lead and minerals, there would come a time when she'd have to purchase more.

'We need more lime,' Ramsay said. He'd washed his face, Laren noticed, and she handed him the bag of food she'd brought.

'You're to eat everything inside,' she told him, taking a small oat cake for herself.

He muttered his thanks and reached into the bag, attacking the food as though he feared it would run away from him. She pretended to study the panes of glass she'd already made, but instead she was watching the lad.

His thin frame bothered her, but worse were the bruises on his face. The boy's father rarely remembered to feed him, for he spent most of his time drinking ale or using his fists against Ramsay. Laren couldn't understand why he stayed with his father, when she'd offered him the chance to come and be fostered with her and Alex. The boy had refused, stubbornly remaining in his own home.

'I need you to stay with the furnace all day today,' she told Ramsay. 'I'll be making large quantities of glass and we won't be able to let the fires go out.' It was a lie, but one that would keep him out of his father's house, at least until tonight.

The wound in her side ached and Laren forced herself to sit for a moment, pushing away the dizziness. It would heal. And as soon as she worked upon her glass, she'd forget all about the pain.

'I've mixed a crucible,' Ramsay offered. 'It's ready to be melted. All it needs are the colour minerals.'

She smiled at him. 'You're the best apprentice I could have, Ramsay.'

His face flushed. 'I'll chop more wood for you.' He returned to work, uncomfortable with the compliment.

She traced her fingers over a piece of bright blue glass she'd made and wondered if it really was possible to earn a profit from her work.

What if it's not good enough? a voice of doubt warned. Her colours might be too dark, not letting in enough light. Although the cobalt had created a nice blue, the silver hadn't achieved the shade of green she'd wanted. No piece of glass could be made in the same way twice, for the ashes varied from the different beechwood trees.

'Have you lit the annealing furnace?' she asked Ramsay.

'Aye. Just now,' he answered.

The annealing furnace had to be a lower temperature than the melting furnace, for the glass had to cool under controlled conditions. She'd learned the hard way that the annealing process was necessary, after a few glass pieces had cooled too quickly and cracked apart when she'd tried to score them.

She stood and took the clay crucible Ramsay had

prepared, adding a small amount of iron to try to create a red glass. It was too soon to heat it, but she set it near the edge of the furnace in preparation.

Although the heat was intense, Laren was used to it. She welcomed the roasting warmth as she turned her attention to some streaked green glass she'd made days ago. From her position behind the fire, she could see Mairin and Adaira still fast asleep.

In her mind she envisioned the Garden of Eden. She would use the glass to form the leaves of the Tree of Knowledge, making it the focal point of the scene. Tomorrow, if she managed to achieve the right shade of red, she could form the apple of temptation.

She lost track of time, heating a cutting tool to a red-hot point before she scored the glass to crack it into the shape she wanted. As she worked, she fell under the spell of creating her glass scenes, watching the shapes transform from the image within her mind into reality.

After she had cut several leaves from the finished glass, she spied Nairna and Dougal at the entrance. Her girls had awakened and Nairna held Adaira in her arms.

Her brother-in-law's face was coated with ash, his face sweaty from the labour. As Dougal stared at her, his expression turned curious. 'You made that?' he asked, pointing to the sheet of glass. 'From sand, just now?'

'No. Days ago,' Laren corrected. 'It takes several days to make glass. Longer, depending on what colours you want.' She put on her gloves, feeling uneasy about the burn scars on her hands, but no one had noticed them. Ramsay had moved to the back of the cavern, trying to remain unobtrusive.

Her side was aching again and Laren took several

breaths to force back the pain. Tonight she would speak to Vanora and ask if she could make a sleeping draught. For now, she hid her misery and asked Dougal, 'Did you bring me any of the beechwood ash? Or am I supposed to scrape it off you?'

His cheeks reddened at her teasing and he pointed outside. 'I filled the wagon with it.'

'You can dump it just outside the cave, if you can manage.'

In the end, all of them worked together to shovel it out. Mairin and Adaira tried to help, but it was more difficult with them underfoot.

When at last the wagon was empty, Laren checked on the melt and adjusted the fires. She used a bellows to increase the heat and Ramsay took his place beside the fire, promising to keep it going.

'It should be ready by midnight,' he predicted. 'I'll add the crucible then.'

'Good. I'll be here first thing in the morning to check the melt.'

'I won't let the fire go out,' he swore. And she knew he'd keep the promise. He was accustomed to sleeping during the day; not once had she lost a melt under his watch.

Laren gave him a solemn nod, refraining from ruffling his hair as she wanted to. Ramsay couldn't bear any form of affection and he'd stiffened on the few occasions when she'd patted his shoulder. When she looked into his dark eyes, she saw the image of the son she might have had.

The vivid pain came crashing back and she bit her lip to suppress it. Nairna sent her a curious look. 'Are you all right?'

Laren nodded. 'I suppose I should take the girls back.

It's late.' She touched Mairin's shoulder and reminded her daughter to hold her sister's hand. After adjusting their outer clothing to keep them warm, Laren took both girls' hands in hers and started to walk back.

Nairna remained at her side and ventured softly, 'I think you should tell your husband about the glass.'

Laren sent the girls to run on ahead and they quickly caught up to Dougal, begging for a ride inside the wagon. When they were out of earshot, she stopped walking, touching her hand to her side.

'I will tell him, Nairna. Just not yet.' The idea of revealing her awkward skills was frightening. It was like exposing the deepest part of herself.

'It would help him to understand why you're gone so many hours of the day.' Her sister-in-law rested a hand upon her shoulders. 'And one day you'll tell the rest of the clan.'

Laren shook her head. 'I know what the other women say about me. They think I'm spineless and unfit to be a chief's wife.'

'I don't believe that.' Nairna shook her head and smiled. 'You're just quiet and shy.'

'No. It's more than that.' Laren reached down and touched the edge of her gown, remembering the threadbare clothing she'd worn years ago.

'My father was a beggar,' Laren admitted. 'He wasn't able to take care of us. Sometimes he would fall under a spell of melancholy and wouldn't get out of bed for weeks at a time.' She pulled her cloak tighter around her. 'We hardly had enough to eat and everyone knew it. My sisters and I wore the cast-off clothes of others.'

From Nairna's startled expression, she guessed that no one had told her. 'The clan knows where I came from. And they know I haven't the ability to lead them.' She shook her head at the incongruity of the idea. Then she looked back at Nairna. 'I may be the chief's wife now, but I'm still an embarrassment.'

Laren quickened her pace, past the white stone that lay on the hillside. 'The glassmaking is part of me, Nairna. If I have this, I can endure their criticism. I can let it flow through me and not let it hurt, because I know what I can make.'

She took a breath, though the confession tore at her heart. 'It doesn't matter if I can't lead the people or be the wife Alex needs, because I know that there's something I can do.'

Nairna tried to offer words of comfort, but Laren didn't hear them. She saw her husband in the distance, waiting for them at the gates.

And when she saw the intense look upon his face, within his expression lay worry and a hint of relief. He embraced the girls, swinging Adaira up into his arms. But though he spoke to them, she didn't miss the way he watched her.

Almost as if he'd needed to see her again.

March, 1300

The soft sound of a stone striking the wood of her mother's cottage awakened Laren from slumber. A secret thrill of excitement warmed her, for Alex was here, just as he'd promised.

Her sisters were asleep beside her, but none of them stirred when she rose from the pallet they shared. Tiptoeing outside, she glanced behind her to be certain her mother hadn't seen her.

The moon shone silver in the clouded sky, and she saw Alex emerge from the shadows. His face and dark hair were damp, as though he'd washed in the stream before coming to see her. In his palm he held small stones, but he let them fall, extending his hand to her. Laren made no sound, but took his hand, following him into the forest.

It wasn't as dark as she'd expected, but as they moved deeper into the woods, she drew closer to his side. The spring air was cool and she sensed the moisture that hung with the portent of rain. Dark green moss covered the trees and she was careful of her footing as she walked with him. A sense of forbidden anticipation built up inside, at the thought of being alone with this man.

Once they reached the clearing, she saw the small circle of standing stones. Ancient and worn, the stones held their own element of enchantment. It was their private place, one where reality faded away and she could forget that he was a chief's son, and she, a poor crofter's daughter.

Here, they could be together with no one to interfere. Never had Alex treated her as though she were beneath him. Right now, he was staring at her with a mixture of desire and regret.

'I have to leave on the morrow,' he told her, his hands drawing her into an embrace. 'My Uncle Donnell wants me to visit the Campbell clan.' There was a heaviness in his eyes, a sense of frustration. He'd been living with his uncle, who had become chief after the death of his father. There was little affection between them, for Donnell continually derided him, claiming that Alex lacked the skill to ever be a leader like his father.

'When will you return?' she whispered.

'I don't know.' His hands framed her face and he touched his forehead to hers. 'He wants me to wed the daughter of their chief. But you needn't worry. I've made my choice of a bride already.'

His fingers moved through her long red hair and within his eyes she saw a rising hunger. A piece of her heart broke away, for if she could, she'd keep him with her. She loved Alex MacKinloch with every breath, with every part of herself.

But she feared they would have no future together, not as poor as she was. And there was a sinking dread that, once he saw this woman, he might forget what there was between them.

For now, she fully intended to savour every stolen moment. His mouth came down upon hers and she kissed him back with all the fervour in her heart. His lips and tongue merged with her own, conjuring up desperate feelings she didn't understand. Against her body, she felt the hard length of his desire. He drew her hips closer, his hungry mouth moving over her skin.

She couldn't catch her breath, her pulse racing. Tonight could be their last night together. Once he left Glen Arrin, she might lose him.

'I love you,' she whispered, her arms twining around his neck.

He lowered her down to the soft grass and she saw the moment when he regained control of his thoughts. Though his breathing was as staggered as her own, he rolled to his side, studying her.

'I want you to be my wife, Laren.'

She tried not to let her feelings overshadow what needed to be said. Closing her eyes, she tried to find the right words.

'Not until you return.' She wanted to believe that he would love her enough, but she didn't want him to later hold regrets.

'Say you will,' he urged again.

She leaned up to kiss him, distracting him with the physical desire that burned between them. It was easier not to think of losing him when his arms were around her.

'You're the only man I've ever wanted,' she answered against his mouth. He took her mouth again, his hands moving over her shoulders, then he brought his palm over her breast.

He let it rest there, waiting to see what she would do. Her nipple rose with a fevered arousal and she felt an answering rush between her legs. She knew, if she allowed it, he would become her lover this night.

His thumb caressed the erect tip and she shifted her legs together at the aching sensation. Temptation warred with good sense and she captured his hand with hers.

'When you return,' she whispered. She could not surrender her innocence to him, not when he might be forced to wed another.

He sat up, leaning her body back against him. 'I've brought you a gift to remember me by.' In her palm, he pressed a small pouch.

Laren unwrapped the leather and poured out a handful of glass droplets. Vivid blue, green and red mingled with white, in a jewelled handful.

'They're beautiful,' she breathed.

'Father Nolan made them. They reminded me of the treasures I'd give to you, if I could.'

The cool glass warmed beneath her fingers and she held one up to examine it more closely. As she studied them, she wondered how they were made. She knew the priest used sand and fire, but no one dared to interrupt him while he was forging his magic.

Alex kissed her again, holding her close. Though she desired him, she was afraid of what the future might hold. And, most of all, she feared losing him.

Chapter Three

A bone-deep exhaustion settled within him. Every muscle in his body ached and Alex wanted nothing more than to find a place to sleep for the next fortnight. But he couldn't.

Despite working since sunrise, they'd done little more than clear away the wreckage. The mood within Glen Arrin was unsettled, for they were exposed, their weaknesses bared to any enemy who happened to draw near.

He closed his eyes, knowing the violence would come. Robert Fitzroy, the Baron of Harkirk, had retreated after the last battle, but Alex had no doubt that the English baron was merely biding his time.

The silence unnerved him more than any direct attack. He sensed, within his blood, that Harkirk would strike again. It was a matter of when, not if.

The heaviness of the clan's fate rested upon his shoulders and he could feel their doubts. He'd heard more than a few whispers today, questioning his leadership. But this was *his* clan. He would do whatever was necessary to keep them safe, even if they were reduced to ashes and sackcloth.

They were his people. His family.

His brother Bram approached, his expression dark, as though he didn't want to bear bad news. 'I've heard talk of several men wanting to leave. They have family among the other clans.'

'I won't let that happen.' Alex adjusted the bandage on his arm, knowing that if a few left, others would follow.

'And how could you stop them?'

'It won't come to that.' He walked alongside Bram through the remains of the keep. 'Tonight I'll speak to them.'

When he passed several of his kinsmen, he didn't miss the despair and hopelessness on their faces as they worked to gather up what remained of their belongings. It wouldn't be easy to convince them, but as their chief it was his responsibility to care for them.

He passed Brodie, who was holding the hand of his three-year-old son. The child struggled to pick up a stone that was nearly as big as he was, his face pursed with effort. Brodie put his arms around his son and helped him to lift up the stone, before setting it down upon the wall.

The fist of grief caught Alex so hard that he blinked back the emotion. It had been almost three years now. Their son would have been the same age as this child. He could almost imagine it in his mind, and when Brodie stood, holding his son's hand, Alex felt the emptiness of his own palm.

It's in the past, he told himself. *You have two daughters. Be thankful for what you have.*

In the distance, Dougal was returning with Mairin and Adaira riding alongside him in the wagon. Nairna and

Laren approached a short distance behind. There was exhaustion in his wife's bearing and he didn't understand why she'd defied him again.

He increased his pace to meet her, when he reached her side, he saw the defensive expression rise up. From the way she clutched her side, she was in pain. He couldn't understand why she would exert herself, simply to get away from everyone else.

'You took the girls for a walk?' he confirmed, nodding toward his daughters, who were tormenting poor Dougal with their chatter.

'Aye. You wanted me to keep them away from the fortress.'

'I meant for you to rest and keep them with you.' He suspected she'd known his wishes; she'd simply chosen to ignore them.

The more he thought of it, the more he realised that they'd been gone for several hours outside. It was freezing and a thin layer of ice coated the loch. Laren wouldn't expose the girls to that kind of cold. When he studied his daughters, he noted that they didn't appear in any sort of discomfort. Their cheeks were rosy, their smiles bright.

'Where did you take the girls?'

She looked startled, as if she hadn't expected him to confront her. 'Just on a walk. Nowhere, really.'

'For several hours?' He moved closer, his gaze narrowed.

'Well, I—'

'Don't lie to me,' he demanded. He reached out to touch the back of her neck and, upon her skin, he felt warmth and a slight perspiration. The aroma of wood smoke clung to her hair. 'You went inside somewhere, didn't you?'

Laren coloured, but didn't deny it. 'Yes. We went to

Father Nolan's cavern.' She backed away from his touch and he let his hand fall to his side. From the fear in her eyes, he knew there was far more that she hadn't said.

'Why?' The cavern had been abandoned for several years, ever since the old priest had died.

'I—I'll tell you later,' she stammered. 'But not here.'

He heard the tremor in her voice, and her blue eyes were downcast. It startled him to see her so uncertain, almost as if she were guilty about something. What was she hiding?

'Send the girls to Vanora and Ross tonight,' he gritted out, releasing her from his grasp. 'I want to talk to you alone.'

Her face flushed with uneasiness. 'I have to prepare food for the girls. They need a meal before they go to sleep.'

It was a feeble excuse not to go. But then his gaze moved down to her hands and he caught the traces of blood upon them.

'You're bleeding again.' It was a foolish observation and it infuriated him that she refused to stop and take care of herself.

'It will stop,' she whispered. 'I'll rest and it will be fine.'

He softened his tone. 'Let Vanora take care of the girls. And let me take care of you.' Without waiting for the refusal he knew would come, he left Laren's side and went to the older matron. Ross's wife sent him a pointed look, but she agreed to look after their daughters.

The afternoon sky darkened, Alex gave orders for Dougal to bring him a horse and supplies for the night. Laren's gaze was focused upon the girls. When she understood that he wasn't giving her a choice, her displeasure was evident.

He didn't care. Right now, he needed to confront his wife, to understand what she was hiding from him.

The more he thought of it, the more he realised that she had never confided in him. Over the past two years, she'd hidden herself away, keeping her own secrets.

Tonight, he wanted to learn exactly what they were.

Alex helped Laren onto the horse, bringing a torch with him as he led the animal into the forest. The light dappled the edges of the leaves, filtering the golden sun amid the oaks and fir trees. Nothing was said throughout the half-hour journey, and when at last he brought the horse to a stop, Laren stared at the circle of stones, her face stricken.

'Why did you bring me here?'

'You know why.' He wanted her to remember the way things had once been between them. The circle was where they had first fallen in love. It seemed like the best place to begin again.

Laren walked forwards, resting her hand upon one of the stones. 'It's been a long time since we were here.'

He'd brought her here every Beltaine, where they had celebrated the feast in each other's arms, in remembrance of their wedding night. But after the children were born, it had become more difficult to get away. Laren was reluctant to leave Mairin and, over time, their circle had been forgotten.

When he turned back to her, he saw that she'd sat down. Her gloved hands resting upon her skirts, as the dying sunlight sank below the horizon.

'You don't have to wear those,' he offered, pointing to her gloves.

'I'm more comfortable with them on.'

Alex didn't argue. He supposed her hands were cold,

now that winter was upon them. While he set up their tent, a thousand questions and demands poured through his mind. He struggled to keep his frustration within manageable boundaries. But the longer she held herself apart, the more he wondered how to begin.

They were alone now, with no one to stare at them or whisper. But Laren didn't even look at him. He supposed her injury was bothering her. His own arm ached, but he was more accustomed to working through discomfort.

Against the fading sunlight, her hair gleamed like reddened flames. Laren was as beautiful to him now as she'd been on the day he'd married her. Her skin was milky smooth, her body slender.

'Do you remember the last time we were here?' he ventured at last.

She leaned against one of the standing stones, her hand pressed to her side. 'It was before Mairin was born, I think.' A softness came over her, and she added, 'We were so young then.'

He came to stand closer to her, and the sun began to dip lower. Abruptly, Laren released a cough that sounded suspiciously like a laugh.

'What is it?'

'You asked me if I found the stones inspiring.' Her mouth tipped into a smile at the sight of the phallic monoliths.

'And did you?'

'Sometimes.' Her face held the softness of the past, like the woman he'd first wed. She held her hand to her wounded side and rested against the standing stone. He reached out and moved a lock of her hair that had fallen against her cheek. When he kept his hand on her face, he saw the sudden confusion in her green eyes.

'There was a time, before we married, when we came here just to be together. Now, you spend every possible moment far away from me.'

She didn't deny it and her silence made him break away.

'I want to know why, Laren.'

'I'm not avoiding you.' It hadn't started out that way, though she supposed it might seem so to him. She'd needed to bury herself in work, to shut out the rest of the world. And when she'd discovered her love of glasswork, she'd sought out every possible moment to work on it.

'Aren't you?'

Laren shook her head. She closed her eyes, the sudden pain of her wound drawing her attention. Her hand felt wet against her side. When she leaned against the stone the earth swayed beneath her feet.

Alex didn't miss the sudden shift in her posture. When he touched her hand, she inhaled sharply at the gentle pressure against her side.

'Show me your wound,' he demanded.

There was anger in his voice and she tried to placate him by offering, 'Vanora gave me a poultice for it and it will heal.'

Her husband stepped in front of her, his dark eyes shadowed with an unnamed emotion while his hand rested upon a sheathed dirk. 'Remove the gown, Laren. Unless you want me to cut it off.'

The sudden image of his blade slicing through the wool made her imagine the layers of clothing falling away until she was naked before him. The vision was strangely erotic. She knew Alex would never hurt her, but the man standing in front of her now was filled with anger and sexual frustration.

He wanted her. She could see it in the tension from his shoulders, in the way his eyes were watching. Laren considered whether or not to simply show him the wound through the torn seam. Yet a sudden sense of rebellion rose up within her. It was his idea to take her away from everyone else, to spend the night alone with her. All day, he'd issued commands and orders, treating her like a child.

But she wasn't at all a child. She was a woman with thoughts and feelings of her own. A woman he'd pushed aside, only sparing her a glance from time to time. And a part of her wanted him to know what he'd been missing these past months.

Instead of revealing the wound, she loosened the ties of the long gown. With her eyes locked upon his, she turned her back to him. 'It hurts to lift my arms over my head. You'll have to remove the gown for me.'

He was silent and she didn't dare turn around. She withdrew her arms inside the sleeves, and Alex came up behind her to help lift the gown away. As he did, his hands grazed the side of her breasts, sending an unexpected jolt through her. He'd done that on purpose. A shiver rocked through her. Once he'd removed the outer gown, she stood in her shift.

The frigid air heightened her sensitivity and her nipples grew taut against the fabric. Alex didn't turn her around, but he pulled back the poultice and examined her wound. 'You have torn the stitches.'

'I'll fix the bandage. It will be all right.'

'No. Let me.' He loosened her shift and slowly lowered the garment to her waist, baring the wound. In the cold night air, she shivered, feeling exposed, but she didn't bother to cover her naked breasts.

Alex removed the wet bandage and the poultice, but as his hands passed over her body she felt the fierce heat and a slight tremble in his palms.

He tore a length of cloth from his tunic and she eyed him ruefully. 'I'll have to mend that later.'

'I don't care.' Gently, he adjusted the poultice against her wound and bound the new bandage around her waist. He kept the pressure tight, but not enough to hurt her. As his hands moved over her flesh, she couldn't help but think of how long it had been since he'd last touched her.

Or since he'd kissed her.

His hands rested at the edges of the shift, when she realised he wasn't going to touch her any more, Laren fumbled with her undergarment. Alex raised it to cover her breasts and then let her go. 'You should be all right until the morn.'

'Thank you.' She hid her disappointment and, once more, felt his disapproval intruding upon the moment.

She crossed her arms over her body; when he stared at her, she didn't have to feign a shiver.

'I'm not going to bother you,' he said, an edge in his tone. 'I'm not so undisciplined that I would take you when you're hurt.'

'I know it.' Even so, her face warmed with embarrassment, as if he'd read her thoughts. Then she realised that not once had she seen his own wound from the battle. 'How is your arm?'

He pulled back the sleeve to bare a reddened gash. The edges were holding together, but when she examined his wound, she could feel the tension in his stance. 'You shouldn't have been lifting stones all day.'

'And what were you doing all day?' he parried back. She

took a step back, for she hadn't anticipated the question so soon.

She closed her eyes, seeking the right words to tell him about the glass. At last, she offered, 'I have work of my own that I do. I—I make…things.' She waited for a heart-stopping moment, hoping he would ask what they were, that he would show interest in her.

'I know you're good at weaving and sewing tapestries, Laren, but I need you to stand at my side, as Lady of Glen Arrin. As the wife I need.'

She didn't correct his assumption, but in his voice she heard the criticism, the disappointment in her.

When she remained silent, he continued talking. 'I know you're uncomfortable in front of so many people, but Nairna could help you. And once we've rebuilt the keep, the pair of you can work together to oversee it.'

'That's not what I want.' The words blurted forth before she could stop them.

'We can't go back to the way it was,' he said quietly. 'I'm the chief now. I can't turn my back on the MacKinloch clan.'

'I wouldn't ask that of you—' her heart felt leaden, but she needed him to understand '—but you're asking me to be someone I'm not.'

'I'm asking you to *try*, for God's sakes,' he shot back. 'Hiding yourself away in a cavern isn't the sort of life you should have.'

She didn't bother to hide her tears, but he couldn't see how he was breaking her apart. To him, being a leader was nothing more than making decisions and addressing the crowds. It was as natural to him as breathing.

To her, it was like being carved apart by knives.

'We were happy before you were chief,' she whispered. 'We had enough.'

'Even if I gave you a castle, it wouldn't be enough, would it?' He raked his hand through his hair. 'Laren, I don't know what you want. I can't read your mind.'

I want you to love me for the woman I am. Not the woman you want me to become. But she couldn't say that. He'd never understand.

When the long silence stretched between them, Alex opened the flap to their tent. 'I'm going to meet with Robert the Bruce in the spring. He might be able to help our clan recover from our losses if we swear fealty to him.'

'Our freedom in exchange for silver?' she mused. 'To fight his battles against the English?'

'What choice do we have?'

'There's always a choice.' She met his gaze and pleaded, 'Don't go to the Bruce yet. I'll speak with Nairna and see if there are goods we can sell to earn a profit.'

'There's nothing we have, Laren. Everything was burned.'

She didn't argue with him, for he would only ask questions if she denied it. On the morrow, she would ask Nairna to help her visit the parish of Inveriston, to try to sell her glass.

She envisioned a stone building facing east with the sun glimmering through one of her windows. The bejewelled colours would cast coloured light upon the floor, illuminating the people.

The vision held her so tightly, she didn't notice when Alex went inside the tent alone. And when she finally joined him, she forgot about the pain of her wound, she was so entranced by the vision of glass and light.

It wasn't until morning that she realised he'd slept on the other side of the tent, far away from her.

May, 1300

The interior of the cottage was cold and dark. It lay on the outskirts of Glen Arrin, far away from the others. The faint scent of dried herbs lingered and she saw her mother Rós's abandoned drop spindle. Laren traced her fingers over the wooden walls, remembering how she'd huddled on the pallet with her younger sisters for warmth.

Some nights, when her father had managed to catch a trout from the loch, they'd feasted together, sharing the succulent fish. She remembered the way he'd told stories, exaggerating the adventure he'd had when trying to secure their meal.

Closing her eyes, she tried to will back the hurt. He'd never been good at farming or fighting, but he'd done his best at both. And he'd been a kind man.

'Laren?' came a male voice.

She turned and saw Alex standing in the doorway. Her breath caught and she had to push back the urge to fly into his arms.

'I thought I might find you here,' he said. 'Father Nolan told me your mother and sisters went to St Anne's.'

She nodded. Not by their choice, but by his mother's hand. Grizel MacKinloch had suspected their courtship and she'd done everything possible to separate them.

'I shouldn't be here,' she whispered. 'It was wrong of me to come back.'

'Why?' His hands moved around her waist, pulling her into a light embrace. 'I haven't seen you in two moons, and you behave as though it's been two years.'

'*You're the tánaiste now.*' *She knew what that meant, even if he was unwilling to acknowledge it. The future leader needed a woman of his own status, someone who could govern the clan.*

'*I won't be chief for many years yet,*' *he said.* '*It's a title and nothing else.*'

'*You have to wed a woman of status. It's expected of you.*'

'*I'll wed a woman of my choice and no one else.*' *There was a hard edge to his voice and she wondered what had happened during the weeks she'd left Glen Arrin.*

Gently, she touched his face. He didn't see her as low-born and something inside her blossomed, knowing that her poverty meant nothing at all to him. He'd never known what it was to go hungry when her father was too proud to ask for food. The other clan members hardly spoke to her at all, pretending as though her family didn't exist. If she were to wed Alex, and he became chief, she could only imagine their outrage. Why should a beggar deserve such a position?

Alex took the edges of his cloak and drew the wool around her, his body heat warming her. She could feel his body responding to her and wanted to lean in against him, letting him know how much she'd missed him.

But this wasn't only about her desires. It was about responsibility to her family. She'd seen Rós's happiness among the other nuns. No doubt her mother would seek to be a part of the religious community. Her sisters were too young to be married, but Grizel had promised to provide dowries for them, if their family stayed away.

'*Come with me,*' *he urged.* '*To our stone circle.*'

She wanted to tell him no, for even a single step would

bring her closer to surrendering her innocence. And it would be that much harder to let him go.

He kissed her and the warmth of his mouth pulled at her, reaching past her inhibitions and fears, until she could deny him no longer.

She followed him into the woods, even knowing she would regret it on the morrow. But her heart belonged to him and, if she would no longer see him again, at least she could have this time.

He shared his cloak with her, his hand holding hers as they walked. But when she saw the circle of torches and the priest waiting, she understood his intent and stopped walking.

'Alex, we can't.' She kept her voice low, not wanting Father Nolan to hear. 'You can't wed me.'

'I can. I swear to you, I'll not let you leave until you're my wife.' His strong arms trapped her in place and he led her over to one of the standing stones. He held up a hand to the priest, silently bidding the man to wait. 'What is it you're afraid of?'

She expelled a breath, staring at the wooded darkness. 'You're going to be the leader one day.'

'Years from now, perhaps.' He turned her chin to face him. 'Before that, I intend to be a husband. Perhaps a father.'

She didn't smile. 'If I wed you, my mother and sisters will suffer.'

She explained that Grizel had ordered her family sent away, offering dowries for her sisters in return. Alex's face darkened with fury. 'Do you believe I'd allow my mother to harm your family?'

He let his hands fall away, struggling to grasp at the

edges of his temper. 'I have possessions of my own, Laren. I can sell them and provide for your family.'

She shook her head. 'They would cut you off. Your uncle would never allow it.'

His brown eyes met hers and she saw a change in them. 'You said once, that I was the only man you wanted. Is that true?'

'Not if it means you have to make sacrifices for me.' Her voice trembled. 'I would never want you to live the way I did, growing up. We were an embarrassment to the clan.'

She lowered her forehead to his chest as though she could draw comfort from him. 'I would never want to bring shame to you. You would grow to resent me, for I could never be the wife of a chief.'

'Do you love me?' he asked. She heard his heartbeat beneath her cheek, and the words seemed to pull apart all her reasons for leaving him.

He forced her to look at him and when she did, she saw something beneath his stoic expression. Though he might be strong-willed, her refusal had wounded him.

'I will always love you,' she whispered. 'Even if you wed another, as you should.'

He took her hand in his, lacing their fingers together. 'I know there's a need within you not to live the way your parents did.'

She said nothing, for it was true. The fierce desire to lift herself out of the poverty, to help her family, burned inside her with a determination she wouldn't deny.

'Let me give you the life you should have had. All I want in return is you. I swear, I'll protect your family and live with whatever the consequences may be.'

Before she could voice an answer, his mouth covered

hers. He kissed her like she was the air he needed to breathe, everything he had ever wanted. She tasted his need, his desire, and as she lost herself in his arms she sensed how deeply it would cut him down if she left him. Even if it was the right thing to do.

Torn between her selfish desire to be with him and the damning consequences, she released her own feelings in the kiss. She clung to him, desperately trying to make him understand how much he meant to her.

The sound of someone clearing his throat only vaguely broke through the spell. Alex pulled back and she saw Father Nolan's reddened expression as he shifted his weight from one foot to the other. 'Shall we proceed?' the priest prompted.

'I'll give it up,' Alex said, 'if being the tánaiste means losing you.'

She saw that he meant it. And though she quailed at the thought of ever being a chief's wife, she couldn't let him walk away from this. It might be a dozen years before Alex would ever have to be the leader. Her doubts began to weaken when she shook her head. 'I won't let you give it up.'

'Will you take me as your husband?' he asked again. 'Will you let me protect you and make a home for us?'

She took his hand in hers, and said quietly, 'I will be your wife.' And I swear that I'll never bring shame upon you, *she vowed silently.* I will find a way to make myself worthy of being yours.

The priest began to speak a blessing in Latin as he joined their hands together. And when the marriage rite was completed, her new husband sent her a smile. 'Begone, Father Nolan. I'm wanting to be alone with my wife.'

Chapter Four

'Bring her to me.' Lord Harkirk lifted his hand and stared at the Scottish chief who stood before him. Finian MacLachor's dark hair was cast with grey, his clothing ragged. Blood trickled from his lip, while his gaze was focused upon the door.

Within moments, soldiers brought forth a young girl hardly more than ten years old. She was sobbing as the men gripped her arms.

'You should guard your women more carefully,' Harkirk said to the warrior. He enjoyed watching the man's face transform with a father's fury.

'Let her go,' MacLachor responded, his voice like the point of a sword.

'Not yet.' Harkirk folded his arms and gestured for the men to take the girl away.

She screamed, 'Da, don't let them take me. Please!'

MacLachor's face turned murderous, and if he'd had a weapon, no doubt Harkirk would have seen him lunge.

He didn't respond to his daughter's begging, but his cold grey eyes grew focused. 'What is it you want?'

Harkirk sat down upon the carved wooden chair, enjoying the man's discomfort. He accepted a cup of wine from a servant, taking a sip to clear his throat. Though he had more than a few Scottish prisoners held captive within his fortress, it wasn't enough. He'd suffered humiliation and defeat from the MacKinloch clan. And his ally, the Earl of Cairnross, had been brutally murdered by Bram MacKinloch.

'I want you to bring me the MacKinloch chief,' Harkirk answered. 'And his brothers.'

MacLachor's face twisted. 'Because they defeated you?'

Harkirk threw the cup of wine across the room, the silver goblet clattering against the floor. 'Because you want your daughter to live. And because I'll give her to my men to enjoy. If you want to see her again, her virtue intact, you'll bring me their heads.'

Although he had the forces to go after the MacKinlochs again, Harkirk saw no reason to risk the lives of English soldiers or the ire of his king. Edward Plantagenet was not known for mercy; though he wanted the Scots beneath his reign, his first priority was to dim the uprisings in the north-west region.

Harkirk calmed his temper, gathering a patience he didn't feel. There was a way to accomplish vengeance, using the blood of Scots instead of his own men. Better to unite the clans against the MacKinlochs, letting them take down his enemy. The king wouldn't care if the Scots murdered each other.

'We can't defeat them,' the MacLachor chief argued. 'The MacKinlochs are too strong.'

Harkirk crossed the room and grasped the man's throat

while his soldiers held the warrior's arms back. 'I watched their fortress burn. Everything they have lies in ashes. Now is the time to strike. And you'll do it for me, if you want your daughter to live.'

His face twisted in a smile. 'You can't protect all of them. A pity your wife is dead. But you have a sister, don't you?' He released the man's throat and ordered, 'You have until the Feast of Saint Agatha to bring me the first head. Or I'll take your daughter's instead.'

Alex brought Laren back to Glen Arrin the following morning. When she departed, the first place she went was towards Father Nolan's cavern on the far side of the loch. Frustration seeped through his mind and heart. Last night, he'd hoped to convince her to try harder, to be strong and stand at his side instead of abandoning him. But he'd begun to realise that Laren wasn't going to change.

When it had just been the two of them and young Mairin, Laren had been a different woman. She'd devoted her time to their baby, spending her free hours weaving. She'd always had an eye for colour, and he'd marvelled at the vivid tapestries she'd woven.

But, most of all, he remembered the way she would stop whatever she was working on and fly into his arms, greeting him with a warm kiss. He'd thrived upon her affection, looking forward to it at the end of each day.

Now, she rarely offered a kiss in greeting or in farewell. He missed that.

He watched Laren disappear along the shores of the loch, her red hair streaming out behind her from beneath the mantle she wore. And with every step she took away from him, it hurt a little more.

Alex took a breath and turned back to the task of setting

down the new foundation. He'd widened the space, making it larger than it was before. The structure of the keep was now the size of a Norman castle, one sizeable enough to keep several families together.

Bram was the first to notice what he'd done. 'This won't work, Brother. It'll take three times as long to build it from wood.'

'Not wood. Stone.' Alex stood up and pointed to the hills. 'We'll need to bring wagons up to the quarry, but this has to last longer. And the danger of fire is less.'

'We don't have the men to build something that large,' Bram argued. 'Has your mind gone soft?'

'It's what our father wanted,' Alex reminded him. When they'd been growing up, he well remembered sitting at Tavin's knee, hearing the promises his father had made. One day, the MacKinlochs would be strong enough to have a castle of their own. As a young boy, he'd looked up to his father, wanting so badly to make him proud.

And though Alex knew he wasn't the chief Tavin had wanted, he could give him this legacy.

'We'll build it in stages, starting with an outer wall.' Alex nodded toward the horizon. 'Lord Harkirk is going to attack again, so we'll need that defence.'

'We'd need twelve walls to hold him off,' Bram argued. From the doubt upon his brother's face, Alex knew he had a lot of convincing to do.

When they passed the stables, he saw that Dougal had built a makeshift shelter for the horses with Callum's help. The two men walked forwards to join them and Alex complimented him. 'The shelter looks good.'

Dougal acknowledged the compliment with a half-smile, but it faded. 'I thought you should know...Brodie is going east, to Perth. He's planning to live with his wife's family at the Murrays.'

'We need every man to stay, if we want to rebuild Glen Arrin,' Alex insisted.

Bram could only shrug. 'You'll have to talk to them.'

Alex didn't answer. He knew he had to bring them together, but would words accomplish anything? Too many had lost so much.

'Tell the others I want to talk with them tonight, then gather a group of men to go to the quarry,' he told Bram. To Dougal and Callum, he instructed, 'Prepare the horses and wagons.' It was going to take the better part of a year to finish a castle, but, if they worked hard over the next few weeks, they could get the foundation and outer wall completed.

Callum drew closer and rested his hand upon Alex's shoulder. Though his younger brother didn't speak, he exerted a slight pressure, as a gesture of support.

'We'll manage,' Alex told him. 'Somehow.'

As his brothers departed, Alex surveyed the damage. Only five huts had survived the fires, and they'd lost fourteen men and boys in the fight—nearly a third of their clan. The grief and frustration threatened to close over him, but he shut out the emotions.

Though he wasn't meant to be chief, he'd sworn a vow to himself that he would prove his father wrong. He'd promised to give everything he could to Glen Arrin, placing the people's needs before his own.

And yet it had all fallen apart.

They couldn't live this way, not with their pride splintered, their homes in ashes. Somehow, he had to gather the people back together. If they could help each other, they'd overcome their losses. But, most of all, they needed to rebuild their pride.

A hardness clenched his throat and his gaze shifted toward the loch and the site upon the hill, marked with a white stone. He couldn't forget his son's death. Not even after nearly three years had passed. He blinked, forcing his gaze away. He knew what his grieving kinsmen were feeling right now, with their family members gone. Work was what they needed, to take their minds off the suffering and to go on.

It was what he had done. Because the moment he allowed himself to stop and think, the numbing grief would close in.

Work was the answer. The only answer he'd found for himself, when Laren had shut him out.

'We'll leave for Inveriston in another day,' Nairna said. 'I'll speak to Bram and he'll arrange it.'

'I can't finish the glasswork by then!' The very idea was appalling. It took a full day and a half simply to make one colour, much less create a flat pane of glass.

Nairna's mouth curved in a sly smile. 'Oh, I don't expect you to finish. We're going to get you a commission. Bring one of your smaller pieces and a sketch of the design you want to do. We'll get the window measurements and they'll pay one-third of the cost up front, plus all of your supplies.'

Laren stopped arguing. She'd never thought about a commission. But the idea of having enough supplies and the chance to craft a window for one of the kirks… Her mind flooded with ideas.

'What if they try to cheat us again?' she asked, thinking of the time before when they'd sent Dougal to sell a piece of glass.

'Dougal sold the glass to a merchant, not an abbot. And what does a lad of four and ten know about silver coins?' Nairna moved to the back of the cavern, sorting through pieces. 'We'll use this one.'

She held up a frame that portrayed the rising sun over the loch. Laren had spent days trying to perfect the orange and yellow shades of glass and she'd experimented with the lead lines to create the effect of ripples in the water.

It was one of the first pieces that she'd been pleased with, a puzzle of glasswork that reminded her of the simple beauty around them.

'You'll tell them that it represents holy baptism,' Nairna went on.

Laren gaped at her. 'But it's just the loch at sunrise.'

Nairna gently set down the glass. 'Not to monks, it isn't. The sun represents the resurrection of Christ, while the holy water washes us clean of our sins.'

'It's the loch,' Laren repeated. She saw no reason to lie, not when the glass was pretty enough as it was.

Nairna put an arm around her and let out a sigh. 'You see, that's why you need me, Laren. We tell them what they want to hear and they will pay us a great deal for the honour.'

'Even if it's not the truth?'

'It's the truth,' Nairna insisted. 'Theirs, not yours.'

She still wasn't convinced, but Nairna had more experience with handling merchants and selling items. With a shrug, Laren acceded, 'I suppose.'

'Leave all of the bargaining to me. You simply measure for the windows and talk about what colours they want. And do *not*, under any circumstances, tell them that it's simply a loch.'

Laren smiled and Adaira came forwards, crawling into

her lap. Her daughter snuggled her face against her chest, and Laren held her close. There was a slight shadow of wistfulness upon Nairna's face and Laren knew her sister-in-law wanted a child of her own.

'I'm glad you're here, Nairna,' she said. 'And I hope we can profit from the glass, however slight it may be.'

'It won't be slight. I promise you that.' Nairna took Adaira from her, lifting the child into her arms. She murmured sweet words to the bairn, nestling Adaira's cheek against her own.

'How is Bram?' Laren asked as they walked around the far side of the loch.

'He hasn't forgotten the years he spent imprisoned.' Nairna shifted the child's weight to her opposite hip. 'And he's angry that Lord Harkirk still holds some of our countrymen captive. He talks of trying to free them.'

Laren shuddered at the thought of the men going off to fight again. She didn't want Alex endangering himself, not so soon after this battle. 'We have to keep our men here,' she insisted. Though she was afraid of the hardships ahead, it would be easier to manage if they stood together. 'They can't go off to fight. Not until we've rebuilt Glen Arrin.'

Nairna squeezed her hand and there was a silent promise between them. They would find a way to earn coins from the glass and pray God it would be enough.

The men were unloading stones from the wagons. Laren watched as they began forming a foundation while other workers built up walls around the outer perimeter of the fortress. She went to join the other women and they worked with the smaller stones, placing them into a dry stone wall. Her side ached, but her girls were eager to join in. They gathered pebbles, tucking them into crevices, believing they were helping.

Laren wiped her brow and cast a glance at the other men. Her husband was directing the construction and he wore nothing from the waist up. Neither did his brothers, nor their kinsmen. They were sweating from the hard labour and none appeared to notice the cool weather.

'I want a drink, Mama,' Mairin informed her.

'I'll get you one.' Laren took the girls by the hand and led them forwards, dipping a wooden cup into a barrel that held water from the loch. They shared it between them and Laren filled it again, intending to take it to Alex.

When she passed by the women, she saw them watching her. Though it made her uncomfortable, she turned back and explained, 'The men will be thirsty.'

'For water?' Vanora scoffed. 'Ross'll be wanting mead or ale.' But after Laren's suggestion, she, too, filled her cup until most of the women trailed behind, approaching the men. It felt awkward to her, having the others follow her example.

As Laren drew closer to her husband, mixed emotions of uncertainty and regret grew, centred inside her. Last night had begun almost as though Alex had wanted to start again, to mend the lost years. But as soon as she'd started to tell him why she spent time in the cavern, he'd focused only on her shyness.

Once, he'd loved her enough that it hadn't mattered. Now, she was afraid that he regretted marrying her. And she didn't know if she could be the wife he needed.

Before she reached her husband, her path was blocked by two of their kinsmen engaged in their own conversation. 'He's lost his mind, that's what,' said Brodie MacKinloch.

'Thinks he'll rebuild out of stone instead of wood? That'll take years and the English will kill us all in the meantime.'

'Who does he think he is?' said the other. 'An English lord?'

'We're leaving in the morning,' Brodie added. 'And unless you want t'be hauling stone for the next year, you'd best do the same.'

Laren didn't move, but the women behind her had also heard Brodie's complaints. The men couldn't possibly conceive of anything beyond the broken-down fortress they'd known for years. Alex was doing his best to rebuild, yet they had nothing to offer but criticism.

She doubted if anything she said would change their minds, but as she passed she sent them a hard look, letting them know she'd overheard their complaints.

When she reached Alex, he stopped working, his face furrowed. 'What is it?' he asked. 'Something with the girls?'

She fumbled with her words, uncertain of what to say. 'I just…wanted to see if you needed anything.' She lifted up the cup of water and Alex took it from her.

He drank, his eyes averted from her. 'Nairna told me that you talked this morning about a way to bring in more money for the clan.'

'Go on.' Laren kept her voice calm, though a cold anxiety filled up her veins. Had Nairna revealed anything to Alex?

'She said that you found some of Father Nolan's glass inside the cavern and that you wanted to sell it to the Inveriston monks.'

Laren's heart nearly stopped, but she realised that her sister-in-law had told Alex only enough to give them permission to go.

He stared at her and the penetrating look made her uncomfortable. 'You knew about the glass, didn't you?'

She gave a nod and her voice barely reached above a whisper. 'Nairna's right. We should try to sell it.'

Her husband set the cup back in her hands. 'A few weeks ago, when you sent Dougal away, was he trying to sell glass then? When he returned with counterfeit coins?'

She lowered her head in a nod. Guilt plagued her, for Dougal had got lost upon his journey home that night. 'I know we should have told you.'

'He won't be going this time,' Alex said. 'Bram will take Nairna and she'll arrange for it to be sold.'

'I want to go with them,' she blurted out, fully expecting him to say no. His gaze shifted to her bandaged side. To appease him, she added, 'If I've healed enough.'

'Why?'

In his eyes she saw more than a question. There was an emotion that he'd locked away and she found herself staring at the hardened face of a chief instead of her husband.

She took a risk and removed her glove. Without taking her gaze from his, she reached out to touch his fingertips. 'Because it's important to me.'

He didn't look down, as she'd hoped, but his hand laced with hers, his thumb caressing the edge of her burned palm.

The aching touch caught the pieces of her heart. She held motionless and, for a moment, it seemed that the crowds of people were no longer watching.

'Then go,' he said. Dark brown eyes stared into hers and she saw the longing in them.

She replaced her glove once more, half-afraid he would change his mind.

'Thank you,' she whispered.

With the spell broken, Alex pointed to the work they'd done. 'We've made good progress on the foundation. Better than I'd hoped. And the outer wall should be completed before the end of winter.'

She was acutely aware of his presence beside her. Once, he might have put his arm around her, warming her body with his cloak. Instead, he kept a careful distance.

'What we build here will be stronger than it was before,' Alex was saying.

'I hope so.'

The brief shadow of uncertainty passed over his face. Though no one could fault his efforts, she knew, as he did, that the people didn't want to rebuild the fortress in stone.

'We need to be safe from invasion,' he continued. 'And I think it's time we sent Mairin and Adaira off to be fostered. We've waited too long already.'

Her heart went cold, though she'd known the time would come. 'Adaira is just a bairn.'

'Do you want them here if Harkirk attacks again? It's too grave a risk.' His hands tightened at his sides. 'I don't want them hurt.'

She knew he was right, but the idea of sending her daughters away was like cutting off her arms. 'They're so young.'

'We could send them further north to the Orkney Islands,' he offered. 'My cousin and the Sinclairs would take them. They'd be safe from the English raids.' His face darkened at the mention of their enemy. 'This war isn't over yet.'

Laren could hardly see, for her eyes were blurred with tears. 'I'd rather wait until the spring. The journey would be safer for them.'

'And what if we're attacked in the meantime?'

'I want to spend these last few months with them.'

'You need to consider what's best,' he argued. 'You're thinking with your heart, not your head.'

'And what if I am?' she shot back. 'Why should I be so eager to send my girls away?' Her stomach hurt at the thought of being so alone.

'Because you don't want them to die.' His voice was cold, with no sympathy at all.

Laren said nothing, trying to blot away the searing memories. It had been almost three years now, but she hadn't let herself grieve. She'd locked away the pain of her son, forcing herself to think of the children who were alive and needed her.

'In the spring,' she repeated. 'Let me have this last winter with the girls.'

He let go of her hand. 'I'll make no promises. If there's even a sign of danger, they go.'

She supposed that was the best she could do. 'All right.' Glancing around, she said, 'Do you want me to see about a meal for the men?'

'I think Nairna has already organised it.'

When Laren looked over at her sister-in-law, she saw that Alex was right. The women were busy cutting up mutton, while others were starting to set up hearth fires for cooking.

'I'll see what I can do to help them, then,' she said, starting to move away from him.

'Laren,' he interrupted. 'Tonight, when I speak to the men, perhaps you could address the women. Hear their concerns and tell me what it is they're thinking.'

'I can't,' she answered immediately.

'I'm not asking you to speak to them,' he reiterated. 'Only to hear them. I don't think that's too difficult.'

In his eyes, she saw the fervent wish that she would suddenly cast off her shyness and become someone else. Someone strong, who didn't hide herself away.

She closed her eyes, wishing she had the strength to try.

January, 1303

The tiny body was cold and rigid within the grave. Her son, her beloved David, was gone.

Laren couldn't voice a single word. He'd been alive for only four days and it seemed impossible that he'd breathed his last.

Hadn't she felt his soft face against the curve of her breast? Hadn't he cried until she'd comforted him, reassuring him of how much she loved him?

Beside her, Alex was silent. The shock of their son's death had been an ill omen, now that her husband was chief. It cast a shadow over them and she felt as though they were a thousand miles apart.

Her body was weakened from giving birth, but she couldn't bear to eat or drink. The numbing grief consumed her. Though Alex said something after Father Nolan completed the final blessing, she didn't hear it.

She walked away from him, needing solitude. She couldn't bear to hear any words of comfort, nor did she deserve his embrace.

Her path led her around the edge of the loch, leaving everyone behind. Even Mairin.

She couldn't cry, couldn't scream, couldn't rage against the Fate that had torn her baby out of her life. All she could do was walk. And when she heard Alex's footsteps following behind, she didn't turn around.

Chapter Five

Laren had just given the girls over to Vanora for an evening meal when Bram approached. 'I saw the glass before Nairna wrapped it,' he said. His voice was low and there was a warning hidden within his tone. 'You're going to tell Alex about this before we go.'

Her face must have revealed her hesitation, for he added, 'If you don't tell him, I will. Be assured of it.'

She hadn't expected her brother-in-law to react so strongly. 'Why does it matter if I tell him now or later? For all we know, it may have no value at all to the monks.' She clenched her fists, her nerves trembling.

'Oh, it has value. And if I know my wife, she'll get exactly what she wants.' He nodded towards Nairna, who was busy speaking to a small group of women. 'I've heard the others talking. They haven't the brains God gave a carrot, but they think you're spending your time in idleness. They've formed a false opinion of you.'

'I don't care what they think of me.'

'It reflects poorly on Alex. If they knew the truth, they

would show more respect to both of you.' Bram reached
forwards and touched her glove. 'You have until morning
to tell him.' The scars around his throat tightened and she
understood that he would uphold the threat.

While Bram returned to the wall the men were con-
structing, Laren let out the breath she'd been holding. She
didn't feel at all ready to reveal this to Alex. Not when he
was fighting to keep their clan together, to unite them in
the rebuilding.

But Bram's words burrowed beneath her skin like a
barb. *They think you're spending your time in idleness.*

She wasn't. The glass she made did have value; she
knew it in her heart. Somehow, she would use it to help
all of them.

The torches flared in the darkness as Alex stood before
the men. Once, there had been nearly three dozen. Now,
they numbered fewer than twenty. In their faces, he saw
discontent and frustration. 'I thought we should join
together and talk,' he began. 'Some of you seem to have
doubts about our rebuilding.'

'It's a waste of energy,' came the voice of Brodie
MacKinloch. 'We haven't the men to build a castle. And
what would we need it for? Our clan isn't important
enough. The English will simply return and destroy what's
left of us, now that the French are gone.'

'If we build our homes of wood, they'll simply burn us
out again,' Alex responded. 'It's a greater waste of time.'

'But faster.' Brodie stood, studying the faces of their
kinsmen. 'You seem to think we're one of the great clans
of the north. But look at us. We've nowhere to live and
hardly any food. If we want to survive the winter, we'll
have to leave.'

Alex saw the agreement dawning over the faces of the men and he had to put a stop to it. 'We've enough to make it through the winter, if everyone shares.' He stood up and met Brodie face to face. 'Years ago, Tavin dreamed of building a great castle, one to defend our people. But we never believed we could do it.'

'Because we *can't*,' Brodie argued.

Alex stepped forwards, using his height to stare down at the man. 'And you're going to let the English defeat us, are you? You're going to run away to your wife's family in Perth, hiding like a coward?' He raised his voice almost to a shout. 'They may have burned Glen Arrin to the ground, but I'll not let them scatter our clan. They will *not* divide us.'

His anger was barely contained, rising into a fury. 'We're going prove to them that we're stronger. And if they dare to attack us again, their blood will fall upon our soil.'

'Alex,' came the voice of his friend Ross, 'perhaps it's better to be practical than to dream of castles and a fortress we can't afford.'

He spun, confronting the older man. 'You don't believe our clan is worth fighting for?'

'We've been fighting the English for years now,' Ross said. 'And they keep coming back. We can't get rid of them.'

'They want us to give up,' Alex said quietly. 'They want us to hang our heads and dwell upon our losses, believing we're not strong enough.' He stared into the eyes of each and every man, letting his words fall upon them. 'But they're wrong.'

He pointed to the hills and mountains in the distance. 'We have wood from our forests. Stone from the mountains. And the labour of our hands. If we don't stand together, more English garrisons will spread across Scotland. We've seen it with our allies and our enemies.' He met Ross's apprehensive look, adding, 'If our clan splits apart, we'll have nothing. Not our friends. Not our clan. Not our freedom.'

An air of silence descended over the men. 'If we rebuild our past mistakes, we'll only repeat them.' He turned to face the foundation of stone, pointing towards it. 'It will take time, aye. It won't be finished by the spring, or even next winter. But if we build it the way it should be created, out of the sweat of our backs and the best materials we can find, it will last.' He turned back to them. 'And it will remain standing when the English are gone from Scotland.'

His words descended upon them and the mood among the men shifted. Alex strode away, having said all he could. He walked through the darkness, hoping he'd convinced them. Along the way, Nairna's dog Caen trotted behind him. Though the animal likely only wanted food, it was good to have at least one supporter of his ideas.

When he reached Ross's house, he scratched Caen's ears. The homely dog licked his fingers, arching with delight from the affection. 'Go back to Nairna,' he ordered.

Caen expelled a whuff of air and went on his way. When Alex entered the hut, he saw Vanora tending the fire while his daughters slept upon a pallet. 'Where is Laren?'

Vanora shook her head. 'She said she'd forgotten something that she left behind on her walk earlier.' The matron lifted her shoulders in a shrug. 'I would have gone after her, except I couldn't leave the girls. I suppose she must have lost track of the time.'

'How long has she been gone?'

'An hour or so.'

A dark fear clenched inside him, for he couldn't understand why Laren would have left the girls alone for so long. It wasn't like her at all. He had visions of her lying unconscious and bleeding from the wound she refused to take care of.

Alex grabbed a torch and strode from the fortress, not bothering to notify his brothers of where he was going. He planned to scour the edges of the loch, praying he wouldn't find her anywhere near the water.

The night sky was clouded and moonless, and his torch cast a flickering reflection against the surface of the water. He ran through the sand, his eyes searching the ground in front of him. His blood pulsed with fear, and as he kept searching he smelled the scent of smoke. Though he knew Dougal had dumped a pile of ashes not far from here, the odour was stronger, almost as if a fire were smouldering.

His senses went on alert and movement caught his eye. Ahead, he saw a dark figure moving. He raised the torch and saw the gleam of Laren's red hair. *Thank God.* He breathed a little easier as she approached. Her eyes were weary, as though something troubled her.

'Where were you?' he asked. 'When Vanora didn't know where you were, I worried that you were hurt.'

'I'm all right,' she said, moving past him.

But he caught her gloved hand and forced her to stop. 'You had a reason for coming out here alone. What was it?'

She shivered in the darkness. 'I was just making sure the glass was ready for our journey. I…wanted to be certain we were taking the best pieces.'

Around her body, he caught the scent of fire smoke. And once again, he saw the faint perspiration on her skin, as though she'd been standing near a hot fire for a long time. She seemed to sense his unease.

'Alex,' she murmured, 'there's something I need to show you.'

From the heaviness in her voice, he didn't know what to think. She was acting nervous, almost as though she were afraid of him.

He followed her along the edge of the loch. Before he realised it, they were standing in front of the small white stone that rested on the hill. Laren started to walk past it, but Alex trapped her hand. 'Wait.'

He didn't want to pass their son's grave without voicing a silent prayer for David's soul. 'I wondered if perhaps you came walking here, to be with him.'

In the moonlight, her face had gone so white, she looked miserable. 'I can't look at it whenever I walk past,' she admitted. 'It hurts too much to think of him.'

Though it had been almost three years since David had died, not a day went by when he didn't imagine how their lives would have been different. This was the son he'd longed for. The boy he'd wanted to follow in his footsteps, just as he had idolised his own father Tavin.

Laren closed her eyes, but she didn't weep. The more he thought of it, she hadn't wept at all when she'd held the infant's body in her arms. Instead, she'd locked her grief deep inside, the way he had.

Not once had he released his emotions, for he'd had to be strong for their family. And though it weighed upon his spirit, he couldn't reveal his pain in front of the clan. It was best to let David go and not to let anyone know how deeply it had affected him.

'He'll never be forgotten,' he said at last.

'No.' She lowered her face, wrapping her arms around her waist.

Though it was dark, he could see the pain on her face. Like a haunted spirit, he sensed her fading away from him. He hadn't meant to hurt her by bringing her here; he'd only intended to honour their son's memory.

'Come,' he said, leading the way. 'You wanted to show me something.'

Laren joined him and they walked through the sand to the entrance of Father Nolan's cavern. He saw the light glowing from the far side and immense heat radiated within the air. From a first glimpse, the cavern appeared other-worldly, almost as if it were inhabited by fey spirits. Apprehensions took root inside him, and when he looked to Laren, her face masked any reaction.

She stopped at the entrance and gestured for him to go inside. When he did, he saw a boy tending the fires, slightly younger than Dougal. Ramsay was his name, Alex recalled.

The boy froze at the sight of Alex and stared down at the ground, his hands clenched with uncertainty.

'It's all right,' Laren murmured. She nodded toward the outside. 'Thank you for keeping the fire going. Go and get some sleep now. You can return in the morning.' She reached into a pouch that hung at her side and handed him some dried meat and an oat cake, that he accepted.

'I started the green melt,' Ramsay muttered, before he crammed the food into his mouth and fled.

Alex had no idea what the boy was talking about, but the interior of the cavern was roasting hot. He removed his cloak and loosened his tunic, walking in front of the furnaces. Rows of pipes were set within one of the openings and inside another he saw clay crucibles.

When he reached the last fire, he turned to face his wife. Laren's blue eyes stared at him and slowly she removed her gloves.

Upon her hands and forearms he saw mottled red skin and burn marks he'd never noticed before. 'My God, what happened to you?'

Alex crossed the cavern to examine her. From the look of them, they were not recent marks. Even so, he was almost afraid to touch the skin, for fear of hurting her.

'When did you burn yourself?' It seemed that there were multiple scars, some older than others.

'The burns are from the times when I caught a heated segment of the pipe. Or when I was careless with the fire.'

Alex stared at Laren. 'You're saying that the glass Nairna wants to sell…is yours?'

She lowered her head in a nod, then raised it again. 'Yes.'

He kept his stare fixed upon her. If she'd said she'd created diamonds out of grass, he couldn't have been more surprised. But it did explain why she disappeared each day for hours on end. And why her hair often smelled of smoke.

And the scars upon her hands.

He couldn't take his eyes off her burned skin, unable to grasp the truth of it. It was as if the woman he'd married had disappeared, leaving another woman in her place. 'When did you learn to make glass?' he asked, keeping his distance from her.

'Almost three years ago.' Her voice was quiet, emotionless. 'Just after we lost David.'

Though she was saying something about how she'd needed to bury herself in work, that she couldn't be around the keep because it reminded her too much of the baby, all he could think of was that she'd harmed herself.

By playing with fire, she'd caused scars that would never go away. She'd taken grave risks, injuring herself, to make glass that she'd hidden in this cavern. The image still didn't fit the wife he'd married.

Laren. *His Laren.* Making glass?

She hardly talked to anyone and seemed overwhelmed at the thought of running a household. How could she transform sand and other elements into glass? It seemed impossible.

He caught her hand, another suspicion taking root. 'There were nights when you said you needed to sleep with the girls.' He kept a firm pressure upon her fingers. 'Did you leave Glen Arrin to tend the furnace?'

Her face paled, but she admitted the truth. 'Yes. After all the work I'd done, I didn't want the fire to go out and lose the glass. I had to do it alone, the first few months after Father Nolan died. I lost many, many melts until Ramsay agreed to be my apprentice.'

There were so many lies she'd told, so many deceptions... He no longer knew what to think of her. Why hadn't she confessed the truth? Why would she build up stories about taking walks, about sleeping with the girls because they were frightened of the dark?

And most of all, why hadn't he noticed? All of the signs had been there.

Mingled emotions fumbled within him, anger and confusion, but shadowed beneath them was the question that bothered him most. 'Why didn't you tell me?'

She looked at her scarred hands, her mood turning sombre. 'Because I knew you'd be angry with me. And in the beginning, nothing I made was good.' She turned her gaze to the heated stones, drawing her knees up to her chest. 'The colours were wrong. The glass cracked apart when I tried to cut it. Nothing I did had any sort of beauty.'

'Then why continue?'

'Because it kept me from thinking of David. I lost myself in the work and it made it easier to bear the pain. It didn't matter to me that I wasn't good enough. It was my escape,' she whispered.

'You used to weave tapestries,' he reminded her.

She shook her head. 'I couldn't touch a loom any more, because the last thing I wove was clothing for the baby. Making glass was different.' She turned back and raised her scarred hands to him. 'I remember each of my mistakes and I won't repeat them.'

He went to her and touched her knuckles, studying the marred skin. He confronted her, unable to let go of the betrayal. 'You lied to me.'

Laren didn't deny it. But she'd been half out of her mind after losing David and had needed solitude. She simply couldn't face the grief or her husband. Being around Alex only reminded her of the tiny infant who had stared at her with solemn blue eyes. The child who would never grow into a man. Even now, the memory of her son's face brought a searing pain to her heart.

Working with the glass had saved her from shattering apart and she couldn't regret the apprenticeship with Father Nolan.

'I'm sorry.' She folded her hands, wishing he could understand. 'But I knew you wouldn't approve.'

'You're right.' He let go of her, rising to his feet. 'It's dangerous and you've already injured yourself.'

'It hasn't happened in a while,' she confessed. 'I take precautions with the fires and it's not as dangerous as you think it is.' She reached for a crucible and added a blend of sand, lime and copper. She slid the clay container into the furnace, using a length of iron. 'If I can sell the glass to the monks at Inveriston, the silver might help us.'

'There are other ways we can earn coins for the clan, Laren.' He crossed his arms, as though he didn't want her to leave Glen Arrin.

She'd expected his response, but not the surge of determination that filled her. 'I may not be as skilled as Father Nolan was, but it's good enough for the kirk.' She walked over to the stone surface where she'd laid out pieces of glass she'd cut and arranged into a wooden frame.

Alex stood with his back to her, silent for a long moment. She waited for his footsteps to approach, for him to see her work. Instead, he held his distance. 'What other secrets have you kept from me?'

'I've told you everything.' But from the distrust in his tone, she could see that he didn't believe her.

He stood at the doorway, his expression unreadable. She tried not to let his cool demeanour hurt her feelings, but it did. It seemed that he didn't even want to look at what she'd done. 'Are you coming back with me?'

She shook her head. 'I can't leave the melts—I've already sent Ramsay away.'

'Stay, then, if that's your wish.' He cast a glance toward the stone table before he left the cavern, but he said nothing more. She'd hoped that somehow his reaction would be different, that he'd find beauty in her work. But all he could see was her lie of omission.

Loneliness clenched her spirit as she neared the entrance to the cave and saw him trudging along the edge of the loch. The moonlight reflected off the silvery surface and Alex stopped at the hillside where their son was buried. For a moment, he got down on one knee, as if voicing a quiet prayer.

Laren closed her eyes and forced herself to retreat back into the cavern. She couldn't allow herself to think of David now.

As she touched the smooth glass, she concentrated on fitting together the broken pieces to decide where the lead lines would go.

She spent the next hour cutting the green glass into pieces, scoring the surface with a hot blade and cracking it apart before filing it smooth. But no matter how many hours' worth of work there was, she couldn't silence the worries in her mind.

Already she wasn't the wife Alex wanted. And now that she'd revealed everything to him, it had made no difference at all. She sat down, resting her head upon one hand. She'd made excuses about her shyness, telling herself that she couldn't be Lady of the clan.

Had she been hiding away with her glass, retreating from the outside world? It was true that the others ignored her, but was it because she'd done the same to them?

She didn't have many friends among the women of the clan. Only Vanora and Nairna, if she were honest with herself, and that was only because she'd spent more time with them. Even if she could overcome her fears, she sensed that the others wouldn't want anything to do with her. Already they believed she spent her time in idleness.

As she tended the fires, her eyes blurred from exhaustion and regret. She didn't know how to mend her broken marriage or overcome her timidity.

The only thing she was certain of was that she couldn't live like this any more.

February, 1303

For over a month, his wife remained distant. Alex saw the wild grief in her eyes and nothing could take away the pain. From morning until night, Laren avoided the castle keep. She hadn't touched the cradle he'd made for David, nor had she put away the baby clothes she'd sewn. It was as if, by keeping the room the way it was on the day their son had died, she could somehow forget what had happened.

At night, she curled away from him on her side, as if she couldn't bear to be near him. As if it were his fault, somehow, that their son was gone.

He never spoke to her about it, for fear that it would unleash the frail bonds that held back his own anger and grief.

Then, one night, he'd found her sitting in their bed, holding the infant gown she'd made for their son.

'It doesn't seem real,' she whispered. 'It's as if I could look back in his cradle and find him there. Sometimes I hear him cry, in my mind.'

His throat closed in, but he remained standing in the doorway. Her words conjured up the crippling grief he held inside.

She folded the gown, looking down upon it. She looked so lost, so broken, he wanted to go to her and hold her tight. To grieve together, the way he needed to.

'I know I have to let him go, don't I?' She turned to him, and the stricken look on her face caught him like a spear in his heart. 'Could you...help me put his things away?'

She wanted him to sit beside her, to fold the tiny garments. To return their chamber to the way it was. Alex started to take a step forwards, but then his gaze fell upon the tiny wooden sword he'd made as a gift for his son.

God help him, he couldn't do it. If he dared to come any closer to Laren, the tight control he had over his emotions was going to break.

In the end, he did the only thing he could. He left her sitting there alone.

Chapter Six

The next morning, Laren didn't see Alex at all. Dougal had said something about him being at the rock quarry with the others and she didn't know if he intended to bid her farewell for the short journey to Inveriston. When she started to walk towards the horses, she looked around for her daughters.

Mairin caught sight of her and raced over. 'Mama, I found these for you.' She placed small rocks in Laren's hand, beaming as though she'd given her diamonds.

'For you,' Adaira echoed, handing her some bruised blades of grass. The young toddler pursed her lips together and Laren bent down to give her a kiss.

When she'd promised the girls that she'd be back by nightfall, she gave up waiting for her husband and mounted the mare Dougal had readied for her. Her side was healing well now and it no longer pained her.

Bram sent her a hard look. 'Isn't Alex coming?'

'No,' Laren answered, 'but he knows about the glass.' When he started to ask another question, Nairna brought her horse over and shook her head, speaking softly to her husband. Thankfully, Bram let it go and led the way toward Inveriston.

All throughout the ride to the parish, Laren agonised over her conversation with Alex. She'd hoped that he would be surprised by the glass, even proud of her. Instead, he'd hardly said a word. The longer she thought about it, the more upset she became.

She'd poured her heart into the glass, giving it life with her breath. It was more than art. It was pieces of herself, destroyed by fire and born again into something beautiful.

Her hands clenched upon the reins of the horse, her cheeks growing colder from the wind. She wished they could go back to their life years ago, when they had lived with only each other. When they could close out the world and lie in each other's arms, content and whole.

She wanted him to love her the way he once had. When just being herself was enough for him.

Regardless of how far they'd drifted, he was the man she wanted. She still loved him, even though he'd become so different. He spent so many hours away from her and the girls, only coming back after he'd traversed every inch of Glen Arrin and talked to every family.

Or had he done so because he didn't want to come home any more? Her head lowered. The wrenching pain of the marriage was pulling her heart in two.

She watched Nairna and Bram riding alongside one another. Though the couple didn't speak, their eyes met from time to time. Their love was strong, their happiness tangible. She wanted that back for her own marriage.

You have to be the wife Alex needs, her mind asserted. *You have to be stronger and face the people.*

She didn't know if she could cloak herself in confidence, becoming another woman. Or if it would mean giving up the glass she loved.

Laren stared at the green hills, watching the mist drift across the trees. Transient and light, the low clouds were hardly visible in the sunlight. The way she sometimes felt among the clan. They didn't see her or know her. The truth was, she wasn't at all happy at Glen Arrin, aside from the time she spent with her daughters or with her glass.

Perhaps she should try to befriend the other members of the clan, not for Alex…but for herself. It might lessen the loneliness that she felt when he wasn't there.

Laren clutched the leather-wrapped package of glass and the closer they came to Inveriston, the more her stomach hurt. *Please, God, let it have value.*

Her nerves trembled as Bram drew their horses to a stop and helped her down. Laren followed them inside the stone courtyard. While as Bram set up the meeting with the abbot, she stared at the interior of the monastery.

Within the chapel, she heard the echoing rise of the monks singing. The space was dark and enclosed, with only a small square window near the top, angled to prevent the rain from entering.

They won't want my window, she told herself. It wasn't at all practical, for they would have to knock down part of the wall to open up the space. The more she eyed the monastery, the more she saw how plain it was. Men who lived and worshipped in such a space would not want colours to distract from their prayers.

Before she could form another thought, Nairna was leading her forwards and unwrapping the leather parcel of glass. While her sister-in-law extolled the qualities of the glass, explaining how the light could enter, Laren studied the abbot. His wrinkled face was impassive, unimpressed by what he saw.

Her gaze fell to the ground. It wasn't good enough, as she'd feared.

But then he spoke. 'Thirty pennies.'

Her gaze snapped to Nairna's in disbelief. Bram's hand came down upon hers in a warning to be silent. His wife smiled at the abbot. 'I would think that a man of God would be ashamed to offer such a price, for something of such quality.'

'We are but humble brethren, with few coins to spare.'

'I am deeply sorry to hear it,' Nairna said, wrapping up the window. 'For I know such a window would bring comfort to many in their prayers. I had hoped that you might wish to commission a window for the new kirk you're building. Our glass artist could create a window of any size, with any Biblical scene that might inspire others to faith.'

She nodded to Bram. 'We'll continue on our journey to Locharr, and perhaps the Baron will want the window for his private chapel.'

Laren squeezed Bram's hand, seeing thirty pennies disappear with Nairna's words.

'Wait.' The abbot reached for the window. 'Let me see it again. It might be that I could obtain some funds from the bishop. And...' his gaze focused upon Bram '...if you believe it's possible to build larger windows, it would make our chapel a more fitting site for the relic we've just acquired.' The abbot blessed himself, saying, 'It's a splinter from the Holy Rood.'

Laren made the sign of the cross, as was expected of her. And though most pilgrims would be overwhelmed by the thought of such a relic, her instincts warned that any splinter of wood could look like another. How would they know if it really was the True Cross or not?

But then, such thoughts were blasphemous. She shouldn't let her doubts affect the faith of others.

She cleared her throat and interrupted, 'Father, seeing as the kirk will be dedicated to the Holy Rood, would you desire a window representing the crucifixion?'

She could envision a three-panelled window with saints on either side, and an image of Christ. Already she was imagining a deep gold glass to create a halo effect, but she would need a special dark enamel to create the shadows of a face. The idea intrigued her, for she'd never tried it yet.

'Who is this?' the abbot asked Bram, and Laren recognised the censure in his voice. This was not a man who would believe a woman capable of creating glass, much less a window that would inspire the people.

'I am the...sister of the glass artist,' she lied. 'He couldn't come, but he wanted me to answer any questions you might have, if you decided upon the commission.'

Nairna sent her a warning look, but the abbot didn't seem upset by her lie. Instead, he looked pleased by it. 'I would like to know how your brother achieves such wondrous colours.'

Laren met her sister-in-law's gaze and remembered Nairna's words. *Tell them what they want to hear.*

'He prays and fasts before he does any melt,' she lied again, and offered, 'Sometimes he is rewarded by beautiful colours in the glass, but there are times when the melts fail. It humbles him,' she explained and saw Nairna roll her eyes.

'I believe we should settle upon our business now,' Nairna interrupted. 'If you wish to purchase this glass for your brethren, the price is one hundred pieces of silver.'

Only the pressure of Bram's hand upon hers kept Laren from screeching at the unholy price Nairna had demanded.

The abbot laughed at her. 'You must be mad.'

Within another quarter of an hour, Nairna had managed to scrape seventy-five silver coins from the abbot, plus an additional fifty pieces to cover the cost of glass supplies. The remaining hundred and fifty coins for the commissioned window would be paid in stages. The final amount to be given upon delivery of the glass.

'You'll need to take the measurements,' Nairna said, nodding to Bram.

Laren handed him a spool of thick yarn, but the abbot declined, saying, 'I will send one of our priests with the measurements, once we've determined the proportions of the chapel. He will also bring a sketch of what we have decided for the subject of the window.'

With the matter settled, Bram thanked the abbot, and Laren joined Nairna in bidding farewell. As they departed with the coins, she sent a last look towards the abbot and caught him smiling at the glass.

She looked away, hardly able to breathe. Her heart pounded so hard, her ears roaring, until she thought she might faint. One hundred and twenty-five pieces of silver. Because of her glass.

By the saints, she couldn't believe it. She could barely manage to hold her thoughts together as they rode away. Nairna and Bram had ridden ahead of her, while she continued behind them. As she rode through the valley, she couldn't stop her hands from shaking.

The wind stung at her eyes, and she followed them for several miles more, before Nairna stopped to wait for her.

When she caught up, the woman threw her hands up in the air and let out a celebratory scream.

Laren couldn't laugh or join Nairna the way she wanted to. Instead, the shock of success left her speechless. She hadn't truly believed the abbot would want her glass or that he would find her work worthy of paying for it.

'What's wrong?' Nairna asked, coming up beside her. 'You should be happy.'

She took her hand and Laren tried to brave a smile. 'It's just…too much. I can't believe he would pay such a sum for a simple pane of glass.'

'It's not simple,' Nairna insisted. 'And when everyone finds out that you were responsible for bringing in such wealth, they—'

'No.' She cut Nairna off. Though she'd have to tell Alex about their success, she wasn't ready to be put on display before the rest of the clan. Trepidation seeped into her veins, freezing up her courage. 'I have to talk to Alex about it first.'

Nairna squeezed her hand. 'You'll be the one to tell him what we've done this day. He'll be proud of you, I know.'

Laren wanted so badly to believe it. But as they began the journey home, her worries continued to grow.

Alex rode hard, Dougal and Callum trailing behind him. Brodie and his family had travelled just past the boundary of Glen Arrin, ignoring everything Alex had said the other night.

Damn the man for giving up so soon.

He pushed his gelding hard, bringing the animal up in front of Brodie, forcing the family to stop. 'I won't let you turn your back on us, Brodie. We're your clan. Your family.'

Brodie's wife sent her husband a troubled gaze, her arms tightening around their young son. 'It's not safe to live here any more, is it?'

'Can their horses travel through walls?' Alex countered. 'Can they burn down the stone?' He could see the flicker of uncertainty on Brodie's face and continued. 'If we had rebuilt Glen Arrin in wood, aye. We'd be vulnerable. But we've made a strong start.'

'We're taking him away from the fighting.' Brodie's hand went to rest upon his son's shoulder. 'He'll be safe.'

'Aye, he will. Here, with his family and friends.' Alex led his horse close enough that he could reach out to Brodie. 'Turn back and look at Glen Arrin, Brodie.'

His kinsman did and, for a time, neither spoke. He wanted his friend to see the vast walls stretching around Glen Arrin, like a shield. 'It's already changed from the place our fathers built. And when we're gone, it will still be standing, for our children.'

He regarded Brodie and saw the indecision on his face. 'What legacy do you want to leave? The memory of a father who fought and won his freedom? Or a man who abandoned his clan, out of fear?'

Finian MacLachor stared at the fortress of Glen Arrin. Though the main structure was destroyed, there were two rows of outer walls being constructed from stone. The men were already working, and the smoke of outdoor fires blended in the cold air. The winter chill cut through his body, but he felt nothing at all.

His sister had begged him not to war with the MacKinlochs. 'You can't be Harkirk's executioner,' she'd said. 'Don't invoke the wrath of another clan.'

Especially a clan they'd been friends with. Tavin

MacKinloch had been like an older brother to him, when they were fostered together. He'd been only a boy, but Tavin had shown Finian how to fish in the lochs, how to hunt and how to charm women into getting what he wanted.

The memory brought an ache of regret. Tavin had been a good man. And though their clans had grown apart with their new chief Donnell, they hadn't raided one another. It was a respectful distance, one he was about to break.

The chainmail armour he wore was heavy, the icy links frigid against his skin. One hostage was all he needed. Someone close to the chief, perhaps their youngest brother. Or a wife. If he took a captive, the brothers would follow. They would hunt down his prisoner and then he would have all of them. His men could capture the MacKinlochs and take their heads to Harkirk.

Finian closed his eyes, the revulsion rising within him. This was Iliana, his daughter. The girl he adored, his only child. Already he could imagine the horrors Harkirk had brought against her and his blood raged at the thought. But when he'd tried to raise a group of men against the English Baron a sennight ago, the soldiers had cut them down. Finian had been the only survivor.

Harkirk's message was clear—rise up against me and suffer the consequences.

The MacLachor people now numbered fewer than fifteen. And the only way to save his daughter was to carry out the devil's work himself.

Moving closer, he dropped near to the ground, keeping hidden. He watched the women and children, searching for the right victim. Regardless of his personal morals, this unholy task had to be done.

And when his gaze fell upon his chosen prisoner, he

knew that Alex MacKinloch and his brothers would not hesitate to fight for her. The only question was how to infiltrate the fortress. It would take time.

Time he didn't have.

Alex rested his hand upon the top edge of the gate house, staring into the distance. The twilight clouds were starting to lift, the mist drifting over the green hills. Brodie and his family had returned to Glen Arrin and it had brought a ripple of change among the people. Although the doubts were still there, he saw them eyeing the fortress in a new way.

He held fast to the hope that they would stand together. Though he believed they could emerge from this crisis stronger than ever, the people had to have faith.

From the valley, he spied a small group of horses. It was Bram and Nairna, returning with Laren. And as they drew closer, he saw a buoyant air of satisfaction in their bearing. Nairna was riding with Bram, while her horse held several bundles of what looked like supplies.

Laren looked uneasy, her gaze lowered to her hands. At the sight of her return, some of his tension eased, knowing that they were safe.

He'd spent most of last night, thinking about her and regretting what he'd said. But damn it all, why couldn't she trust in him? Why had she felt the need to hide herself and her deeds, as though he would punish her for them?

After the travelling party grew closer, Alex descended the stairs of the gate house, going to greet them. He closed off his troubled thoughts and waited as his wife approached. Laren's face revealed her own uncertainty as she dismounted, while Nairna had a broad smile upon her face. Bram's wife was nearly ready to explode with her news, but she grabbed Laren's hand and pushed her forwards. 'Tell him!'

Alex looked into Laren's blue eyes and she admitted at last, 'We sold the glass. Nairna negotiated one hundred and twenty-five pieces of silver from the monks.'

'Can you believe it?' Nairna gushed. 'The abbot had never seen work like hers before.' Without giving either of them a chance to speak, she lifted up the sack of coins and added, 'We stopped to buy more food and supplies for the clan along the way home.'

Nairna's excitement should have been infectious, but he was more concerned over Laren's face. She didn't look as happy as she should.

Alex went to help unload the bundles and Laren joined at his side, her gaze downcast. He walked alongside her, slowing his pace until Nairna and Bram had continued on with the coins. When they were alone, he stopped. 'Something's troubling you.'

He waited for her to speak, and Laren lifted her gaze to his. Her expression held worry instead of joy. 'I'm glad I was able to help the clan,' she said at last. 'I was hoping we could sell the glass.'

'And?' He waited for her to say more.

'And I'm not upset about the glass. I'm happy, truly.' She knotted her fingers together. 'I'm upset about the way you left me last night.' Her blue eyes were filled up with emotion, her face struggling to remain passive.

He didn't know what to say to her. It wasn't possible to dismiss the deception, for it had revealed a deeper fissure in their marriage. Even Nairna and Bram had known about the glassmaking before him and it bruised his pride to know it.

'I don't want us to go on like this,' she murmured. 'It hurts too much.'

He didn't know what she meant by that, but he didn't like it at all. It sounded as if she'd rather be alone than married to him.

'I don't know what I've done to make you shut me out,' he said at last. 'But you never talk to me. You tell me nothing of your thoughts, nothing of what it is you want.' He touched her gloved hand and pulled it off, uncovering her scarred hand. 'I can't read your secrets.'

'We don't know each other any more, do we?' she whispered, her eyes filling up. 'It's not the same as it once was. And I don't know how to change it.' She replaced the glove he'd removed and pulled the edges of her cloak around her.

She was right. Ever since David's death, they'd become different people. They'd grown distant, leading separate lives within their marriage.

When she'd been shot with the arrow, it had been the awakening he'd needed. He'd let the years slip away from him, along with his wife. And he didn't want that.

'We should go back,' Laren murmured. 'It's late, and I don't want to leave Vanora with the girls for too long.'

Alex pulled back, uncertain of whether she was truly worried about the children or whether she didn't want to be alone with him.

'Before I take you back, I need to know something.'

Laren waited in silence, and he reached down for the nerve to speak the words he didn't want to voice. 'I know you never wanted to be Lady of Glen Arrin. But I can't change my responsibilities as chief.'

She gave a nod, waiting for him to continue.

'You're not happy here,' he stated. 'Not with me. Not in this life.'

A tear spilled over from her eyes and, inside, he felt an answering emptiness. Alex kept his hands upon hers, demanding an answer. 'Do you want to remain married to me, Laren?'

She was quiet for a long moment. It dug into his heart and he was afraid he already knew what she would say.

Instead, she answered, 'I don't know.'

The misery in her eyes left him without anything to say, hurting him worse that he'd imagined it could.

And with that, she took long steps, leaving him behind.

Laren didn't know what the right decision was any more. Her heart bled, for in spite of everything, she did love him. But she sensed that Alex was the one who wanted to end their marriage. He must have thought about it, to even voice the question.

The truth was, she didn't want to be apart from him. Not at all. But he ought to have a wife who could lead at his side, someone confident and a helpmate.

Now that her glass had sold, she would be spending more time than ever with the furnaces. It would take months to make the pieces she needed. And after seeing Alex's reaction last night, she didn't believe he would support her decision. She simply didn't fit his vision of a wife.

During the past three years, he hadn't been the husband she'd needed, either. When they'd faced the worst moment of their lives, he'd abandoned her, leaving her to grieve alone. She resented the fact that he spent every moment with the clan instead of with her and their girls.

Laren wiped at her cheeks, reaching deep for the courage to mask her emotions. When her girls saw her, she didn't want to answer any questions about why she was crying. Footsteps trailed her, but she didn't look behind.

She was too busy trying to hold back her feelings, to keep herself in control.

A hand caught her arm and spun her. She collided with Alex, who locked her in his arms. He looked furious, his jaw tight. 'What do you mean, you don't know?'

She was so shocked by his sudden behaviour that she couldn't speak at first.

His hands came up to her face, threading his fingers into her hair. 'After all these years, you don't believe our marriage is worth fighting for?' In his eyes, she saw a fire that hadn't been there before. It rekindled her courage and she took his hands in hers.

'It's worth fighting for, aye. But I'm not the same woman you married, years ago. I'll never be that girl again, because a part of me is buried on the hillside by the loch.' She let go of the tears then, gripping his palms tightly. 'I can't be shaped and forced into the woman you want me to be.'

She stripped away her gloves, letting them fall to the ground. 'This is who I am, Alex.' She let go of his hands, but remained in his arms.

'I never asked you to be someone else.' His breath was warm against her face and he was fighting to let her speak. 'But I don't know who you are now.'

'Do you want to?' she whispered.

His dark eyes transformed with an intensity she never expected. 'Aye.' He leaned in, as though he were about to kiss her. But his mouth hovered a breath above hers. 'But there can be no more lies between us, Laren.'

'And you need to spare a few moments of your time for us,' she finished. 'Instead of coming home late at night, when we're asleep.'

Against her ribs, his palms slid down, as if to determine

whether or not her wound had healed. Her cheeks grew warm, her body responding to his heat.

'We're not through talking about this,' Alex murmured against her lips. When he broke away, she felt a building sense of anticipation. 'We have to join the others. But tonight, you're going to show me your glassmaking. I want to know everything you've kept from me.'

She didn't speak, feeling shaken. She hoped that this would be a new start for them, that they could somehow heal what had been lost. The wind drifted against her skin in a cold whisper, and he released her, leading the way back to the fortress.

Inside the gates, Alex struggled to mask the response Laren had evoked. He was dimly aware of the women's excitement as Nairna showed them the food she'd bought with Laren's silver coins, along with a few ells of cloth. Bram had taken the remainder of the money into his own safekeeping, and they intended to keep it hidden from the others until they'd traded and purchased what else they needed.

Laren murmured words to him about seeing to their daughters and disappeared from his side. Alex stood back from the rest of the clan, absorbing the transformation. Though he was thankful for the change in their fortune, he had to decide what to do about it now.

Bram leaned in to speak to Nairna and his wife nodded, handing him a large flagon. A moment later he approached, offering Alex the container. 'Nairna and I wanted to offer this wine to you and Laren to share this night.'

'Your wife sent you to do her matchmaking, did she?'

'You'd be right.' Bram handed him the flagon. 'I don't know if Laren told you, but the abbot has commissioned her to build more windows for their new kirk. He's promised one hundred and fifty pieces of silver.'

Alex couldn't find the words to form a reply, he was so taken aback by the amount. Never in his wildest imaginings could he have foreseen that the glass would have such value.

'She'll have to begin work on the windows immediately,' Bram said. 'But for this night, Nairna and I both thought you should enjoy your own celebration.'

'There's no need for wine,' Alex said automatically.

A slight twitch formed at the edge of Bram's mouth. 'But drink loosens the tongue, doesn't it? And Laren's not the sort to say much.'

Alex eyed his brother, understanding breaking through him. 'I asked her to meet me at Father Nolan's cavern.'

'Nairna and I will watch over your girls.' Bram sent his brother a conspiratorial smile. 'And I'll make certain your wife joins you this night.'

Laren's stomach was tying itself into knots of anxiety with every step she took towards the loch. Bram had offered to escort her there, but she'd refused. She didn't know what Alex wanted from her this night, but she was prepared to do as he wished.

She followed the curve of the water, avoiding the white stone on the hillside. A thin layer of ice coated the edges and she used the moonlight to guide her path. When she reached the far side, she saw the cavern illuminated from the glow of the furnaces.

Alex was already waiting at the entrance. His hair was darker, wet as if he'd washed in the loch. The tunic he wore was a fresh one, a muted blue that she'd sewn a few months ago.

He extended a hand to her and she entered the cavern, feeling anxious about his intentions this night. Upon the floor, she saw that he'd spread a woollen blanket over the earth floor. He poured two cups of wine and handed her one. Laren drank far too quickly, needing the liquid courage. The sweet wine had a light flavour, one she'd never tasted before.

'It's from Burgundy,' Alex told her.

Laren slowed down as she drank more of the wine and felt its warmth permeating her body. 'It's good.'

He poured her another cup, then pointed toward the furnaces. 'I sent Ramsay home. He warned me not to let the fires go out.'

'He's very particular about his work.' She noted that he'd set out several melts, some of which were ready to be blown. She removed her mantle and adjusted the ties in her hair, binding it away from her face.

'Some have said that he's...different from the others.'

From the way her husband hesitated, Laren understood what he meant. She walked over to check on the crucible of green molten glass. 'He is. The boys tease him because he often will become obsessed with a small detail.' She smiled, remembering the first time she'd met him. 'He'll spend hours, counting to himself until he knows it's time for the crucible to go inside the furnace. He has a brilliant mind, but most people don't understand him. They think there's something wrong with him, because he chooses to be alone.'

When her husband's expression sharpened upon her, Laren hid her discomfort. 'But he's done well as my apprentice.'

Alex walked over to examine some of the pieces of green glass she'd cut. He picked one up and held it to the light, but said nothing about it. Laren set several pipes into one of the furnaces to preheat. When she was finished, she turned back to her husband. In the faint light of the fires, his features were arresting. Dark eyes stared into hers and he made her uncomfortable. 'Bram told me about the commission.'

She took a breath and faced him. 'I'm going to make the windows. The clan needs the silver.'

'Do you want to make them?'

'More than anything,' she replied. She willed herself to take a step closer to him and he led her to sit across from him on the blanket.

For a time, he simply looked at her, and the only sound was the pop of the firewood as it cracked and burned. She waited for him to speak, prepared for his anger.

Instead, he reached down to the earthen floor and chose a handful of small pebbles. He rolled them between his fingers, then he reached out to place them in her palm.

'What are these for?'

'I used to throw these at your home at night. To awaken you,' he said.

She fingered the tiny stones, remembering. 'I hardly slept on the nights when I knew you were coming to meet me.' When she looked at her husband, she couldn't read his features, couldn't understand why he'd given her such a token.

She opened her palm and returned the stones to him. 'What are you doing, Alex?'

'I told you I didn't know who you were any more.' His dark eyes hid any feelings he might have had. 'So I thought we should start at the beginning.'

The words reached inside her and touched a part of her heart that had been cold for so long. He was right. If they wanted to rebuild any part of their marriage, they had to start again. Laren let the stones fall back to the sandy floor of the cavern and rose to her feet. She walked to the entrance of the cavern, bringing the blanket with her.

Alex followed and she laid the blanket on the ground, lying down to look up at the night sky. 'Do you remember when we used to go to the stone circle and look at the stars?'

He stretched out beside her, his body only a hand's distance from hers. 'Some nights were freezing.'

'Like tonight,' she agreed. When he didn't move, she slid closer to him until they lay side by side, the heat of his body warming her. For long moments, they stared up at the sky, although there were no stars visible.

As the moments drifted by, her heartbeat seemed to quicken. She was aware of his strength and his masculine power. Would he pull her close and kiss her, the way he once had? But instead, he remained quiet. She studied him with a sidelong look, noticing the way his face held years of tension. Whether it was the burden of leadership or frustration with her, she didn't know.

His hand bumped against hers and she laced her fingers with his. Though he did nothing more than hold her palm, Laren feared the gesture would lead to more. Although she wouldn't consider turning him away if he wanted to make love, she didn't feel ready for more intimacy. Her feelings were too uncertain.

When he made no other move, she let go of his hand and rolled to her uninjured side, facing him. She wanted him to let go of his inner frustration and forgive her for the secrets.

'I'm sorry I kept the glassmaking from you,' she said.

She wanted him to face her, to see whether he felt anything at all towards her, whether there was any hint of love remaining.

But instead of warming to her, Alex compressed his mouth into a line. 'So am I.'

She waited for him to say something about the glass, to reveal any of his shielded emotions. But there came nothing at all. With her apology, she'd darkened his mood once again.

She stood and returned to the stone work surface, resting her palms upon it. Her throat felt thick, heavy with hurt. But this was her own fault and she couldn't take back the years they'd lost.

Alex came up behind her and drew her to face him. His expression held a solemnity that worried her. 'Are there other secrets you've held back from me?'

She shook her head. 'Nothing. I swear it.'

He rested his hands upon her shoulders, letting his touch slide down to her forearms. Her skin prickled with the unexpected caress and when he lingered upon her burn marks, she felt embarrassed by the ugliness. She wished she could eradicate the years of pain and scarring, becoming the innocent girl she'd been so long ago.

But then, that wasn't possible, was it? She was for ever changed, just as he was.

Without speaking, she took his hand in hers and brought him to lie beside her on the blanket. She curled up against him and he pulled her body closer, both arms wrapped around her. It felt so good to be in his embrace, that she fought the unexpected tears that rose up.

Although he'd never left her, she hadn't known how much she'd missed the feel of his skin against hers. How much she'd missed him.

And there came the grain of hope that somehow they would manage to resurrect all that had been lost between them.

March, 1303

Laren stared at the wall, unable to sleep. It had been two months since David had died, but none of the pain had dissipated. She'd buried her grief, using her glass work to keep her spirit from shattering apart.

Alex worked among the clan during the day, and on the days when she wasn't with her furnace, he avoided her. Even now, in their bed, he slept on the opposite side, turned away from her.

Her hands were raw, the skin burned when she'd touched the wrong part of the pipe. It was a careless accident and the pain made it impossible to sleep. She didn't care. The burns were a physical penance she endured, for it kept her mind off her lost child.

Without warning, Alex reached out in the darkness, his hand touching hers. Out of reflex, she jerked her hand back, for the slightest touch was excruciating against her burned skin.

His hand moved away and the silence was damning. He didn't know. He'd tried to touch her and she'd responded as though she didn't want him.

'Alex?' she whispered in the darkness.

But there came no answer.

Chapter Seven

Later that night, Laren rose from sleep and went to tend the glass. She hoped she hadn't let the melts go too long, but it appeared that they were still viable.

While Alex slept, she took the heated pipe and dipped it downward into the crucible containing the green glass. When she had a ball of molten glass the size of her fist, she began turning the pipe. Over and over, fighting the pull of the earth, she blew a breath of air into the pipe, resting it against her cheek for a moment.

'I thought you were going to sleep,' came her husband's voice.

Laren moved to the marble surface of the table and rolled the glass against it, shaping it into a cylinder. 'I'll sleep when I've finished this piece.'

She returned the glass to an opening in the furnace, resting it against a metal support as she turned it. When it was hot again, she shaped it, adjusting the size and ensuring that the glass was of equal thickness. Then back again to reheat it.

Her hands were shaking against the pipe; she couldn't stop the voices inside that reminded her of how very little she knew and how many mistakes she'd made in the past. Alex had never seen her work before and his presence made her anxious. She wanted him to see the beauty in it, to understand why she loved it so.

She continued turning the pipe, watching the glass expand and grow. And somehow, within the golden sphere of fire, she found a steadiness. She had blown glass a thousand times, until it was instinctive. This time would be no different.

'Why do you keep putting it back in the fire?' Alex asked.

'It cools in less than a minute,' she replied. 'I have to keep reheating it or I can't shape it.'

When she'd blown the glass into the size she wanted, Laren sat at her bench and rested the pipe upon a long table with the glass hanging off the end. She took her iron jacks and used the tongs to gently pinch an indentation into the hot glass, even as she kept it spinning.

'It looks like you're making a goblet,' Alex said.

'Not quite.' She adjusted the necking and explained, 'I can't take the glass off the pipe without this.'

She eyed him for a moment. 'Since I've sent Ramsay away, could I ask for your help?'

'I don't know anything about glass, Laren.'

'No, but you've a strong arm. Take that pontil there and dip it into the hot glass,' she said, nodding toward one of the heated pipes. 'I need a small amount, about the size of a robin's egg.'

He reached for the pipe, pulling it from the flames. The tip was red hot, and he lowered it into the crucible of green molten glass.

'Turn the pipe as you dip it,' she instructed, 'and bring it over to the marble table. Don't stop turning the pipe.'

He did as she asked, following every instruction she gave him to adjust the shape of the glass and press his own pipe to the surface of her glowing cylinder. With both pipes on either end, Laren adjusted the necking. With a light tap against the pipe, the piece of glass separated, leaving Alex holding the hot cylinder with the pontil.

She sent him a smile of relief and took it from him, continuing to work with the glass. Perhaps Nairna had been right. It might be that he wouldn't discourage her glass making. She held on to the intense hope as she finished the glass and placed it within the smaller furnace to anneal.

'Won't it melt again?' Alex asked.

She shook her head. 'This furnace is at a lower temperature. It allows the glass to cool slowly and it's stronger that way. In another day, I'll make it into a flat pane. Then I can cut it into pieces for my windows.'

She held up a piece of glass the colour of the green hills. 'It will look like this when it's finished.'

'Show me some of the other work you've completed,' Alex ordered. He stood beside the glass she'd begun cutting and Laren went to the back of the cave for some of the cloth-wrapped windows she'd made.

Though she supposed the windows were good enough, the old fears crept back to stifle her courage. These pieces were hers. Her vision, her colours that she'd made after Father Nolan had passed away. It was possible Alex wouldn't like them and she didn't want to see the disapproval on his face.

When she unwrapped the first window, she revealed a scene she'd done of a shepherd tending his sheep upon a hillside. She'd struggled to get the right shades of green and her early attempts at the lead lines weren't as good as she'd hoped.

She waited for him to speak. To say something about her work.

He examined the glass, touching the lead lines. But he revealed nothing of his thoughts. 'Show me the others.'

Laren obeyed, unwrapping one window after the next. With each bit of glass she revealed, it felt as though she were baring herself before Alex. She waited for some comment, some sort of criticism of her work.

Instead, he merely nodded.

It hurt in a way she hadn't expected. Her spirits sank further, but she hid her disappointment.

'Can you leave the fires now?' he asked.

She nodded. 'Ramsay will return soon—they should be all right until he arrives.'

'Good.' Alex held out his hand to her, and started to lead her from the cavern. It was still dark outside, with only the torches of Glen Arrin in the distance to guide their way.

'Where are we going?' she asked Alex.

'I'll show you.'

They returned home and he continued walking past each of the houses, to the foundation of the new fortress. Surrounding it was a wall that rose up to her knees. But what surprised her was how wide the diameter of the wall was. They had changed the structure, bringing the walls much further out. The men had been working on it all day, and they would have the remaining stones in place within a sennight if they continued at this pace.

Although there was a new gate area already formed, Alex put his hands around her waist and lifted her over the wall. It was dark within the space, but in the distance, the sky had lightened, transforming night into dawn.

'It's larger than the previous keep,' she commented. 'But why is the wall so vast?'

'We're putting it up in stages,' he said. 'And it won't be a wooden keep. It will be a castle.'

She didn't know what to say. A castle would be a visible threat to the English, inviting an attack. And with all the unrest and the raids, she sometimes wished they could go and hide in the forest, invisible to everyone.

'It will take years to build this,' he said, 'but it will be worth it in the end.'

She sat down on the low stone wall, drawing up her knees. 'You want this, don't you?'

'My father dreamed of it. It's something I can build in his memory.' He sat with his back to hers, letting her lean against him.

Though the morning light was the barest shade of lavender, as the sun slowly rose, she saw the vast work spread before her. These were his dreams, his desires.

She turned slightly, lowering her feet and resting her cheek against his back. Alex faced her, his hand upon the wall. 'The glass was beautiful,' he said quietly. 'I could see the fire and beauty you imprisoned within it.'

She never expected the compliment. And yet, the heaviness in his voice made her wonder if there was more to what he was saying.

'Finish the commission, if that's what you truly want,' he continued. His gaze returned to the framework of the castle. 'I have work enough to occupy myself here.'

And although he'd just given her the freedom she wanted, Laren sensed the distance stretching further between them.

* * *

'She's returned,' Bram said, his face twisted into a frown. 'May God help us.'

'Who?' Alex saw the unrest in his brother's face and knew the answer before he spoke.

'Our mother.'

Alex resisted the urge to cross himself. They had enjoyed a peaceful few weeks while their mother had taken sanctuary with Kameron MacKinnon, Lord of Locharr. As their ally, Lord Locharr had come to their aid on more than one occasion. The older man had more patience and understanding than any other person he'd met…and since he'd welcomed Grizel into his home, Alex rather thought the man deserved sainthood.

But if Grizel MacKinloch was returning home, it meant trouble.

'Where is she?'

'Waiting near the gates with her wagons. She's already given Ross an earful about the keep. I thought I'd warn you.'

Alex expected no less from his mother. No doubt she would have opinions about how they should have put out the fires and saved the keep. He crossed through the fortress and stopped to gather his two daughters. With Adaira and Mairin holding each hand, he went to greet her.

Possibly the distraction of the girls would keep Grizel from lashing out at the others. He didn't need his mother stirring up unrest with her harsh criticisms.

The older woman had already dismounted and Nairna was walking at her side. From the sulking expression on Grizel's face, Alex could tell that she was working herself into a mood.

'Well. It's about time you came to welcome me,' she said

in greeting, her gaze falling upon the girls. 'I suppose that wife of yours has disappeared again.' Her nose wrinkled in distaste.

Alex's knuckles clenched into a fist, recognising her baiting. 'Laren is involved in another task,' he responded. He gave his mother the required kiss of welcome and bade his girls do the same. Grizel inspected the children, but said nothing to them. With his permission, the girls joined Vanora, who was busy blending mortar for the day's work. They began making towers of stones, staying out of harm's way.

'Why are you here, Mother?' Alex asked.

'I thought it was my home, if I remember correctly.' She smoothed her skirts and strode forwards, her eyes drinking in the sight of the remains. 'And since Lord Locharr told me the state of things, I thought I'd best return and help you.'

He doubted if she intended to do anything except criticise, but he kept that opinion to himself.

'I can see that you've destroyed everything Tavin worked for.' Her face tightened in a frown.

'The English destroyed it.'

'Only because you were foolish enough to steal that Frenchwoman away from Lord Cairnross.'

'It was a rescue,' he corrected. 'Lady Marguerite asked us for sanctuary and we granted it.'

'And you see what that's brought you.' Grizel waved her hand at the repairs. 'Now you've wasted time building walls instead of a proper tower. Tavin wouldn't have wanted this.'

He didn't waste his breath arguing further. His mother thrived upon conflict; she liked nothing better than to engage in a verbal match.

'My Lady Grizel, I'm grateful to see that you've returned,' Nairna interrupted them. In a voice as sweet as cream, she continued, 'Would you walk with me and we can discuss how we could best use your skills?' Nairna took Grizel's hand in hers, leading her away from the others.

Alex made a mental promise to gift his brother's wife with a length of silk, as soon as he could arrange it. If Nairna could keep Grizel occupied, it would make the repairs far easier.

While Nairna retreated with his mother, Alex stared over at the loch. After Laren had returned to the cavern early this morn, he hadn't seen her since. He didn't know if she'd remembered to eat or whether she was already caught up in making the glass.

He'd never seen anything like it, in all his life. It was like watching sorcery, in the transformation from sand into molten glass. When she'd spun the pipe, putting her breath within the glass, all traces of the shy, quiet wife had disappeared. She'd revealed an inner strength and power, a confidence in her skill.

He hadn't known that she was capable of such feats; now he wondered who the woman he'd married truly was. Because of her glass, she'd brought untold wealth to them, silver coins that would help them rebuild every last stone of Glen Arrin. He was grateful for it, but it meant that she would spend hours of the day away from everyone.

Alex felt torn between his wife and his responsibilities as chief. He worked alongside the people, hour after hour, until he collapsed into his bed at night. And he could foresee no changes in the near future. It exhausted him, just thinking about it.

If she worked on her glass all day and night, would he

even see her at all? It was impossible to transform a marriage if they never spent any time together.

Alex lifted a stone and laid it upon the wall, that Callum had spread with mortar. His daughters were laughing as they stacked smaller stones and knocked them down again. He watched them, and their smiles warmed him. Mairin, though only four years old, was starting to look more and more like Laren. He watched as she tightened her lips, adjusting the stack of stones to build it higher.

Her small fingers moved with an exact manner, so careful was she. He moved closer to the girls, kneeling down. 'What are you building, Mairin?'

'It's a castle, just like yours.' She sent a glare toward her younger sister. 'But the English keep knocking it down.'

Adaira beamed and pushed the stack over, laughing as it fell into pieces. 'Again!' she demanded.

Mairin rolled her eyes, but granted her sister's wish by building the stack again. While she worked, Alex asked, 'Did you know about your mother's glass?'

His daughter wrinkled her nose. 'We're not supposed to go in the cave. We might burn ourselves if we get too close.' She sent him a tentative smile. 'I like the blue glass best. But I have to be a big girl and keep Adaira away from the fires. She'd burn right up. Or the witches might get her.'

Alex hid his smile and said, 'You were good to take care of her.' He touched her hair, bringing her into an embrace. Adaira moved in, her small arms joining them. With a tight squeeze, he accepted their affection as the precious gift it was.

'It's pretty, isn't it?'

'Aye. There's magic there.' He suddenly thought of the glass droplets he'd given Laren, so many years ago. Had she kept them at all? He hadn't seen them in so long, he supposed they were gone.

A sudden noise caught his attention from outside the fortress, something that sounded like an approaching horse. 'Stay here,' he warned his girls. He crossed the area, moving to the first stone wall that was partially completed. Shielding his eyes from the sun, he looked for the source of the sound.

Nothing. Not a single movement from anywhere. But he knew what he'd heard. And if it were Dougal or another clansman, they'd have revealed themselves. His instincts sharpened and he scanned their surroundings for the invisible threat.

'I'm hungry, Da,' Mairin informed him. 'Don't you think we should eat something?'

He nodded, taking her hand in his. 'We'll fetch some food and bring it to your mother.' He didn't like the idea of Laren working alone, even if her apprentice Ramsay was there. Though her cavern was hidden on the far side of the loch, it didn't mean his wife was safe from an attack.

Mairin dashed across the fortress toward Vanora's house, while Alex trailed her. Adaira put her hand in his, emitting a stream of girlish chatter. When his elder daughter emerged with a sack of food, Alex brought both of them close. His claymore was strapped to his back and he had another dirk at his waist, if he needed to defend them.

He said nothing to the girls, but, as they walked, his eyes searched the horizon for any movement or sound. Adaira made him stop several times as she watched a bird hopping upon a tree branch or a fish splashing within the loch. He hoisted her on his hip when she grew tired, her arms settling around his neck. As he drew closer to the cavern, he could smell the smoke from Laren's fires.

He listened hard, but the sound was gone. A part of him wondered if he could have imagined it. But then, his hearing was acute and he was well attuned to the signs of a forthcoming raid. It might have been an enemy scout, sent to determine their weaknesses.

Or perhaps he was feeling troubled by the long silence from the English. He'd expected an attack long before this and it was starting to make him uneasy. Since he hadn't heard the sound a second time, he dismissed it as nothing but his imagination.

When they reached the entrance to the cave, he set Adaira down. Laren was inside alone, working with a long pipe. To his surprise, he saw that this time the cylinder was rotating outward, becoming a disc. With deft fingers, she whirled the pipe until it flattened out.

The girls stared at her, their faces awestruck. It was like watching a sheet of sapphires form before his eyes. She rolled the spun glass repeatedly, until it was about ten inches in diameter.

Then she transferred it to the annealing oven and turned back to face them, smiling at the sight of the girls. 'I'm glad to see you.' She kissed them on their cheeks, but when she lifted her eyes to Alex's, her expression grew guarded. 'Is the rebuilding going well?'

'Well enough.' He shifted Adaira's weight to the other hip. 'My mother returned.' Laren showed no response, though he knew she wasn't fond of Grizel. 'Nairna found a way to keep her busy.'

'Drowning kittens, is she?' His wife turned back to another crucible, checking the colour of the melt.

'Grizel isn't that bad.'

Laren raised her eyebrows. 'Not to you, perhaps. But

we'll leave that subject for a time when little ears aren't listening.'

Mairin pointed to a piece of glass in the shape of a partially opened flower bud. It hung from a piece of rope, suspended above the fires, and Alex hadn't noticed it last night. 'Do you think there are any witches in there? Mama said it's a trap for them.'

When he sent his wife a questioning look, Laren shrugged. 'If there are any evil spirits lingering, I don't need them near my glass. It belonged to Father Nolan. I keep it because it reminds me of him.' Her face softened in memory as she reached up to touch it.

'Mama, I'm hungry,' Mairin informed her. 'We brought food for you.'

A grateful look passed over Laren's face. 'I haven't had time to eat.' When they sat down and opened the sack Mairin had brought, Alex started to pass out the food his daughter had selected. To his chagrin, she'd brought a container of honey, oatcakes and every sort of sweet Vanora had in her possession.

'Did Vanora pack this?' Laren asked.

Mairin shook her head. 'I did. I packed my favourites.'

Alex sent his wife a private look and a shrug and he saw the amusement on her face. He should have known better than to let Mairin choose the food. Adaira selected a sweetened cake and then toddled over to him, planting herself on his lap. He helped her break off pieces and while they ate, Laren said, 'It's been a long time since we've shared a noon meal as a family.'

He didn't know if she meant it as a compliment or a criticism. 'I can't stay for too long.' There was so much work to be done, his absence would be noticed.

Should he leave Laren alone again? It bothered him that

he hadn't located the source of the sound he'd heard and it was difficult to release the suspicions. The last thing he wanted was to leave his wife unguarded while an enemy was nearby.

Alex was about to set Adaira down when he suddenly felt something warm and wet against his tunic. He pulled Adaira back and she continued to puddle upon the sand.

He grimaced and set her down. Laren saw what was happening and a smile of amusement perked at her mouth as she chided her daughter for the accident. 'Wait here, both of you, while I see to your father.'

He didn't hide his disgust as he stripped off his tunic. Fortunately, he'd caught the mess before Adaira soaked his trews.

Laren took the garment from him and rinsed it in the loch, scrubbing it with sand. 'It will dry soon enough.'

While she cleaned the tunic, Alex scooped up some water, washing off his skin. Rivulets of water spilled over his hard muscles and Laren found herself staring at her husband. He stretched and shivered from the freezing water. Her eyes followed the water that pooled over his skin, trailing downwards.

He saw her staring and sent her with his own frank gaze. Dark eyes moved down her face, past her breasts, to her hips. Unable to help herself, she reached out and touched his cool skin, wiping away a droplet of water with her fingertips.

Alex didn't move, but he caught her wrist and held it to his skin. 'After the girls are asleep, meet me here again tonight.'

He pressed her fingers over his ribs, guiding her hand around her waist. Though his skin was icy cold from the water, she leaned in to warm him. His hand cupped her face and she stood before him, his nose resting against hers.

Though he hadn't done anything at all, Laren's breath was shaky, her body seeking his nearness. He was watching her with unveiled desire and she wondered when he would take her to his bed. She'd expected it last night, but he'd surprised her by holding back.

His fingers stroked the side of her face and she lifted her mouth to his, claiming the kiss that he hadn't given.

At the first touch of her lips, he opened to her, his firm mouth seeking. She'd forgotten this, the way he made her pulse race. Though he kept the kiss gentle, she wanted more from him. She wanted to lose herself in his arms, to let him drive out all the demons of their past.

When he pulled back, he let his hands remain around her waist. 'Tonight,' he repeated. She nodded and when he released her, she nearly stumbled, feeling foolish that he could still make her weak-kneed. 'Will you be all right with the girls, or shall I take them back with me?'

'They can stay. Ramsay will be along soon and he'll take over the fires.'

Alex donned his wet tunic, shrugging off the discomfort as he turned back to the fortress. Though it was cold outside, he showed no sign of it as he walked away.

When Laren returned to the cave, her girls busied themselves playing in the sand near the entrance. And as she worked to make more sheets of coloured glass, she thought about how alone Alex was. He worked endlessly on the building and it was weighing upon his spirits.

But never did he talk to her about his own worries. He kept those thoughts closed off, as if they revealed a weakness he didn't want to show.

* * *

Laren set down her cutting instrument and stared at the afternoon sky. A cold rain began to drizzle and the girls had moved inside the cave for shelter. It was starting to grow darker and she needed to bring them back home before it grew too late.

'Come, girls,' she said, lifting Adaira into her arms and wrapping her younger daughter beneath her cloak. She used the other side of the cloak to shield Mairin from the rain. As they hurried back to the fortress, she glanced behind her and saw a hooded man, mounted on horseback. Her heartbeat quickened, for he'd emerged from the woods near the loch. Not far from her son's grave, if she guessed correctly.

Who was he? And what did he want? From his clothing, it appeared he'd come from another clan. Was he a messenger?

She hastened back to the fortress, but he didn't follow. It seemed that he was watching her and she wondered why. When she reached the interior of Glen Arrin, she breathed a little easier. It was raining hard now, and most of the men had abandoned work for the day, seeking shelter inside their huts.

She brought the girls to Vanora's home and the older matron welcomed them inside, fussing over their wet clothes. Alex was speaking with Ross and in the corner sat his mother, Grizel.

The woman's dark hair was pulled back from her face, a sour expression on her mouth. Her gown was spotless and she wore a woollen wrap to keep out the cold. 'Come and give your *seanmhair* a kiss,' she ordered the girls.

They glanced at Laren, who had no choice but to nod in

agreement. The girls weren't fond of Grizel, but she hoped Mairin could manage to control her impulsive tongue.

After the girls had greeted her, Laren came forwards and bent to give the matron a kiss of welcome, but Grizel turned her cheek aside. 'I meant the children, not you.' Bitterness lined her mouth and she nodded towards the outside. 'I see you're neglecting your home and family again.'

'I see you're as pleasant as ever,' she retorted. As soon as she had spoken the words, she wanted to bite her tongue. She knew better than to fight with Grizel, but there were times when her patience was sorely lacking.

'If you would spend half the time looking after your responsibilities, you'd be a better wife to Alex. Why he ever married you, I'll never know.'

'That's enough, Mother.' Alex broke away from his conversation with Ross. 'If you've nothing better to do than offer insults, you can return to Locharr.'

'I'll not. This is my home, where I belong.'

Laren moved as far away from Grizel as she could manage, but already she could feel the tension stretching through her. The girls were picking at their food and Adaira began to whine.

'Hush now,' Laren soothed, picking up her youngest and stroking her hair. 'You just need to rest, sweet one.' She began speaking words of comfort, ignoring Grizel's proclamations about how her boys never fussed a day in their lives.

She tried to block out the words, but the longer Grizel went on, the more she needed an escape. When the girls finally fell asleep, she walked outside, heedless of the rain.

She heard footsteps behind her and saw Alex following. Laren didn't stop, but continued trudging through the mud until she reached the outer wall. She rested her hands upon the wall, staring at the ruined foundation where they had once lived. 'I couldn't stand it any more,' she told her husband.

'She's always been that way. Nothing you say can please her.'

Laren turned to face him. Rain was pouring down over both of them, but she'd rather stand outside and be frozen than endure another moment of Grizel's company. 'Tell me that we won't be living with her for long.'

Alex came up beside her and sat, shielding her from the rain with his cloak. 'We'll finish as soon as we can.'

'Good.' She shivered beneath the makeshift shelter. 'Alex, I saw a horseman near David's grave.'

His arm came around her shoulders, as if to guard her. 'When?'

'Not long ago. Just as the girls and I were returning.'

He stood and let the cloak fall away. His hand caught hers and he walked back with her to the low wall overlooking the fortress.

'He was hooded. I couldn't see his face, but he looked like another clansman, not an English soldier.'

'Harkirk could have hired a clansman to gather information,' Alex responded. She could feel the tension in him, the restlessness of a man who would do anything to protect them.

'Go back to Vanora,' he ordered. 'Bram and I will search the forest. If he's still there, we'll find him.'

Chapter Eight

Night fell and Laren hadn't seen Alex or any of his brothers returning from their search. She kept glancing at the door, hoping to see him enter. When the hours stretched on, she thought of his earlier request for her to meet him at the cavern. No doubt he would want her to remain here, after the stranger's appearance.

Ramsay. The thought came out of nowhere. Her apprentice would have gone to the cavern to tend the furnaces. He'd be there alone and knew nothing about the threat.

She needed to send word to him, to bring him back to the safety of the fortress. But whom could she send? Alex had taken Bram and Callum with him, and she didn't know whether Dougal had gone as well.

'This house is too cold for my old bones,' Grizel complained. 'The fire's not hot enough and you ought to patch the holes in the walls.'

'The fire is as hot as we can make it,' Vanora said. 'Sit closer, if you're cold.'

'If I sit any closer, I'll go up in flames,' the old woman

retorted. From the amused look Vanora sent towards her husband Ross, she wouldn't be at all disappointed.

Ross looked pained at Grizel's tirade of complaints. It occurred to Laren that he would be more than willing to leave the house for a short time. He was her best hope of bringing Ramsay back.

She reached for her cloak and beckoned to the older man. 'May I speak with you for a moment?'

He looked eager for a reprieve and rose, reaching for his own mantle. When they were outside, he asked, 'What is it?'

Though he already knew about the horseman she'd seen on the far side of the loch, he knew nothing of her glass-making. She chose her words carefully. 'Ramsay MacKin-loch went to Father Nolan's cave, on the far side of the loch. He doesn't know about the horseman. Could you go with me and help me bring him back to Glen Arrin?'

Ross started to shake his head. 'Alex doesn't want you leaving my house.'

'I know. But Ramsay is only eleven years old. He needs someone to take care of him.'

'Eleven is old enough to know better.'

'Please, Ross.' She touched his arm. 'I worry about the boy. And he'll be waiting for me to...' she hesitated, then amended '...to bring him a meal. His father often forgets to feed him.'

The older man appeared reluctant, but at last he took a torch from one of the sconces in the fortress. 'Walk with me to the edge of the loch and show me where I can find the cavern. Then swear to me that you'll return to your daughters.'

'I promise.' She joined the older man, walking slowly outside the gates. The night was so dark, she could hardly see anything without the torch. 'Follow the shore line around the curve,' she directed. 'Then about a half a mile with the trees to your right. He—he keeps the fire burning to stay warm. You'll smell the smoke.'

Ross lifted the torch and turned back to her. 'I'll fetch the boy and bring him back.'

'Thank you.' She waited as he trudged forwards, watching to be sure he'd gone the right direction around the loch. Her cloak wasn't warm enough and she held the edges tight, turning back toward the fortress. The faint light of the torches guided her way, but she heard the snapping of ice behind her.

The hairs on the back of her neck rose and she knew instinctively that someone was there. She had no weapon with her and the gates were further ahead. For a moment, she remained motionless, hoping that the darkness would make it impossible for the intruder to find her. Holding her breath, she questioned whether to remain in place or try to reach the fortress.

When the footsteps drew closer, she broke into a run. A hand reached for her cloak and caught it, jerking her backwards. She lost her balance and let out a scream, just as a hood blinded her. The suffocating darkness choked her; when she tried again to scream, a hand covered her nose and mouth.

Oh God, not this. She struggled against her attacker, trying to break free of him. His strong arms held her trapped and she was starting to lose consciousness from lack of air. Dizziness and a ringing in her ears made her knees weaken.

She didn't know who the man was or why he was trying to take her hostage, but she wasn't about to let him seize her without fighting as hard as she could. Letting her weight go slack, she fell to the ground. Laren tried not to move, hoping that he would relinquish his grip enough for her to make an escape.

His hold relaxed against her throat and she cried out, 'Alex!' as loudly as she could. A fist cuffed her jaw and she saw stars, her head reeling.

Then, without warning, the hands released her. She heard her husband and Ross fighting and the sound of swords clashing. Laren kept low to the ground, unable to see anything. She struggled to remove the hood, and when at last she saw the flare of Ross's torch her attacker was gone.

'Stay with Laren,' she heard Bram say. 'We'll find him.'

Both he and Ross disappeared into the woods. Laren pressed her palms against the frozen earth, fighting for a deep breath.

Alex helped her up, gathering her into his arms. She was shaking so hard, she couldn't seem to stop. 'I'm s-sorry,' she stammered. 'I never meant to leave. I wanted Ross to warn Ramsay—'

But he only held her tight, stroking her hair and murmuring that it was all right. 'I'll take you home.'

'Not yet,' she pleaded. 'Take me to the cavern. I need Ramsay to be safe.'

Alex gave no answer and she suspected he would ignore her request, forcing her to return to Ross's house. He took her hand and led her back to the fortress, but when they reached the gates, she was startled that he took a torch and brought her back again.

At her questioning look, he said, 'It's important to you, isn't it?'

She nodded, still stunned that he would listen to her. Along the walk, she huddled close to him and his arm remained around her waist. With each step, she drew comfort and strength from him.

Never before had she endured a terror like this one, nearly becoming a prisoner. She knew full well what happened to the captives who were taken by the English. She'd seen Bram's scarred back, and even Callum had not once spoken a word since his rescue. As a woman, she would have been used and discarded. The thought sent a new wave of fear within her and she tightened her grip around her husband.

'Do you think he was sent by Harkirk?' she asked him.

'Undoubtedly. If you were his prisoner, he knows I'd stop at nothing to get you back.' The ruthless tone in his voice made her shiver.

When they reached Father Nolan's cavern, the fire had died down to coals. There was no sign of Ramsay. Alex brought her near the meagre heat, resting his hands on her shoulders. 'I thought you said he would be here.'

She nodded. 'He was supposed to come.' But now that he was absent, she wondered whether something had happened to him or whether he'd broken his promise.

Her husband added wood to the furnace and a shower of sparks rose up towards the cavern ceiling, tiny pieces of light in the darkness.

'Thank you,' she whispered to Alex, 'for saving me.'

His gaze was stoic, revealing no feelings at all. She didn't know what he was thinking right now, but she wanted a moment to be in his arms, to take comfort that she was safe, no longer at her captor's mercy.

Alex drew her against him and touched his forehead to hers. 'I'll kill any man who touches you.'

She rested her hands upon his heart and felt the rapid pulse beneath her fingertips. He was so warm and right now she wanted to forget about what had happened to her. She felt breathless standing so near to him, but he made no move to touch her.

'You gave me pebbles last night,' she whispered, 'to remind me of the beginning.'

His expression remained neutral, but he gave a nod. She rested her cheek against his strong chest, her own heartbeat echoing his. Right now she needed him to take away the fear, to drive it out of her mind. Though he'd come for her, saving her from captivity, she needed more from him than an embrace.

She wanted the physical closeness they'd once had, when he'd taken her body beneath his, sending her into the mindless frenzy of lust. But if she dared to offer herself to him, would he turn her away?

'We should return,' he said quietly. 'Vanora will wonder what's happened and I need to know if Ross and Bram found the intruder.'

A bleakness passed over her, though she knew he was right. This wasn't the time or the place for a coupling. But she needed him so badly right now, to reassure her that she was safe. Her body ached for him, her sensitive flesh growing moist.

And he sensed it. 'What is it, Laren?'

She didn't have the words to say it. But there was only one way to find out if he needed her as badly as she craved him.

His wife let her cloak fall to the ground, her blue eyes staring at him as though she wanted to tell him something, but was afraid to speak.

And then she reached for him, her lips seeking his. He kissed her, feeling the tension mount higher within him. Nothing could have shaken him more than seeing the intruder try to take his wife. He hadn't seen the man's face, but he'd heard Laren scream.

He'd hardly been aware of his actions, but he'd unsheathed his sword, intending to murder the man who had hurt her. She'd cowered upon the ground, curling up with pain.

Even now, her cheek was reddened from where the man had struck her. Alex traced his fingertips over the bruise, wishing he could take it away.

He was fighting the urges that rose up in him, the desire to claim Laren with his body and assert his possession. Her sweet mouth was coaxing him beyond the boundaries of his control, and when her hand moved down to the ties of his trews a thunderous lust rose up.

Her palm cupped him, her long fingers guiding up his erection.

Saints, he didn't know if he could stand this. He'd meant to court her slowly, to somehow rebuild their marriage so that she would trust him again. But his manhood was roaring with need and his own hands were shaking to keep himself under control.

'Take me,' she pleaded. 'Make me forget what happened.' She was lifting her skirt and when she raised her leg over his hip, all rational thought left him.

It had been so damned long. Too many months had passed since he'd been with her intimately. And on the rare times they'd shared sex, it had been calm and quiet. Nothing at all like the desperate way she was clinging to him now. Her mouth was all over his, her tongue seeking him.

He led her back to the wall of the cavern, pressing her shoulders against the stone. He tried to gentle his kiss, to slow her down, but the next thing he knew, her hand was guiding him inside her.

At the feeling of her wet heat surrounding him, he cast aside any attempts to take her gently. She was panting, struggling with their height difference while she tried to make love to him.

Alex lifted her up, bringing her legs around his waist, still buried deep inside. She leaned down to kiss him and he thrust against her, hearing her moan. It took his willpower apart, and he gave himself up to the moment, penetrating her, letting the rhythm sweep over him. Her panting rose to a fever pitch and he reached for her breast with one hand, teasing the hardened tip as he lifted her, sheathing himself deep within.

She went liquid against him, her body squeezing his shaft, and he surrendered to the heady sensations pounding through him. When she cried out at the friction, he felt himself growing thicker, trembling close to the edge. He pumped harder, marking her, until at last she slumped against him, spent in her own fulfilment. He felt his own release coming and emptied himself inside her, his body slick with sweat.

For a time, he kept her propped against the wall, cupping her bare bottom. She shivered and leaned in to kiss him again.

There were no words between them now. She'd needed him and, though he'd taken her physical offering, he didn't know what to say.

In the end, he lowered her down, straightening her gown and his trews.

And he felt utterly confused by what had just happened.

When they reached Glen Arrin, Walter stood outside his home and raised his hand, beckoning for them to come near. The older man had taken in Callum and Dougal, as well as a few others, when they'd lost their homes.

'What is it?' Laren asked.

Walter's face shifted with worry. 'I found the lad outside. Ramsay asked me to tell you he was sorry he couldn't come.'

'He's with you now?' Relief filled her to know that Ramsay wasn't at home with his father. 'Is everything all right?'

'His eyes are swollen shut,' he admitted. 'His father had beaten him. I found the boy near the loch, putting ice against his eyes. He was talking about some fires and begged me to find you.' The old man shook his head and sighed. 'I brought him back here and made him sleep.'

'He's not going back to his father,' Laren insisted. 'Alex, promise me. Ramsay's been hurt enough.'

Her husband's expression was grim; though she knew he was distracted by the attack tonight, her apprentice couldn't defend himself from a grown man.

'The boy can stay with me,' Walter offered. 'He won't be needing much space.'

'For now,' Alex agreed. 'But, Laren, before I speak to Ramsay's father, we need to find the man who attacked you.' They took their leave from Walter, and Alex led her forwards until they saw Bram and Ross approaching.

'He's gone,' Bram said. 'We'll have to continue the search in the morning.'

'He's like a spirit,' Ross added. 'Disappeared without a trace.'

'He's not a spirit.' Laren shivered, remembering the man's strong grip. Alex drew her to his side and, after agreeing to search again in the morning, Ross and Bram returned to their homes.

Her husband was staring at her and Laren flushed, remembering the way she'd thrown herself at him earlier. She didn't know what had come over her, but she didn't regret touching her husband. He'd made her feel alive again and she didn't regret seducing him.

But there was trouble brewing in his eyes. 'I don't want you returning to the cavern,' he said. 'Not after what happened tonight.'

She frowned, not understanding. 'Alex, I have to finish the commission. I have to return to the furnaces because I can't make the glass here.'

He pulled her into a tight embrace. 'The commission be damned. You were nearly kidnapped tonight. I almost lost you because you left the fortress.'

'I won't be alone,' she argued. 'Ramsay will be there and—'

'You're not going back,' he repeated. 'We don't need the silver. Your life is more important than glass.'

She'd never seen him like this and it startled her to see him so adamant. She started to speak again, but he cut her off. 'I'm not leaving you alone again. You'll stay here at Glen Arrin and you and Nairna can organise the women with the rebuilding. There are some tasks that both of you can do and it will keep you protected if you're here.'

She grew cold, suddenly realising what he was saying. 'You're asking me to give up the glassmaking.'

'No.' His hand came around the back of her neck, softly, but firm in his grasp. 'I'm not asking.'

Gone was the passionate husband and in his place was an iron-willed chief. He was entirely serious in his command.

'I'll take Callum with me, as a guard,' she offered. 'I won't do my work alone.'

'You won't do it at all. It's not safe for you to be by yourself, so far away from Glen Arrin.' He took her hand in his and started to pull her back inside Ross's house.

'Alex, no.' She refused to move another step. 'I'm not going to fall into Nairna's shadow. I've been given a task that I promised I'd complete.'

'Do you know what would have happened to you, if he'd succeeded in taking you hostage?' His voice went low and she sensed the danger beneath it.

'Yes,' she whispered, her voice trembling. 'I know how they would have used me.'

'And do you think I would *ever* let a man touch you in that way? I don't care what the glass means to you. You can let it go.'

Inside, she was torn apart by his words. She'd thought that, by bringing in so much silver, he would respect her skill. That he would encourage her glassmaking, being proud of the way she'd earned them wealth.

All her life, she'd been treated like the beggar her father was. Never had she possessed any sense of pride; she'd grown accustomed to everyone looking down upon her. And now that she'd finally proven that there was something more, that she could be a woman worth something, he wanted her to let it go.

From deep inside, a dormant anger intensified, rising higher until it cracked apart. 'I can't give up my glass, any more than you can give up being chief. It's who I am.' She was crying now, but he hadn't softened even once. If anything, his stubborn will had grown more rigid.

'You'll have to,' was all he would say. Then he took her hand and guided her inside Vanora's house. When the matron and Grizel both asked questions, their voices rising and arguing as they exclaimed over what had happened,

Laren didn't speak a word. Instead, she went to lie beside her daughters, sleeping as far away from Alex as she dared to go.

Laren didn't speak to him all the next day. Alex had sent more men to find the intruder, but they'd found only traces of blood and the horse's tracks disappeared near the stream. There was no way of knowing where the man had gone or when he would return. At least he'd managed to wound his enemy.

Though he tried to continue working on the outer wall, his thoughts were consumed by Laren. She'd avoided him that morning and he sensed the resentment simmering beneath her mood.

He tried not to care. Aye, she was angry about not being able to work on the glass, but this was about her safety. Though rationally he knew it was impossible to keep her in his sight at every moment, he'd been caught off-guard last night. When he'd seen her fighting her attacker, he'd nearly lost his mind. The visceral need to protect her, to surrender his own blood for hers, had surged inside him.

And later, when she'd reached for him, needing the physical comfort of his body, he'd thought they were starting to mend their broken marriage. All this morning, he'd remembered her touch, the sounds she'd uttered when she experienced her climax, her legs tightening around his waist.

Alex grew aroused just remembering it and it only added to his dark mood. He busied himself with hefting stones from the wagon to the outer wall, trying to drown out his needs with the punishing work, but he couldn't help but be aware of Laren. She'd done as he'd ordered, walking behind Nairna and helping the women to gather thatch and smaller pieces of wood for the new homes they had to build.

Deliberately, she walked past him once and he noticed the scent of wood about her. She didn't speak, but the gentle sway of her hips captured his gaze. When she glanced beyond the fortress, he sent her a silent warning.

Upon her cheek, he saw the reddened mark that was beginning to bruise. It angered him even further, wishing he'd been able to kill the man who'd touched her.

Laren started to walk towards the gates, and at her open defiance, Alex dropped the stone he was holding and crossed the space. 'Where are you going?'

She stood tall and stared back. 'To fetch water from the loch. Or am I not allowed to do that either?'

'Not alone.' He gestured for her to walk forwards and she picked up a wooden bucket, while he trailed behind to guard her.

She stepped on to the outer layer of ice, moving towards the unfrozen portion. He didn't like her venturing out, not when she could slip or fall into the icy water. Without asking, he seized the bucket and started to get the water for her.

Laren watched him, her gaze infuriated. 'And now I'm too helpless to even dip a bucket into the loch?'

He slammed the bucket down, his fury erupting. 'What do you want from me, Laren? You were nearly taken last night, and you expect me to grant you freedom to go where it pleases you? He's going to come back. And I'll be damned if I'll let you be his captive.'

'Instead, I'm your captive,' she said. Her voice was cold, full of her own ire. 'Do you plan to tie me to your side, so

I can't escape you? Or perhaps you'll bind me to your bed and use me as it pleases you?'

'You were the one who wanted me last night,' he shot back. 'I was going to leave you alone.'

Her expression was brittle and she was near to tears. 'I wish you would. At least then I could be of some use, if you'd let me make the glass.'

He took a step back, feeling as if she'd struck him. He didn't understand why she was so insistent on returning to the cavern. They didn't need the silver as badly as she believed they did.

'If the furnaces weren't so far away, it would be different.' He tried to appease her and continued, 'Perhaps in the spring, when it's safer, you could return to the work if it pleases you.'

'You truly don't understand, do you? This isn't like my weaving or sewing. It's not the same at all.' She reached down for the bucket, her arm straining with the weight of the water.

She was right—he didn't understand. And the angrier she grew, the more he sensed that this was about something else entirely.

He took the bucket and tossed it aside. Taking her wrist, he guided her forwards, moving towards the cavern. She said nothing, but matched her pace with his, even though it meant she had to run slightly.

When they reached the entrance, the furnace fires were out, the interior cold. She went to her work table and sat before it, her hands clenched tight.

'What is this really about, Laren?'

She picked up a piece of glass and rubbed its surface. 'You're not being reasonable about this. I understand that you don't want me to work alone. But you can't lock me away.'

'And why can't I?' He moved to sit across from her. 'If I want to keep you safe from harm, why does that make me a monster?'

'It doesn't. But I can't give up this commission.' She pressed a clear glass droplet into his hand. The smooth surface grew warm within his hand and she said, 'Working with the glass gives me a purpose. It's something I can do that no other woman of this clan can. With it, I can prove to them that I'm worth something. That I'm not a beggar, like my father was.'

In her eyes, he saw twenty years' worth of pain. He'd never thought much about her family's poverty—he'd seen only the woman who had stolen his heart.

She rose from the bench and went to stand at the entrance. 'Don't keep me a prisoner, Alex. Let me do this.' The desperation in her voice and in her eyes gave him pause. He wanted to keep her within the fortress, where no one could hurt her. Why couldn't she understand that he needed to protect her?

'You'll stay at Glen Arrin, until we're sure that the threat is gone,' he said.

'And after that?' she whispered.

He wanted to refuse. But he sensed that if he took this away from her, she would grow to hate him.

He didn't know what the right decision was. She was staring at him with a blend of hope and doubts. Finally, he acceded, 'Only if Callum agrees to guard you.'

It was the only compromise he'd make. And even then, he didn't like it.

The light in her eyes and the fierce joy took him aback. She threw her arms around his neck, and though he rested his hands upon her waist, he didn't hug her back. He felt as though he were bargaining to save his marriage and it infuriated him that she would push him to that boundary.

As he took her back to Glen Arrin, he wondered what he'd just agreed to.

Finian lay upon the ground, blood staining the frozen grass beneath him. Though it had been nearly a sennight, the wound upon his arm kept reopening. The skin had turned red, and he'd been shaking with fever for two days now. He'd finally accepted that he couldn't stay here any longer; he had to return home to tend the wound.

When he heard a horse approaching, Finian struggled to rise. Dizziness plagued his vision, but when he saw the rider his tension eased. It was a priest, travelling on horseback. Not a threat at all.

The priest drew closer and when he spied Finian, he dismounted. His dark robes trailed the ground and he folded his hands within the long sleeves. '*A charaid,* you're bleeding. Will you allow me to help you?'

Finian nodded, easing himself to sit up. Though the ground still swayed beneath him, he allowed the priest to unwrap his sodden sleeve.

'A sword, was it?' The priest opened up a pouch he carried and withdrew a folded piece of linen from inside. He pulled back Finian's sleeve and tore a piece from it, swabbing at the blood. 'You're lucky you didn't lose that arm. I won't be able to stitch it for you, but you are welcome to join me as I journey to Glen Arrin. I'm certain one of the women there would help you.'

'Glen Arrin?' Finian repeated, unable to believe what he was hearing.

'Aye.' The priest smiled. 'There is a glass artist there

whose work is nothing short of miraculous. The abbot has commissioned a window from the MacKinlochs and I'm bringing the plans to them.'

Finian barely listened to the man's words, for when the priest tightened the linen around his arm, the pain made it impossible to answer.

'Will you come, then?' the priest asked again. 'The MacKinlochs would be glad to help a man in need.'

But Finian only shook his head. Though the MacKinlochs hadn't seen his face on the night he'd attacked, as soon as they saw the wound upon his arm, it would reveal his identity. 'No, thank you, Father. I'll return to my family.'

After he thanked the priest for his kindness, the man smiled. 'A family is a blessing indeed. God go with you and your loved ones.'

A bleakness reached out to him, squeezing Finian's heart. For there was no one to guard his daughter now. And he simply didn't know how he could save her.

The autumn was fading into harsh winter as Laren finished panes of glass in all different colours, preparing for the design she would have to make. Callum had kept his word, patrolling the area surrounding her cavern. She'd felt uneasy about Alex's brother, for never did he speak. She worried that he resented having to guard her, for he ignored her attempts to give him food or to make him feel more at ease. Truthfully, she hoped that her husband would lift the requirement, now that there had been no further attacks.

One morning, before she could go to the cavern, Laren spied a priest arriving on horseback. He was dressed in dark robes of a simple wool, with a hood to cover his head.

When he approached, he stopped the horse a few paces before the gates. He lowered his hood, studying the fortress as if wondering if he were in the right place. He tucked his hands inside his long sleeves and ventured forwards, leading the horse with him.

Laren guessed he was one of the priests from the abbey who had come with the plans she needed. She drew close to Nairna and her sister-in-law crossed over to speak with him. The man appeared tired and frail from his journey, but he managed to smile and greet them.

'You came from the Abbey of Inveriston, I presume?' Before the priest could voice a reply beyond a simple nod, Nairna continued on. 'You'll want a meal and some mead to refresh yourself. And perhaps you'd honour us by saying Mass in the morning?'

'Of—of course.' The man appeared taken aback by Nairna's bold questions, but eventually he managed to introduce himself. 'I am Father Stephen.'

Nairna sent him a broad smile. 'You are welcome here.' Now that he was dismounted, she explained in a low voice, 'Laren can discuss the glass with you and show you the sample pieces. The others don't know about it yet. We'll go to the cavern and you can give her the plans you brought.'

'The cavern?'

He appeared confused, but Laren clarified, 'Where the glass is made.' It was far better to hold a conversation there, where no one would eavesdrop.

The priest lowered his head, nodding his agreement as he followed them towards the shores of the loch. Laren studied the priest, unsure of whether or not to admit that she was the glass artist and not her false brother. He didn't appear to be biased against women. As they walked towards the cavern along the edge of the loch, she weighed it over in her mind, wondering whether or not he would retract the commission.

But he was a man of God, and she already felt terrible for the lie she'd told the abbot. If this priest would be staying with them for a few days, it would be impossible to keep the truth from him.

When they reached Father Nolan's cavern, Laren stopped outside the entrance. 'I want to be truthful with you,' she confessed. 'It was I who made the glass, not my brother. I should have been honest with the abbot, but I was afraid he would not allow me to take the commission.'

The priest appeared troubled. His eyes narrowed, but before he could argue with her, Laren insisted, 'There is no reason why my glass should be any different than a man's. And the abbot was pleased with the work I gave him.'

She led him and Nairna inside the cavern. 'If you are not satisfied with my work, I will return the coins.'

He gave a slight shrug, giving no hint of his opinion. Laren withdrew the sheets of glass she'd made in various colours, offering them for his inspection. While he and Nairna looked at them, she opened the annealing furnace to see if the cylinder of glass that she'd made earlier was ready to be flattened.

The priest had stopped talking, his eyes intent upon Laren as she scored and cracked the cylinder in half. Though it made her uncomfortable to be watched, she understood that this man would report everything back to the abbot.

Don't be nervous, she ordered herself. *You've made sheets of glass hundreds of times.* She placed the two halves of glass, curved-side down, into a cooler part of the furnace to soften into sheets. When she turned back to them, the priest was staring at her with wonder.

'Do you have the plans for the windows?' Nairna asked. 'Laren needs them to continue her work.'

His expression faltered for a moment, but then he opened the pouch at his waist, searching through it. A moment later, he withdrew a sheet of parchment and handed it to them.

Laren studied the sketch, her mind forming ideas for the different colours. She already had blue and green sheets for the crucifixion scene, but she would need more brown and gold. The hardest element would be the faces. She simply didn't have enough experience with painting enamel upon glass.

'I might have them ready for you in the early summer,' she predicted. 'But I'll need the measurements for the kirk windows.'

'Would you like to measure them yourself?' he offered. 'I could escort you there.'

She thought about it, but Alex was unlikely to let her leave Glen Arrin. With no other choice, she suggested, 'It would be best if you could have your priests build the frame and bring it to me.'

He was speaking to Nairna again, asking questions about the rebuilding efforts, and Laren turned her attention to another crucible of sand, lime and beechwood ashes.

After a quarter of an hour, the priest touched her hand gently.

'Did you hear my question?'

She coloured. 'No, I'm sorry. I was trying to decide which melts to begin next.' Glancing outside, she realised it had grown late. 'I should get back to my daughters.'

The priest's hand rested upon hers a moment longer and his expression grew troubled. Uneasiness rippled through

Laren, for no man had ever touched her, save Alex. She glanced around and realised that Nairna had already gone back to Glen Arrin. Callum was still outside and she didn't know if he was guarding them.

Father Stephen was looking at her intently. 'Do you want me to walk back with you?'

She shook her head slowly, her mind in disarray. His hand was warm upon hers and an unsettled feeling rooted in her stomach.

He meant nothing by it, she told herself. He'd held her hand while he spoke, that was all.

But it was the first time another man had noticed her. And when she turned back to the entrance of the cavern, she saw her husband standing there. Watching.

August, 1303

Alex found Laren huddled in their bed, though it was the middle of the day. When he opened the shutters to let in some light, she closed her eyes against the sudden brightness.

'Are you ill?' he asked.

She stared at the wall, her face so pale, he didn't know what to think. Though it hadn't been a full year since their son had died, he might as well have buried his wife. She rarely spoke to him any more.

Only a few months ago, they'd tried to put the pieces of their marriage back together. She had allowed him back into her bed for a time, but the emptiness in her embrace made their lovemaking hollow. He couldn't seem to break past the grief that closed her off from him. The warmth and love within her had died away, like a candle extinguished with no warning. And gradually, he'd stopped touching her at all.

He sat down upon the bed, feeling helpless. 'What can I do?' His voice sounded wooden, even to him. He reached out and rested his palm against her hair. Laren took his hand in hers. She moved it away, and at first he thought she didn't want him to touch her. But instead, she slowly brought it lower, beneath the coverlet.

Until she rested it upon her swollen womb.

All the words fled Alex's mind, for he was caught between joy and fear for the unborn life. He traced the rounded shape. Although it was small now, it would transform Laren's body over the next few months.

'When will the bairn come?' he managed to ask.

'In the early spring.' Her voice was emotionless and, had he not seen the glimmer of tears in her eyes, he'd have thought she didn't want it.

Slowly, he raised her to sit up, and brought her into his arms. 'It will be all right,' he said. 'I promise you.' The birth of this child was an unexpected blessing, one that might heal his wife's grief and fill her arms.

'You can't keep that promise.' Her voice was filled with uncertainty. 'If it happens again—'

'It won't. God wouldn't do that to us.' He wrapped his arms around her, trying to reassure her. But she didn't move, keeping her hands at her sides. 'Laren, I'll take care of you.'

Long moments passed, but she wouldn't look at him or return the embrace. In the end, he lowered his hands and stepped back. Not once would she look at him.

Leave her alone, *his mind insisted.* She doesn't want you right now.

Alex closed off the aching hurt inside of him. When he reached the door, he turned back to look at his wife one last time. Her hand rested upon her womb, her body curled inwards...as if she could guard the unborn life with her own.

Chapter Nine

'Return to the abbey,' Alex ordered the priest, resting his hand upon his dirk. 'Immediately. You will not say Mass tonight or in the morning.' And, God willing, the man would stay in Inveriston.

'If that is your wish.' Father Stephen bowed his head, but there was no humility or embarrassment in the man. He behaved as if there were no shame in what he'd done. Callum trailed the man, as if to ensure that he obeyed Alex's orders.

Once the man had reached the far side of the loch, Alex turned back to Laren. 'Why was the priest holding your hand?' He kept his voice neutral, but he could see the flustered air upon Laren's face. She stared at a piece of glass as though it were the most important thing in the world.

'He wasn't holding my hand. He was just…offering to walk back with me.'

'With his hand on yours.' Although most of the priests were celibate, Alex wasn't such a fool as to believe all of them were. And he'd seen the man touching Laren with more than kindness in his eyes. She was *his* wife. And, priest or no, he'd slay any man who dared to lay a hand on her.

He reached out and captured Laren by the waist. The scent of wood smoke clung to her and a long lock of red hair rested over one shoulder. Alex leaned in, bringing her into his embrace. He held her, the softness of her hair resting against his mouth.

She pulled back to stare at him. 'He brought me the plans for the commission and that was all. You've no reason to be jealous.'

He didn't care that he was behaving like an overprotective husband. The need to reassert his claim, to remind her that she was his, took precedence over all else. 'Haven't I?'

Though she slept beside him at night, for the past fortnight she'd remained on the opposite side with their daughters between them. What he wouldn't give for their own chamber, a place where he could remove the barriers of sleeping children and reach out to her again.

'The damned priest has touched you more than I have in these past few weeks.'

She looked uncomfortable in his arms. 'You've been busy with the rebuilding.'

Aye, he had. He'd worked all day and deep into the night, determined to get the walls up as soon as possible. Though there had been no more attacks, he didn't believe they were safe. And if he had to work himself to the bone to finish their defences, he'd do so.

'It will be finished soon,' he swore, letting her go. 'A few more days, at the most.'

She nodded, but when she started to retreat back to the glassmaking, he reminded her, 'Nairna arranged a feast to celebrate *Oidhche nam Bannag*. She'll expect you to be there.'

His wife's face brightened with embarrassment. 'I should have helped her with the preparations. I wasn't thinking about what day it was.' She glanced back at the furnace, frustration lining her face. 'Will you go and fetch Ramsay to come and watch the fires?'

'Aye. Then I'll return and wait for you.' He wanted her to walk with him to the celebration, to pretend to be his lady, even if it was just an illusion. After Laren had been attacked, he'd been so focused on catching the intruder, he'd neglected her again. He saw her upon waking and when he drifted off to sleep at night, but that was all.

It was no way for a man to reconcile with his wife.

Snowflakes drifted on the wind, and after Alex left the cavern, he realised he didn't know where to look. Possibly in Walter's house or among the other boys. He supposed Ramsay could be anywhere.

But when he reached the outskirts of Glen Arrin, he spied the lad waiting. Ramsay shrank down, as if trying to make himself invisible. He huddled in the cold and Alex recognised one of his old tunics that Laren must have given to the boy. It hung down over his wrists and the saffron colour was faded and worn.

Alex studied the boy's face, but thankfully he didn't see any fresh bruises. He made himself a mental reminder to find out where Eoin was, since he hadn't seen Ramsay's father in a sennight. Though Walter had taken the boy into his home, it was a temporary solution. Ramsay deserved a permanent place to live where he would be warm at night, with enough food to eat. Perhaps when the keep was finished, he and Laren could foster the boy themselves.

'Laren has asked you to come and tend the fires,' he told

the boy. 'But if you'd rather attend the celebration tonight, we can—'

'I've no wish to go.' Ramsay got up and started running toward the cavern, as if he couldn't stand to make any further conversation.

Alex followed the boy, and when he arrived back at the cave he saw Laren emerging. Her hood had slipped down to reveal her hair and snowflakes melted against her cheeks. Ramsay was already inside the cavern, adding firewood to the furnaces.

Laren walked a short distance with him and when they were out of earshot, she reminded him, 'I would never, ever betray you. Not with any man.'

He drew her to his side. 'It's not you I distrust. It's the priest.'

She fell silent as they walked towards the fortress. In the distance, torches flickered amid the fortress construction. A large bonfire blazed in the centre of the enclosure and people were starting to gather around. Monroe pulled out his pipes and began to play a lively tune while some of the folk began to dance.

When they entered the space, Alex saw that Nairna had cut fir branches, tying them in different places around the fortress. Laren's pace slowed as she studied Nairna's greenery. 'It reminds me of the way we used to decorate our home.' With a furtive smile, she said, 'My sisters and I used to collect fir branches and holly. We gave each other stones and sticks and pretended they were gold bracelets or beautiful gowns.'

'Did you ever receive real gifts?'

She nodded. 'Mother would try to make us something warm—a hood or hand coverings. Father would set snares for rabbits; if he was lucky, we had our own feast.'

Alex led her inside the fortress and she looked around for the girls. 'Where are the children?'

'Look there.' He pointed to a small circle of young girls. Grizel was addressing them solemnly and placed the bannag stone in the lap of each girl as they took turns representing St Brigid, who first held the Christ Child. 'My mother said the children will enjoy a celebration of their own. Dougal plans to tell them stories inside one of the huts.'

Laren seemed content at this, and when they drew closer to the music, he remembered that they'd danced together a time or two. He took her hand and led her away from the others, just as Monroe changed the tune to a softer one. The pipes held a haunting note of wistfulness and his wife's face softened. She'd always loved music.

'Dance with me,' Alex said, pulling her near. She hesitated, glancing around at all the people, but he took her hands and wound them around his neck. 'There's no one here except you and me.'

'There are nearly thirty people,' she protested.

But he leaned in close, touching his nose to hers. 'Don't look at them. They won't even notice us here.' He lowered his hands to her hips, moving her in a slow circle.

Laren's breath faltered at the touch of her husband's hands. He was right. The rest of the clan seemed to melt away like frozen snow, until there was nothing left but him. His dark eyes reached inside her, reminding her of days long ago.

Against her hips, she felt his arousal and his mouth moved down to hover above hers. He didn't kiss her, but warm breath mingled against her lips. 'Do you remember the first night we celebrated *Oidhche nam Bannag* together?'

The snow had stopped falling and her body was growing warmer as he wrapped his cloak around her, pressing her back against the stone wall. Though the colours had faded, she recognised the woven wool that she'd made for him, years ago. 'You kissed me for the first time.'

His palm came up to the side of her face, caressing her cheek. There was a sinful glint in his eyes, of a man who wanted to assert his claim upon her. The priest's words had conjured a jealousy she'd never seen before.

Beneath the cloak, his hands moved over her flesh, seeking bare skin while his mouth bent to hers. 'You're mine, Laren,' he said against her lips.

Before she could answer, Ross approached them. The man's face held a knowing grin and he told them, 'There will be wagering games tonight. Nairna has asked each family to offer a prize.'

'We will offer something,' Alex answered. When he'd gone, he said to Laren, 'What about a piece of your glass?'

'No.' The answer came without any need to think. She wasn't ready to reveal the glass to the others.

'It wouldn't have to be a large piece. Perhaps some small coloured pieces that you have left over.'

'I'd rather we kept it a secret.' Though she knew it had to be revealed sooner or later, she wasn't quite ready to show everyone else. It made her nervous to think of everyone staring and whispering about her.

'Why? You said you wanted to prove yourself to them. This would be your chance to show them what you've done.' Alex let go of her and she walked alongside him towards Nairna. 'Once we deliver the finished panels to the abbey, they'll have to know where they came from.'

'Not yet,' she said, increasing her pace. If she told them now, she was certain they would come to watch her work. She didn't want curious eyes interfering with her concentration.

The further she moved away from Alex, the more the cold bit through her garments. She huddled with the edges of her mantle pulled around her. With no other place to go, she moved towards the crowd of people.

But to her misfortune, Nairna saw her. 'I was hoping you'd come,' she exclaimed, with a wide smile. 'Now, we need a few more women. Vanora, you should join us.'

'What do you need?' Laren wondered if there was more food to be distributed or something to do with the children.

Nairna wouldn't answer, but kept gathering women until she had twelve in a line. 'Now, then.' She turned back to the men. 'Which of you thinks he's man enough for one of these women?'

Only Vanora's hand clamped over hers kept Laren from fleeing. In her worst nightmares, she couldn't imagine why Nairna would do this to her. Everyone was watching and she wanted to die with all the eyes upon her.

A number of husbands stepped forwards, thankfully, including Alex. Most men looked curious, rather than outraged.

'What is she doing?' Laren whispered to Vanora.

'Wait,' the older woman said. 'Watch and see.'

When the men had come to stand before them, Nairna asked, 'What gift will you give to a woman of your choice? Go and fetch it.' While the men had gone, Nairna arranged for each of the women to be blindfolded.

Laren didn't like the sensation of being sightless in front of so many people. As each minute dragged on, she felt more and more uneasy about standing here. After a time, the darkness made her dizzy and lightheaded while she imagined everyone watching her.

But a moment later, her blindfold was removed. Laren blinked as her eyes adjusted, then she saw an array of small gifts within a basket.

Nairna walked to each of them, showing them the contents, then directed each of them to choose a gift for themselves. Laren saw them select dried flowers, a clay container, lengths of wool and even a barley cake coated in honey.

When the basket came to her, the only gift remaining was a flask containing a fermented liquid. Possibly mead, she guessed. But she knew from Alex's stiff expression that he had not given the gift.

Vanora opened her clay container and found it full of ashes and sand. 'What sort of man would offer up such a terrible gift?' The matron shook her head in disgust. 'A fool, I'd wager.'

But Laren knew. Her husband had given it, for she was the only woman who would understand it. They were her tools, the ingredients needed for glass.

As Nairna bade each woman to try to choose the man who had offered the gift, there was teasing as the men denied or agreed that they had brought it. When Vanora's turn came, she held up the container of sand.

'Whoever gave this must have been a man who wanted to tease his wife. I'll guess that Ross gave it.' With a smug grin, she added, 'He never did like to spend his hard-won coins.'

But Ross shook his head, grinning that she'd guessed wrong. 'You should know me better, woman.'

When it came Laren's turn, her hands were trembling as the eyes of the others stared at her. She held up the flask and said, 'I believe Ross gave the mead.'

Nairna turned a questioning look to the older man, who

nodded in agreement. 'My own wife doesn't know what's closest to my heart,' he sighed. Then he puckered his lips to Laren, making kissing sounds while the others roared with laughter.

'Will you take his kiss and the mead, or another gift of your choice?' Nairna asked.

Laren shook her head, feeling the nervousness starting to take hold. 'I'll take the container of sand. And the man who gave it.'

The laughter of the crowd fell silent when Alex came forwards. Though Vanora pressed the container in her hands and took the mead in exchange, Laren hardly noticed. She saw only her husband coming for her and, in his eyes, there was fierce desire.

He took her hand in his, leading her away from the others.

The wind was bitterly cold as they walked along the edge of the loch. Alex held Laren's waist, his cloak draped over both of them. Laren had grown quieter, but he hoped her tension would ease when they reached the cavern with the furnaces. One advantage was the intense heat when they were lit.

When they reached the entrance she stopped him. 'Let me send Ramsay home. Wait while I speak with him.'

He heard her quiet tone as she talked to the lad. Within a few minutes more, the boy left the cavern, his gaze still fastened upon the ground. His skin was flushed with heat—at least he would be warm enough until he reached Glen Arrin.

Alex caught the boy by the arm before he could go far. 'I know you've been staying with Walter, these past few nights. Has he been treating you well?'

The boy gave a single nod, looking nervous at the questions.

'And what of your father? Has Eoin bothered you since that night?'

Ramsay clutched his arms, but shook his head. The boy's hollowed posture and broken spirits made Alex wish he'd known of the abuse long before this. The guilt weighed upon him, but he promised himself that nothing would happen to Laren's apprentice again.

'If it's your wish, you needn't return to your father's house. I'll see to it.'

The boy stared at him as if he didn't know how to respond. Then, with a quick nod, he fled the cavern and started on the path toward Walter's.

'Thank you for looking after him,' came Laren's voice. She sent him a quiet smile before she turned back to the fires, stoking them higher. He watched as she examined a clay container that held a melt. The colour had started to shift from saffron to a pink tone.

'Not too much longer,' she said, sliding it back into the furnace with an iron rod. 'An hour, perhaps.'

When she turned back to him, Alex spread his cloak upon the ground. Laren hesitated, her face flushed as she held her hands out before the furnace, warming them. He saw the way her gaze was fixated upon the fire and wondered if it hadn't been such a good idea to bring her here. She seemed distracted by the glass.

When he came up behind her, she stiffened. 'I didn't like what Nairna did tonight. Being in front of so many people…' Her voice trailed off, her eyes upon the floor. 'I know she meant nothing by it, but I felt so awkward.'

'You haven't been around the clan very often in the past fortnight.'

She turned to him, discontent rising in her eyes. 'I know it. But I have to stay with the glass, if I want to finish it for the kirk windows.'

Alex said nothing, for it was her decision to leave them, seeking out her work to give her comfort. His mood shifted into one of frustration. By giving her the freedom to complete the commission, it seemed that she'd slipped even further away from him.

'How much longer will it take?' He moved to the far end of the cavern, near the pipes that were preheating.

'Months,' she admitted. 'Ramsay is learning to blow the glass, but he needs another year before his pieces will be good enough.'

It meant another few months when he would hardly see her at all. He turned back and she was sitting at the stone table, arranging pieces of coloured glass. 'I don't like living this way,' he admitted.

Her hands stilled and she raised questioning eyes to him.

'I don't like seeing you only at night. And when I do, you're already asleep.'

She remained seated, watching him. 'The work is exhausting.'

He crossed back to stand before her. 'I wanted to bring us back to the way things were, before David died. But that can't happen, can it?'

Her face grew pale, knowing what he meant. 'What do you want from me, Alex?'

'I don't think it's something you can give.' Her glass-making required her to spend hours away from them. And it wasn't possible for him to see her throughout the day, not when she had to stay with the furnaces.

'I'm not giving up the glass.' She stood up, facing him.

'I didn't demand that, did I?' He fought back the resentment, the frustration building up inside. 'But what kind of a marriage is this, if we're always apart?'

She stared at him in distress. He felt as though he'd struck her down, but he didn't know how else to say it.

'What would you have me do?' she whispered.

'I don't know.' He raked a hand through his hair and strode away. 'There's nothing you can do, is there?'

She remained silent. For long moments, he heard nothing. Then her footsteps approached and he felt her hand upon his shoulder. When he turned to her, he saw that she'd unbound her hair. The long red strands held a slight wave to them, from the earlier braids. Then she reached back and loosened her gown.

His mouth went dry when he saw her lower the sleeves and the bodice, baring her breasts. She lifted his hands to touch the warm weight of them and he understood. She was trying to offer herself, to pacify him by giving him her body.

But the act was meaningless without her heart. He didn't want her like this. Lowering his hands, he faced her. 'This won't fix what's broken between us.'

A wrenching hurt filled up her blue eyes, but he didn't apologise. She fumbled with her gown, covering herself. 'I can't seem to please you any more, can I?'

Alex stepped forwards and picked up one of her glass pieces that lay on the table. It was a colourless scrap she'd discarded, the edges jagged and raw. He rubbed the hardened surface for a moment before he let it fall back.

'I don't know what happened to the marriage we had. You're not the same person you used to be.'

'No. I'm not.' She folded her arms across her waist, as if she could hold back the bruised feelings.

'From the moment we buried our son, you left me,' he said. 'You hid yourself away with your glass, and I had no wife at all.'

A glimmer of anger tightened her features. 'I wasn't the only one who hid myself away. When I came home at night, you weren't there. How many times did you eat with other families, coming home only when we were asleep? You spent more time with the clan members than your own family.'

'I'm their chief. It was my responsibility.' Didn't she understand that he hadn't known what he was doing? He'd spent time with the other families, trying to unravel the needs of the people.

'Was it?' she asked softly. 'Or were you avoiding me?'

Her accusation was dangerously hard. And a little too close to the truth. He hadn't known how to help her through the pain when he'd never handled it himself. It seemed easier to pretend nothing was wrong, to go on about their lives as usual.

'I'm not avoiding you now.' He came close and stood before her.

She looked so vulnerable, so upset, he didn't know what to say. He'd brought her here, hoping to make things better.

'Laren, what should we do?' he asked at last. A hollowness filled him up inside, for he couldn't find the right words.

'When we were younger, no one wanted us to be together,' she said quietly. 'You came at night, so my parents wouldn't know. And no one could keep us apart.' She raised her eyes to his. 'We loved each other too much.'

He reached for her hand, remembering those days. Her palm rested in his and she touched his palm with her other hand. 'I don't think you love me now, the way you did then.'

'No,' he admitted. 'Both of us have changed.' He kept his voice neutral, hiding the blunt pain he would never reveal to her. 'It can't be the same as it was. But it can be stronger.'

Her hands moved to rest over his heart. For a time, she thought about what he'd said. Then she answered, 'Sunset.'

He moved back, uncertain of what she meant. 'Sunset?'

'When the sun goes down, we both come home. I'll leave Ramsay with my glass. And you'll leave your work. The stone can wait a few hours.'

He cast a glance towards the furnace, wondering if she could keep that promise. Often, she'd forgotten the time when she was caught up in her glassmaking. Still, it was worth trying. 'All right.'

She laced his hands in hers, tilting her face upwards. 'It's worth fighting for, Alex.'

Glen Arrin—1298

Alex stared at his father's body as the men lowered it into the shallow grave. One by one, the men placed stones over Tavin and the brutal finality made him walk away.

The truth was, he didn't want the other men to see him weep. He wasn't a child and his mother would only cuff him if she saw tears.

When he reached the hillside, he started to run hard. His lungs heaved and his cheeks were wet, but at least there was no one to see. He didn't know where he was going, but he had to get away from everyone else.

Near the top of the hill, he saw a forest clearing and a circle of standing stones. Alex vaguely recalled seeing

*them once before, but the limestone blurred before his
eyes. He sank to his knees, leaning against a stone as he
wept. His father was dead and two of his brothers as well.*

*He'd tried to stop Bram from leaving, but his older
brother had grabbed a sword and gone running toward
the English soldiers. Callum had followed, while Alex had
remained behind like a coward. If he'd gone, maybe they
would still be here. But they had disappeared, like so many
of the other men.*

*'They're dead,' his Uncle Donnell had said. 'Nothing
to be done about it.'*

*Alex pressed his forehead against the stone, his hands
shaking. He barely heard the soft footsteps behind him, but
saw Laren standing there. Like a quiet spirit, she stepped
closer, and her own tears were wet against her cheeks.*

*She spoke not a word, though he remembered that her
own father had been numbered among the dead. Though
he'd known who she was, it was the first time she'd ever
approached him. Rarely did Laren speak to anyone, though
she was one of the most beautiful girls in the clan. She
seemed embarrassed by her family's poverty, though it
meant nothing to him.*

'Do you want me to leave?' she whispered.

*Alex shook his head, resting his forehead against the
stone. There were no words he wanted to speak right now,
but he supposed she understood that. He'd loved his father
and had wanted so badly for Tavin to be proud of him. The
emptiness stretched out, filling him with regret.*

*Laren touched her hand upon his shoulder, offering a
quiet comfort. He'd turned and locked his arms around
her, both of them grieving. Though she was hardly more
than a stranger to him, she held him in her embrace and it*

felt right to have her there. The warmth of a human touch made it easier to endure the wrenching pain of loss.

After that day, there was an invisible bond that drew him to her. He'd sworn that when he came of age, Laren would be his wife—her and no one else.

Chapter Ten

Finian MacLachor's arm burned from the wound he'd sustained. Though it had stopped bleeding long ago, the wound wasn't healing well. His arm had swollen up to twice its size and he shuddered at the task that had to be done.

It had been a risk, trying to steal the chief's wife—one that hadn't worked. Alex MacKinloch had slashed his sword in the darkness and Finian had misjudged the distance. He'd been fortunate enough to escape with his life, for the MacKinlochs had spent several days tracking him. He'd kept to the lochs and streams, using the water to hide his footprints. And when he'd returned to infiltrate Glen Arrin a second time, he'd watched over the MacKinlochs for a night and a day, gathering information. They hadn't even known he was there, that brought him a slight consolation.

His brother Brochain was heating his dirk within the fire, bringing the point and blade to a fiery heat. 'This is going to hurt like hell, Finian.'

'And if you don't do it, I'm going to die of the poison that's already in me.' He held up his arm, bracing himself for the worst.

A gasp shuddered from him as Brochain plunged his blade into the swollen wound, letting it bleed out the yellowish pus that was festering inside. Then his brother packed the wound with healing herbs their sister had prepared. Finian didn't know if he passed out or not, but the next thing he was aware of was Brochain using the flat of the blade to cauterise the injury.

A cry tore from his mouth as the blistering pain ripped through him. And when it was done, Brochain passed him an animal skin of ale.

'This isn't strong enough,' he told Brochain, drinking heavily.

'You'll live,' his brother pronounced.

Finian lifted the animal skin again, wishing to God that it were possible to get drunk faster. His face tightened as he eyed the remains of their land. Although the homes were untouched, there were so few MacLachors left alive that it might as well have been abandoned.

'What are you going to do about Iliana?' Brochain asked.

Finian stared into the fire, knowing that there was little hope for his daughter. His attempts to attack both Lord Harkirk and the MacKinlochs had met with failure. The Feast of Saint Agatha was rapidly approaching and he doubted if he'd meet with any success.

'Gather some of the men. We'll try for a MacKinloch hostage one last time. Take anyone you can find.'

'Even the children?' Brochain sent him a dark look. It

wasn't at all what Finian wanted. But what choice did he have?

He drained the rest of the ale. 'Even the children.'

At dusk, Alex spied Laren walking towards him. She'd kept her promise over the last few days, leaving Ramsay to work on the fires while she returned at sunset. The first outer wall was now finished and the second nearly so. Alex leaned up against the inner wall, waiting for his wife. Against the descending sun, her hair gleamed like fire.

Even after five years of marriage, she was as beautiful to him now as she'd been the first day he'd met her. But she appeared tired, her face wan. In her hands, she carried a leather-wrapped bundle and he wondered what it was.

When she reached his side, he greeted her with a kiss. Although she was shy to show him affection in front of the others, gradually she'd become used to it.

'What did you bring back?' he asked. 'Something for the girls?'

She glanced around, as if looking to see who was watching. 'And for you. But we should go to a place where the others won't see.'

It was glass, then. He'd suspected as much. 'I'll bring Mairin and Adaira to the edge of the loch. Will that be secret enough?'

She nodded. 'I'll wait for you there.'

Before she could go back, he caught her hand. 'We can only stay for a short time, Laren. Tonight we're going to have a competition among the men. Both of us should be there.' If all went according to plan, they would have walls up around the keep later tonight. Alex had ordered the men to cut large pieces of wood for the framing, and it was piled up in readiness. 'We'll feast with the others later.'

After she left his side, he went to fetch his daughters. Mairin and Adaira were hungry, but when he told them that their mother had a surprise for them, their curiosity overcame their whining.

'What is it, Mama?' Mairin demanded, racing towards the edge of the loch where Laren was waiting. 'What did you bring us?'

'Cake?' Adaira suggested. 'For me?'

'No, not cake,' Laren said. She unwrapped the leather bundle and Alex spied a row of twisted pieces of glass. One end was a solid teardrop, while a wisp of melted glass spiraled upwards like a swirl of honey.

'What are they?'

Laren took one and passed it to him. 'Drop it hard against the stone and watch.'

He took the soft end and eyed her. There was mischief brewing in her eyes and, from the way she pulled the girls behind her, he suspected that she was playing a trick upon him.

Gingerly, he let go of the bit of glass. As soon as it struck the stone, it exploded with a loud crack. He jerked back from instinct and unsheathed his dirk.

Laren started laughing at him. 'Were you trying to kill it?'

He rolled his eyes. 'By God, woman, what *was* that?'

Mairin burst forwards. 'I want one! Let me try!' Laren gave her a twist of glass and her daughter happily smashed it against the rock, giggling when it exploded in a shower of dust.

'When you drop hot glass into cold water, it makes these sometimes.' She reached into a fold of her cloak and showed him droplets of colored glass. 'Like the ones you gave me.'

She'd kept them. He didn't know why, but knowing it brought a warmth inside of him. While his daughters smashed more of the glass droplets, Laren joined them in laughing. Her face was flushed and the bright smile on her face caught him like a kick to the lungs. He hadn't seen her so relaxed in a long time.

When they'd finished smashing the glass, Laren took the girls in each hand and Alex took Adaira's other palm. He eyed Laren and together they lifted Adaira up by her palms, swinging her forwards until she squealed.

When they reached the fortress again, he saw that Nairna was lighting the torches.

The aroma of roasting meat filled the air and his girls sniffed appreciatively, reminding him of how hungry they were. As soon as she saw all the people waiting, he saw the happiness freeze up on Laren's face. She held on to the girls' hands as if they were a shield.

Alex saw the look of fear upon her face, but a moment later she released the children, murmuring for them to go and sit with Vanora. He saw her approach Nairna and the woman sent Laren a grateful smile. 'I'll need ten women to help me pass around the food,' she predicted. 'Could you gather them and ask for their help?'

Laren nodded and seemed to steel herself for the task. One by one, she went to several women, asking them for help. Before long they had passed out wooden platters containing slices of roasted pork, paired with carrots, turnips and nuts. Two barrels of ale were opened and the atmosphere transformed into one of celebration.

When Laren joined him again, she didn't look well.

Alex made her sit down and eat something, but she picked at her food. 'Are you all right?'

His wife nodded and, when she met his gaze, admitted, 'You asked me to try harder. To be the wife you need.'

He understood that she was trying to behave like the Lady of Glen Arrin. He reached over and squeezed her hand. 'If you can find a bit more courage, we're not done yet.' It was time to begin the competition and choose teams.

He led Laren forwards, bringing her to the centre of the fortress. The clansmen set aside their food and Alex waited until he had their attention. 'We wanted to host this celebration tonight in thanks for all that you've given to rebuild Glen Arrin. It's time to begin framing the keep and I wanted to offer a competition to anyone who wishes to join in.' He pointed towards the new foundation, that had been laid in stone.

'A prize of three cows and two sheep will be awarded to the winning team of men who can construct their side the fastest. My brothers and I will form one team, while we need three more teams to complete the remaining sides.' He continued explaining the rules, before the men began dividing up into groups.

Several of the women went to wish their husbands luck and Alex saw Bram pull his wife into a deep kiss. The two of them were so wrapped up in each other, he doubted if they'd notice if the walls came crashing down.

But Laren had already retreated from his side, back to their daughters. He didn't miss the looks of reproach on the faces of many women. There was a coolness there and his wife kept her gaze downcast.

He'd never really noticed the way they treated her like an outsider. It bothered him to see her in that way. Had it always been like this? He tried to remember if she'd had close friends when they were first married and he wasn't chief of the clan. He didn't know.

She sat with Adaira on her lap, Mairin snuggled close, but there were no women joining Laren to talk.

When he gave the signal, Alex worked alongside his brothers, building the framework while the teams on the other sides raced to build up their wall faster. As the hours passed, the lower walls of the castle keep began to take shape.

His arms were aching from holding the beams in place while Dougal climbed a ladder to hammer in the pegs. From behind him, he caught a slight motion. And then one of the beams slipped.

Alex threw himself at Bram, knocking his brother to the side as the wood struck the place where he'd been standing. Thank God, no one was hurt.

But when he got back to his feet, he saw that Laren had rushed forwards. 'What happened?' Her face was tight with worry and he pulled her against him, offering her comfort.

'I'm all right,' he told her. 'The beam slipped.' Her hands came up to touch his back, but the embrace was tentative, as if she suddenly realised that others were watching them.

When he released her, she let out a shaky breath. 'How much more is left to finish?'

'A few hours more and we'll have the four walls framed. After that, we'll choose our winning team and end the work for the night.' He took her hands, adding, 'You look tired. If you want to take the girls back to Ross's, you needn't wait on me.'

She studied him for a long moment. Then she said, 'I'll put the girls to sleep. And then I'll wait.'

* * *

Laren had made it halfway across the fortress when Alex's mother Grizel crossed the space to speak with her. 'You should know better than to go near the men when they're building. You might have been killed just now.'

'The beam had already fallen,' she pointed out.

Her mother-in-law let out a sigh. 'Your judgment seems to be lacking at times. And it's clear that you have no inkling of the responsibilities of a chief's wife.'

The woman's criticisms were like dull razors, cutting into her confidence. Though Laren tried to ignore Grizel, the longer she remained silent, the more her mother-in-law found fault with other things.

'You should have organised the feast tonight,' Grizel continued. 'I don't know what it is you spend your time doing…sleeping, I suppose. Like your father always did.'

'I'm not my father,' she shot back. Inwardly she cursed herself for rising to Grizel's bait.

A light entered Grizel's eyes at the prospect of an argument. 'No, but you've the same blood. Why you ever thought you'd be a good wife to Alex is beyond my ken.'

'I loved him,' she whispered. 'And he loved me.'

'Love has nothing to do with a strong marriage. If you were a better wife to him, you'd lead at his side. Though I imagine you think it's best to keep bearing children. Why, if your son had lived—'

'Don't speak of him.' Laren turned on Grizel, tightening her grip on Adaira. 'Don't ever speak of him.'

When the older woman's lip started to move, Laren cut her off. 'Save your words. You've said enough this night.'

She increased her stride, forcing Mairin to walk faster. Angry tears welled up inside. Worse, she couldn't even have a moment alone, for the woman was staying with them. The walls of the keep couldn't go up fast enough as far as she was concerned. She tucked the girls in, wishing she could crawl under the coverlet and ignore Grizel for the rest of the night.

But voices rose from outside, breaking through the stillness. 'Did you hear that?' she asked Grizel, listening hard.

'It's nothing. Just the men working,' the woman responded. 'Now, as I was telling you—'

'Stay with the girls,' Laren ordered. She knew she'd heard something. Though she hoped that she was being fearful over nothing, she still moved to take one of Ross's dirks. The blade was heavy in her hand and she wished the men would return.

'There's nothing there,' Grizel insisted. 'Now put that down and—'

Laren stepped outside, clenching the weapon in her hands. When she heard nothing but the sigh of the wind, she wondered if perhaps Alex's mother was right.

And then she heard rustling sounds. Movement, coming from outside the fortress.

With her heart pounding, she ran back to Alex, where four walls of the keep stood in various stages of completion. Ignoring the celebration, Laren found her husband, just as he was announcing the winning team.

'I heard movement coming from the trees,' she warned him. 'I don't know if it's a raid, but they're near the loch.'

Alex alerted the others and the men grabbed weapons, just as a group of a dozen men emerged through the gates, their shouts resounding in the darkness.

Two of them moved towards the livestock, while others went after the grain. The sounds of fighting tore through the celebration, iron blades clashing together as the MacKinlochs defended their home.

'MacLachors,' she heard Ross say.

'I thought they were our allies.' Laren didn't understand it. If they'd needed grain and supplies, they'd only had to ask. Alex would have welcomed their labour in return for food.

'They've a new chief, so I've heard.' the older man replied. 'Likely a young man causing trouble.'

Laren stayed clear of the fighting, but in the distance, she spied two of the men moving towards the hut where her girls were sleeping.

No. She ran hard, fury rising from the pit of her stomach as she went after them. Her lungs burned, the fear snaking into her gut. If they dared to harm one of her daughters, she'd hunt them down.

Alex came running behind her, his claymore drawn with both hands. 'Stay back,' he warned, but Laren ignored him. When a raider moved towards her, she swung the dirk. He dodged her slash and, with his spear shaft, struck a blow to her hands. The weapon dropped away and she had no choice but to retreat.

'Get inside, Laren,' Alex warned. He swung the claymore, the long blade slicing towards the man's head. 'If you lay a finger upon my wife, you'll find it on the ground, along with your severed hand.'

Laren moved behind him, holding her torch aloft, in case the man broke free. Alex held the claymore in both hands before he charged at the man, swinging with precision. 'Why did you come, MacLachor?'

'For the bounty on your heads.' He held the spear up, blocking Alex's blow, but when the claymore cut into the wood, Alex couldn't free his weapon. Instead, he twisted the blade, disarming his enemy.

He threw himself atop the man and caught him by the throat. 'What bounty?'

'The one offered by Harkirk.' The MacLachor man fought to free himself, his fingers digging against Alex's palm.

Laren grew cold at the thought. If what he said was true, then they were in more danger than they'd believed.

'How much did he offer for me?' Alex jerked the man to his feet, tightening his grip. When there came no answer, he unsheathed the dirk at his waist. 'Tell me, damn you.'

His enemy's gaze went blank, in anticipation of death. 'Our chief's daughter is Harkirk's hostage,' he admitted. 'The Baron says he'll take your life for hers.'

Instinctively, Laren glanced behind at the shelter where her girls were sleeping. Harkirk had the MacLachor chief's daughter in his keeping?

Now it was clear. The man who'd attacked before must have been a MacLachor, trying to lure Alex. And tonight, they'd struck with the last of their men, in a desperate act.

She saw her husband's attention flicker for just a moment, then he dived to the ground. An arrow lay embedded in the wood just where his head had been. The MacLachor used his chance to escape; within seconds, he'd disappeared into the darkness of the trees.

'Get inside,' Alex ordered, opening the door for her. From the torn look upon his face, she knew that he had to go with his men, to pursue the remaining MacLachors.

'I'll keep you safe,' he swore. There was a look of hesitation on his face, before he returned to the centre of the fortress. Laren stood at the entrance to the hut, watching as he went off to fight.

When Alex was gone, she knelt down to touch the arrow. It might have killed him just now. Her hand shook as she ripped it free of the wood, staring at the pointed tip. If he hadn't moved in time, she might be sitting here with him dying in her arms. She shivered, wishing her husband hadn't left her. Waiting was nearly as bad as watching him fight.

She forced herself to go back inside, where she found Grizel standing in front of the girls, her face pale. In her hands, the older woman held a spear she'd snatched from Ross's belongings.

'Are they all right?' Laren whispered.

Grizel nodded. 'They slept through the raid.'

Laren's knees were shaking and she went to stand near the hearth. Despite the heat of the fire, she couldn't stop shivering. Then she looked over at Grizel, who was setting the spear aside. 'Thank you for watching over them.'

The older woman turned away in silence, staring at the flames. Her mood had shifted into a solemn regret and Laren wondered if Grizel was remembering how her husband Tavin had been killed in battle.

'You should be glad to have daughters,' the old woman said. 'At least they won't grow up to fight in raids. Or be taken as slaves.'

'I hope not.' Her thoughts lingered upon the MacLachor's claim that Harkirk had taken their chief's daughter captive. And she wondered what would happen now.

'You don't look well,' her mother-in-law remarked. 'Did you remember to eat?'

She nodded, but her thoughts returned to Grizel's comment about being glad to have girls. She did love her daughters, but sometimes she couldn't help but wonder what their son David would have been like. He'd have been three years old, had he lived.

She clenched her gloved hands, trying to blot out the memories. But her mind persisted in the painful visions.

Would David have dragged a wooden sword around, pretending to be like his father? Would he have laughed and held on to her hip when he needed her? She vividly remembered the warmth of his small body nestled against her breast when he'd been born.

Until the terrible morning when his body was cold and lifeless upon hers. She'd never known what had caused him to die, and it hurt so much to remember it.

'You're weeping,' Grizel said suddenly.

Laren hadn't realised. She wiped the tears away and lowered her head. 'It's been a difficult night for all of us. We should get some sleep.'

But as she curled up on her side, she felt as though a splinter were piercing her heart.

When Alex returned later that night with Ross and Vanora, Laren awakened instantly. Perhaps she hadn't been sleeping at all, but when he entered, she stood up and guided him back outside.

Without speaking a word, she wrapped her arms around his waist and held him. He gripped her back, taking comfort in her embrace.

'They're gone,' he murmured. 'All except a man who died from one of Callum's arrows.'

'You let them go?'

He pulled back to study her face. The torchlight cast a honeyed glow over her face and he said a silent prayer of thanks that he'd been able to come back to Laren.

'Aye. I may regret showing them mercy.'

She rested her hands around his waist. 'What are you going to do about the bounty?'

'Nothing.' It was beyond his control anyway. If Harkirk wanted to hire assassins to try to bring them down, so be it. It was the reason they'd built strong walls to defend Glen Arrin.

'Aren't you afraid?' She touched his cheek, rubbing the stubble that abraded her fingertips.

'No.' He couldn't afford the luxury of fear. The greater issue was Glen Arrin and how to keep the rest of them safe.

She studied him with uncertain eyes. 'You nearly died tonight.'

'I nearly die every time I fight,' he pointed out. 'It's always a risk.'

But she took no reassurance from his indifferent tone. Instead, she looked even more upset.

'It's late,' he told her. 'We'll sleep and talk about it in the morning.'

She drew back from his embrace. 'Alex, if there's a price on your head—'

'Leave it be, Laren.' He didn't want to talk about it or dwell on it. His body was physically exhausted, his mind restless.

'I'm afraid for you,' she admitted.

He wouldn't allow himself to feel any fear. And though she was wanting him to tell her that it would be all right, the truth was, he didn't know. With the state of unrest among the clans, he had enemies enough who'd be willing to attack. The last thing he wanted was to bring more danger upon the MacKinlochs.

He locked away the errant thoughts. Instead, he guided Laren back inside to lie down with their girls. She tried to get him to sleep with her, but he remained seated, resting his hand upon her hair.

His girls were sleeping, their hair tangled up, their

shoulders moving as they breathed. He couldn't imagine a man like Harkirk holding a young girl captive. No doubt the MacLachor chief was out of his mind with fury.

Though he'd wanted to ignore the threat of the English, he'd be forced to deal with them soon enough.

It felt as though the grains of his life were spilling out, all too quickly.

Chapter Eleven

Another fortnight had passed and the wooden keep was nearly finished. Though Alex had wanted to build up the walls with stone, he'd conceded to the men that it would be faster to put up a temporary structure and build the castle around it later. Within another day, they would have a place of their own for sleeping. He wanted Laren and his daughters out of Ross's home, for they needed their own space.

The threat of the MacLachors had set all of them on edge. It had fuelled the men into working harder, finishing their walls and strengthening the defences. Another attack was imminent, and he didn't know if it would come from Harkirk's forces or the MacLachor clan.

He had to do something. Ignoring the problem wasn't going to make it go away.

He walked toward Laren's cave, his leather shoes crunching upon the frozen ice puddles on the ground. He wore a shaggy, fur-lined mantle, and his breath formed clouds in the wintry air. A few sparse flakes of snow drifted in the air.

When he saw Callum standing at the entrance with his bow, he nodded a dismissal to his brother. Though he was grateful that Callum had agreed to watch over Laren, he knew that it couldn't last much longer. His brother deserved better than to stand guard, hour after hour.

The heat from Laren's furnaces was welcome as he entered the cavern. She wore only a gown and perspiration lined her neck. Her hair was bound back and in her hands she held a long metal pipe. A bubble of glass formed from the end and he stopped, spellbound at the sight of her magic. With breath and fire, she formed a cylinder of glass, the colour of rubies. She kept her entire attention focused upon the glass and it gave him the distraction he needed.

Quietly, Alex took one of the cloth-wrapped pieces of glass that she'd finished long ago and set it outside the cavern to take back with him. Though it was not a piece she'd meant for the new kirk, he had another purpose for it. And Laren wouldn't like it at all, if she knew of his intentions.

Only when she had finished the piece, setting it within the annealing furnace to cool, did she turn around to greet him.

'It's beautiful,' he told her and was rewarded by a slight smile.

'I love red,' she admitted, 'but it's the most difficult colour. I wish there were a way to make it so that it wasn't so dark. It doesn't let in the light the way other colours do.'

She moved over to the stone work surface where pieces of cut glass lay spread out. He could see the emerging figure of the crucifixion, and in the surrounding scenes were stories that revealed the Garden of Eden, Moses parting the Red Sea and an image of the Virgin Mary.

But none of the saints or apostles had faces yet. It made him wonder if the gift he'd planned for Laren would be welcome or not.

'My cousins will arrive soon to take Mairin home with them,' he told her. 'A messenger came this morning. She'll go north, as we planned.'

Laren set down the cutting implement and when he drew closer, he saw the exhaustion on her face. She'd been working since dawn, just as he had. She rested her hands upon the stone table, but she looked unnaturally pale. 'I know she has to go, but I wish she could stay.'

'She'll be safer.' He came up behind her and rested his hands on her shoulders, trying to reassure her.

Laren didn't answer, but kept her head lowered. It was then that he noticed something wasn't right with her bearing. She looked shaken, almost unwell.

'What is it?' he asked her.

Without warning, Laren's knees folded and he caught her before she could fall to the ground.

His heart quickened when she remained limp into his arms. She remained unconscious for only a moment or two and he helped her to sit on the bench beside him, with her head lowered.

'Take deep breaths,' he ordered. As he rubbed her shoulders, he noticed her pale colour. It made him wonder if she was no longer taking care of herself. 'Are you ill?'

'No. I'll be all right.'

Even so, he wasn't convinced. He leaned back against the table, keeping her in his arms. She didn't relax and seemed to grow more tense, the longer he held her. At last, she said, 'Alex, it's all right. I was just dizzy for a moment.'

'Has it happened before?'

She lifted her shoulders in a shrug. 'It's nothing to worry about.'

'I don't like seeing you faint. You could have hit your head.'

Although Ramsay was there most of the time, there were times when she worked alone inside the cavern. 'I'll send Dougal to you in the morning,' he said. 'You could finish your work sooner with both him and Ramsay to help.'

She shook her head. 'Your brother is more interested in horses and animals than glass. I'll be fine as I am now.'

But he didn't agree at all. She was growing more and more tired with every day that she worked. Even this morn, she'd struggled to awaken. Alex helped her to stand up and held his hands around her waist. 'You're working too hard, Laren. I can see how weary you are.'

'I promised to finish the windows for their new kirk by the early summer,' she insisted. 'No one else can do the work.'

He didn't understand her haste, for there seemed to be plenty of time. And despite her protests, he intended to find more people to help her. If nothing else, it would ease his mind to know that she wasn't working alone.

'You don't need to bury yourself in glassmaking, Laren,' he said.

'I need to finish it,' she insisted. 'A few months more and I can send the windows to the abbot.'

He didn't doubt her words. But there was an agitation in her voice, one he hadn't expected. 'Something else is bothering you.'

She rested her hands upon the stone table, revealing her scars. With her eyes closed, she admitted, 'Nairna came to me today, asking for advice. She wants a baby.' Laren reached for a piece of cut glass, arranging it in the mosaic that was forming the window. 'It doesn't seem fair that I've been blessed with our children, when she would give anything for a single bairn.'

'I'm certain she and Bram will have a family, soon enough.' With the way his brother and Nairna spent all their hours together, he supposed it was only a matter of time.

'Perhaps.'

He moved his hands to her shoulders, feeling the knots of tension in her neck. As he massaged her skin, her hands grew still.

'I brought something for you.' He reached inside his cloak for the gift he'd brought her. Holding it out, he said, 'I wanted you to have this.'

Laren held on to the cloth-wrapped package. 'What is it?'

'Something you need.'

She sent him a curious look and untied the package, letting the cloth fall open. Inside were three slender brushes. The handles were made of a smooth wood, sanded to a silky finish. The delicate bristled tips could create a fine painted line and he'd bought her the brushes, knowing it would help her paint the faces of the saints.

She set the brushes down on the table and the look on her face was near to tears.

'Did I do something wrong?'

She shook her head. 'They're exactly what I needed.' A teardrop rolled down her cheek and she stared at the table.

He didn't know why on earth she was weeping. She couldn't do the intricate shadows on the faces without the right tools. 'Why are you crying?'

'I don't know,' she sobbed.

'Are you tired or hurting?'

She wiped the tears away. 'No. I don't know what's the matter with me.' She stood up, holding the brushes in her hands. 'It was kind of you to give these to me.'

He didn't know what to say, so he gave a nod and started to leave. Laren caught him by the hand before he could go. Her fingers laced in his, and she came closer. 'The keep will be finished tonight, won't it?'

'Aye.' He held her fingertips lightly. 'The men worked on it, day and night, to finish early.'

'Because you're afraid of another attack,' she predicted.

He inclined his head. 'We all know it will happen. But we don't know when.'

She paled and he said, 'I'll do whatever I have to, to keep you safe.' His hand moved to the back of her neck, in silent reassurance.

She raised her eyes to him and they grew shadowed with suspicion. 'You wouldn't give yourself over to Harkirk, would you?'

'It's not what I want.'

But she saw through his words and started to shake her head. 'Don't, Alex.'

'I'll have to confront him, soon enough. This can't go on.' Though he had no intention of being a martyr, he didn't want his clan or family to be hurt on his behalf.

'What will you do?'

He made no reply, not wanting to upset her more. Instead, he caressed the tension from her neck, wishing he could soothe away the worry.

'I don't want anything to happen to you, Alex,' she murmured. 'Your daughters need you.' She lifted her blue eyes to him, winding her arms around his neck. 'I need you.'

He held himself motionless, her quiet confession

reaching beneath his skin in a way he didn't understand. He could feel the softness of her body pressing close and it sent a rush of sudden desire through him. The last time they'd been together she'd seduced him, sending him past the brink of reason until all that existed was her.

Laren took his hands and drew them around her waist, bringing their bodies close. She tilted her head up and in her eyes he sensed her desire. He wanted her now, so badly he was shaking from it. But she was so pale, so fragile, he didn't want her to think that she had to yield to him.

'Will you kiss me?' she whispered.

He cradled the back of her nape and shook his head. 'If I touch you right now, I won't stop.'

'I don't want you to stop.' She pressed the length of her body against him and he couldn't have stopped his response if he tried. His hands moved down to her hips and when she moved against him, it was a sensual caress against his arousal.

As his mouth claimed hers, she yielded sweetly, her tongue meeting his with its slick warmth. Alex drew it into his mouth, caressing her with his own tongue, mimicking the act that he wanted to do with her.

When he pulled back from the kiss, he was fighting to keep his breath steady. The temptation to remove the layers, to feel her bare skin against his, was taking him apart. 'You're not feeling well,' he said, letting go of her. 'I'll send Ramsay to tend the furnaces, and you can come home and rest.'

But Laren stepped in his path. 'I don't want you to go, Alex.'

Her husband was so taut with sexual need that she sensed that he was on the edge of losing control. Beneath her fingertips, his heartbeat was hammering.

Laren reached beneath his tunic, using her bare hands to touch his skin. 'I haven't seen you the past few nights. You've gone back to the way things were before.'

'Our defences aren't finished yet,' he argued back. 'If the English or anyone else attacks us again—' He broke off, shaking his head. 'I have to be certain everyone is protected.'

'How long will it take?'

He shook his head. 'I don't know. The outer framing of the keep is finished, but the stone will take many more months.'

She'd wanted to believe that they had started over, that things would return to the way they'd been. Instead, it seemed that he would spend all of his time away from them, just as before. Nothing at all had changed.

'I'm doing this for you,' he said. 'And for our daughters.' He gripped her hard, not allowing her to pull away. 'I have to know that I've done everything I can to keep you safe.'

Her hand moved up to his face, lingering upon him. 'It's lonely at night,' she whispered, 'when you're not there.' She felt a desperate need to bind him to her, to rekindle the lost feelings.

If he left her to fight Harkirk, she was afraid of losing him. It was hard enough falling asleep at night without him there, but if he were to die, especially now...

Alex closed his eyes, his hand covering hers. His mouth moved over her palm, as he brought her fingers down lower to his throat. She leaned up to kiss him, needing him to let go of the tight control.

His mouth hungered over hers while his hands bunched over her gown. She forgot all about her earlier dizziness as he distracted her with the kiss. It sent a spiral of awakening sensations through her skin, until she needed more.

'Alex,' she whispered. 'I'd rather have a husband in the flesh, than a husband who's never there.' She drew his hand to her breast in an unmistakable invitation.

He rested his mouth against her cheek, his hand cupping her fullness. She felt the tension trembling within him, the fierce needs that he wouldn't voice. She wanted to push him past the brink, binding him to her so he would realise what he was missing when he spent so many hours away from her.

It had been so very long since she'd joined with him. She wanted him to trust her, to let her ease the burden of leadership. He kept everything hidden, but she could see the stiffness in his bearing. She lifted his tunic away and massaged his shoulders, trying to soothe the rigid strain in his muscles.

His body had changed over the past few weeks, the outline of hardened muscle caused by lifting so many stones. Though he'd never been soft, she marvelled at his strength, running her fingertips over the heated skin.

He captured her hands, lowering them to her sides. 'I don't trust myself to be gentle right now, Laren. It's been too long.'

'Just be with me,' she urged. She reached up to loosen her gown and her clothing fell away, his hands moving over her skin in reverence. Her breasts were sensitive and when he lowered his mouth to her nipple, she gasped in response. She tried to remove his trews, needing his length against her.

With his hands, he parted her legs, and she stiffened at the sharp reaction he provoked. When his fingers brushed against her hooded flesh, she let out a soft cry, feeling the moist response between her thighs.

'Do you remember the first time I took you?' he murmured.

She could hardly stand up as his fingers caressed her folds. 'In the stone circle, just after our wedding.'

'I couldn't get enough of you that night.' He used their clothes to form a softer surface on the sandy floor of the cavern and guided her to lie down. 'I couldn't believe that you were mine at last.'

'I couldn't believe that, out of all the women you could have had, you chose me.' She pulled him down to lie atop her and Alex's body covered hers. For a moment, she rested beneath him, wishing she could hold on to him.

His hands moved up her legs, his mouth grazing a trail, followed by his fingers. When he reached her womanhood, he touched her again and the sudden response was more intense than anything she'd felt before. Her wetness coated his fingers and she grew embarrassed by her reaction.

'Alex, don't go to Harkirk.' She lifted one leg around his waist and he drew his hard length against her. 'Stay with me.'

'I won't hide like a coward,' he insisted. 'We're going to finish this. And when it's over, you'll not have to worry about an English invasion again.'

The fierceness of his tone took her aback. He lifted her bottom, sheathing himself deep within her body. She couldn't stop the moan that he forced from her throat. He found the place that brought her such pleasure, withdrawing his shaft to her entrance. Hovering there, she felt his thickness stretching her, while he used his thumb to bring her closer to the edge.

Sweet Mary and the saints, the long weeks without him were making every sensation fuller. He knew just how to touch her, just how to make her desperate with need.

And when he thrust against her, it was like being touched everywhere at the same time.

She ground her hips upwards, trying to force him to move faster. Instead, he slowed down, taking his time to torment her. Aching for him, she reached for his hips and he rewarded her with a thick thrust. And when the rigid pleasure started to break through, she cried out as the waves shattered her body, turning her molten, like the hot glass.

He pressed her knees against her chest, driving his shaft against her, his penetrations making her body tremble. She couldn't catch her breath as he quickened the pace, thrusting within her liquid depths. A dark warmth emanated from deep inside, spiralling harder. She found herself fighting against him, struggling to keep a thread of sanity amid the rush of sensations. The pressure inside was building, her body straining for him.

'You're mine, Laren. No matter what happens to me, no man will ever bring you this.' He thrust harder and the harsh rhythm pushed her over the edge. She couldn't do anything except surrender to the blinding feelings that kept pressing her higher. Not once did he let up with the driving rhythm, taking her harder than he'd ever done before.

He'd become the conqueror, and she, his slave. Then his hot mouth covered her breast and she came apart again. White-hot, shimmering fires of release rocked through her and she gasped at the way she was meeting him, thrust for thrust. After a few more penetrations, he let out his own growl and released his seed within her.

Never, in all their years of marriage, had he ever let go of his control so completely. But his words terrified her. *No matter what happens to me.*

He wouldn't tell her what he was going to do and it frustrated her that he'd withheld that part of himself.

'Come back to the keep with me,' he whispered, kissing her deeply. Laren's fingertips reached up to her lips, as though she could hold on to his kiss.

'Soon,' she promised. 'I'll wait with the furnaces while you fetch Ramsay.'

As he withdrew from her body and got dressed, she felt the shielded distance descending once more. Though she'd granted him the physical release he'd needed, it wasn't enough.

And she didn't know how to break through to him.

When he'd gone, Laren tried to stand, but her knees buckled beneath her. The familiar dizziness broke over her like a wave, and she lowered her head, fighting to steady herself.

You should have told him, her conscience warned. She hadn't had her woman's flow in nearly two months and her breasts were tender. The familiar signs of pregnancy were there and she supposed this new child would be born the following autumn.

It surprised her that Alex hadn't guessed already. Anything and everything made her cry. The tears came without warning; today had been particularly bad. Nairna had been trying for so long, wanting a child, and Laren had fought to hold back her emotions.

It seemed so unfair that Nairna should want a child so desperately, while her own fertility was effortless. She'd said nothing, not wanting to hurt her friend.

But she had other reasons for not telling Alex. She was achingly tired all of the time, and nausea plagued her from the moment she woke up until she fell asleep at night. It was so unlike her other pregnancies, she felt afraid for the first time in her life.

He would worry overmuch, likely confining her to bed. And then how would she finish the glass?

Just a little longer, she thought to herself. A few weeks more and the troublesome symptoms would subside. She'd finish the windows and then tell him about the new child.

Her hand moved down to her womb and she voiced a silent prayer that the bairn would somehow survive.

Chapter Twelve

Finian stared into the dying coals of the fire, his spirits as sunken as his cheeks. He didn't remember the last time he'd eaten. And he didn't know what to do. Their raid had failed. He'd underestimated the strength of their fighters and seizing a hostage no longer seemed possible. This task rested upon his shoulders and damned if he had any idea what to do now.

'Finian,' came the voice of his brother Brochain. 'English soldiers have arrived.'

He jerked to his feet, resting his hand upon the hilt of his sword. 'What do they want?'

'They came from Harkirk. They said they had a message from the Baron.'

His brother held out a cloth-wrapped bundle, and bile rose up in Finian's throat. By the Holy Virgin, what was this? He set the bundle upon a table and peeled back the layers of cloth. In the centre, he saw the ragged gown that had once belonged to his daughter.

The implication, that her clothing had been taken from her...that the soldiers were using her...it was too much.

He closed his eyes, the rage building up until he could hardly think. His brother stared at the gown, his face white. 'Is that Iliana's?'

'Aye.' Finian clenched the gown, trying to keep control over his stomach. He couldn't bear to think of any man laying a hand upon his daughter. Whether or not his fears had come to pass, the message was clear.

His time was running out.

The interior of the new keep was warmer than Laren had expected. It seemed that every member of the MacKinloch clan had gathered inside the Hall. Though it was built of wood for now, already the men had begun laying stone to surround the wooden interior. She slipped inside the chamber, keeping in the background as she searched for her girls.

She saw them seated beside Alex at the far end of the room. He was talking to Bram while Nairna was busy organising food. Laren rested her back against the wooden wall, trying to stay out of the way. The scent of cooking meat wafted through the air and she swallowed hard to quell the nausea.

She needed to sit down, to calm her stomach and the lightheaded feeling, but there were no benches or chairs. The people milled around, drinking and talking, and she felt the familiar nerves creeping up. The desire to leave the crowds was rising up and she fought her instincts.

Instead, she focused on the walls of the keep. The fresh scent of cut wood was welcome and she ran her hands over the surface. Though it would be one day be lined with stone, at least they would have a dry roof over their heads for tonight.

She kept to the outer perimeter, pasting a smile on her face that didn't belong there. As she neared Alex, she saw Vanora standing not far from the children. The older woman was responding to something her husband had said; when Laren greeted her, Vanora didn't seem to have heard her.

'He's been waiting on her, but she's not here yet,' the matron was saying, with her back towards her. 'I don't know why he's gathered us together, but it has something to do with Laren.'

Laren was held motionless, not understanding. She'd thought this was about a celebration, a welcome for the people to be glad of the new keep.

The sickening feeling in her stomach twisted again. She was close enough to Alex that he could now see her and when she saw the wrapped package, her heart plummeted.

No. He wouldn't.

'Many of you have asked where we've found the silver to fund the rebuilding of Glen Arrin,' Alex said in a voice that carried over the crowd. 'I believe you deserve that answer now.'

Though she supposed Alex intended it as an honour, she didn't want the others to look upon her early efforts in glass making. They weren't good. The colours weren't right and the panes could shatter with the slightest scratch.

Alex revealed the coloured glass and she saw the image of the Madonna and Child that she'd created a year ago. The faceless Virgin was nothing more than a hooded woman, her arms cradling a precious bundle.

'This was made by Laren,' Alex explained. 'She sold her glass and brought the silver to us.'

It took only seconds for every face to turn and look at her. And when she saw her husband's eyes, her own filled with tears. She didn't hear the words spoken by her clansmen. She fled outside the keep, needing to get out. For her husband to bare her soul in front of everyone felt like a betrayal. Why had he done this? He *knew* how much she hated being the centre of attention. Nothing hurt her more than to be stared at by others. She couldn't bear it.

Outside, the snow mingled with rain, but she felt none of the cold. All of it was clustered inside her heart, for she'd never wanted to reveal herself in this way.

'Laren.' She heard Alex's voice behind her. 'Come back inside. They need to know the truth about why you're gone so many hours. And you need more people to help you.' He tried to bring his arm around her waist, but she pushed him back.

Behind him, she saw curious faces and heard their whispering. Whether it was good or bad, she didn't want to know. And when he tried to prompt her again, she turned and ran, unable to face them.

Alex waited for another hour before going after Laren. He wanted to give her time to calm down, to accept what he'd done. He'd never understood her secrecy. There was no reason not to tell the others about her glass.

After he'd shown them her work, the people had been fascinated, offering compliments Laren wasn't there to hear. Each one of them had come forwards to touch it. They asked questions he couldn't answer and he suspected many would want to watch her work.

Others didn't believe him. They refused to acknowledge her skill until they saw it with their own eyes. The realisation made him wonder if, perhaps, he'd acted in haste.

But he'd wanted to get help for her. She couldn't complete the task alone, regardless of what she believed.

'Glass or no glass, she's not been much of a wife to you.' Grizel came forwards and Alex saw his girls walking beside his mother.

He sent her a sharp warning look. 'You've no right to speak of her in that way. Especially around them.'

'Why not? They know their mother is never there.'

He didn't miss the way Mairin's eyes filled with tears. She wrenched her hand away from Grizel and glared at her grandmother. 'My mother's glass is wonderful. You're just jealous because you can't make anything!'

His daughter went running toward the loch shores, around the outer edge towards the cavern. At the loss of her sister, Adaira began bawling.

'Leave us, Grizel,' Alex warned. 'You've done enough.' He comforted Adaira, lifting her into his arms and rubbing her shoulders.

'Well. I've a right to express my opinion, don't I?'

'You've no right at all to say anything against my wife. And if you want a place to live among us, you'll find a way to make it up to Laren.' He strode away, not bothering to say another word. Her sharp tongue would only earn her the brunt of his temper if he was foolish enough to remain near her.

With long strides, he caught up to Mairin. The young girl was smashing stones into the water, tears staining her cheeks. 'I hate our *seanmhair*,' she wept.

'Grizel is sorry for what she said.' The lie slipped from his mouth, even though he doubted she was sorry at all. His mother's bitterness poisoned the atmosphere around her, until it was impossible to live anywhere near her.

'She told me this morn that I'm going to be sent away.' Mairin looked up at him, her eyes worried.

He came closer to her and rested his hand upon her shoulder. His daughter was taller than his waist and it seemed strange, suddenly, that she'd grown so quickly. Her reddish hair was losing its baby golden tone and was growing darker.

'It's only for fostering, Mairin. You'll go north, to the Orkney Islands. My cousin has agreed to it.' When more tears streamed down her face, he hugged her tightly. 'It will be safer there, you'll see.'

'I don't want to go,' Mairin insisted.

He dropped a kiss upon her tousled hair. 'You'll meet new girls and boys to play with. Perhaps a future husband.'

Her face wrinkled in horror at the thought of a boy and he suppressed a laugh. 'Come and let's find your mother,' Alex said.

He hoped that, by now, she would be more amenable to the idea of having additional apprentices. At first, he'd thought Dougal would be the best choice, but it was Monroe, one of the younger boys, whose eyes had lit up at the prospect. Even when the others had finished looking at the glass, he'd continued to study it, touching the surface as if he couldn't quite believe it was real. The only question was whether Laren would allow the boy to join as another apprentice.

Before they reached the cavern, he saw her returning from the far side of the loch. Mairin raced into her arms and Laren lifted her daughter on to her hip, speaking softly to her. When she reached Alex's side, she took Adaira from him and cuddled the baby girl in her arms.

To him, she uttered not a word. He could almost feel the air of invisible frost around her, though she would say nothing in front of the girls. He couldn't read her face, unable to discern her thoughts.

But when she started to enter Ross's home, he stopped her. 'Did you forget that we're sleeping in the keep this night?'

She coloured, but before she could say anything, Mairin blurted out, 'Will we have our own bed, Da?'

'Not yet. But if there's time, I'll try to make one for you soon.'

His admission didn't dim the girl's excitement and Mairin eagerly pulled Laren forwards toward the wooden structure. Once they were inside, he arranged for some straw mattresses and blankets for the girls. Laren put them both to bed in a warm corner of the keep.

Only when they were asleep did she finally rise and move towards the other side of the keep where he'd arranged for them to rest.

'You're angry,' he said, catching her by the arm.

She didn't speak, but her hands were clenched at her sides. He could feel the emotions simmering deep inside her and doubted if any words he spoke would assuage her.

'I won't apologise for what I did. They needed to know.' He tried to touch her shoulder, but she closed her eyes as if in pain.

'Four of them followed me to the cavern. They wanted to watch.'

He moved in front of her, forcing her to face him. 'What you do is nothing short of magical. It's understandable.'

'I don't want them watching me.' She lowered her voice to a whisper. 'I started one of the melts, but they kept asking me questions. I feel as if I've lost my sanctuary.'

'What are you afraid of, Laren?'

'I hate it when they stare at me. I imagine what they're

thinking, that what I do isn't good enough.' Turning her head slightly, he saw the glitter of tears. 'Even though I know it is, I can't stop remembering the things they used to say about my family when we were growing up. Now I'll have to endure their stares every day.'

He leaned in until their bodies were close together. She let out a shuddering breath when his chest pressed against her breasts. 'I never believed any of those things. You weren't to blame for your father.'

'He did the best he could,' she whispered, 'but it wasn't enough.' She moved to face him and in her blue eyes he saw the pain. 'I shouldn't care what they think of me, should I?'

'They were intrigued by your skill. Not even Father Nolan could make glass the way you do. Monroe asked if you would allow him to help you and Ramsay.'

'I don't understand why,' she said. 'Why would you tell them now, instead of after I've finished the windows?'

'Because you need help. And because I want you to stay closer to the fortress.'

Her eyes flashed with anger and he held up a hand. 'Hear me out. I'm not forbidding you to make the glass windows. You can cut the pieces here, in the keep.'

'But the glass—'

'You have enough colours to do most of the work.' He'd seen the dozens of panes for himself. 'Ramsay and Monroe can make the glass and bring it to you here.'

She stared at him. 'What aren't you telling me, Alex?'

'I'm leaving with my brothers in a few days. I won't let Harkirk be a threat to us any longer.'

The winter wind swept across the hills, drawing grey clouds that threatened snow. The priest from the abbey,

Father Stephen, had returned a day ago to check on Laren's progress, but just as before, Alex didn't allow him to stay longer than an hour. He didn't want the priest anywhere near his wife.

When he entered the cavern, he ordered Monroe and Ramsay to go back to the keep. 'I want to speak to Laren alone.'

While Monroe wasted no time, Ramsay finished putting a clay crucible into the furnace and looked to Laren for permission. 'Go on,' she said. 'It won't be ready for hours yet. You can return after sundown.'

Alex moved to the table, resting his hands on either side, waiting for Laren to look at him. Her hands faltered upon the glass and she set down her cutting tool.

He saw her grow waxen, her fingers trembling. She closed her eyes and sank down upon the bench, lowering her head to her knees as though she were light-headed.

'What is it?' Immediately, he went to her side, kneeling with his arm around her waist for support.

'It's the same as before. If I stand for too long, I feel faint.' He didn't like hearing it, for the long hours were taking their toll. He touched her face, seeing the circles beneath her eyes.

'You need to slow down,' he said. 'The kirk won't be finished until the summer. There's time yet; you've no reason to work all day, every day.'

Instead of his words reassuring her, Laren buried her face in her hands. 'I have to work at this pace or it won't be finished.'

'I don't need you working yourself into exhaustion for it. We don't need the silver.'

The desperation in her expression made him fear that,

once again, she was hiding something from him. 'Laren,' he warned, 'what is it?'

She grew silent, taking long breaths before she lifted her face to his. 'I'm going to have another baby.'

The unexpected joy that flickered upon his face suddenly halted. 'You aren't happy about this child, are you?'

His accusatory tone bothered Laren. It wasn't as if she didn't want the bairn. She loved her children and welcomed the thought of a new life.

But she was deeply afraid that this child wouldn't live. She hadn't yet felt any movement and the harsh symptoms were taking their toll upon her body. She didn't know what to tell him and her silence was damning.

The look on his face made her feel as though she'd buried a dirk in his gut. 'Is it that you don't want to bear any more children of mine?'

She wanted to utter no, that it wasn't that at all. But if she admitted the danger, he wouldn't let her near the glass. The urge to hold in her secret was so strong that she almost held her silence. But when he turned away from her, she sensed that, if he left her, nothing would be the same ever again.

'Wait,' she said. 'You're wrong.'

For so long, she'd held her worries and fears inside, not wanting to burden him. It had become as natural as breathing, no matter that the pain bled through her.

He needs to know, her conscience urged. *If you don't tell him, you'll lose him.* And God above, she couldn't bear to think of it.

'I'm afraid,' she said softly.

He turned back to her and the look on his face was a mixture of anger and hurt. 'Afraid of what?'

'Of losing this child.' She dug her fingers against the stone table, forcing herself to look at him. She let him see the raw grief, the despair that she'd carried over the past two years.

But still Alex didn't move. He was waiting for her to tell him more and she fumbled for the words.

'I'm so tired,' she confessed. 'And I never seem to get enough sleep. The thought of food makes me sick and I keep getting dizzy. I've fainted many times and I've never felt this way before. Not with any other pregnancy.'

She spilled out her fears and, at last, confessed, 'I haven't felt the child move. I'm afraid this bairn is already dead inside of me.' The tears spilled over her cheeks and when he saw them, he took a few steps closer. He knelt down before her, resting his hands on either side of the bench.

In his eyes, she saw the shadows of his grief. She reached out to him, putting her arms around his neck. The warm male skin gave her comfort and his arms tightened around her.

'I didn't want you to grieve,' she whispered. 'I don't know if I'll lose the child or not. But I didn't want to burden you.'

He pulled back, fury in his eyes. 'You're my wife. Not a burden.' His hands pressed away the tears, framing her face. 'When David died, you wouldn't talk to me for days.' His wrath spilled over and he said, 'It wasn't only a son I lost that night. I lost you.'

She was shaking, her grief rising up and overflowing. 'I blamed myself for his death. Every night I wondered what I'd done wrong. Why he was taken from us.' She buried her face in his shoulder, not caring that she was dampening his tunic with her tears. 'I couldn't be with you when it was my fault.'

'Do you think I believed that?' He leaned in close, his cheek touching hers.

'I believed it.' She swallowed back the tears, trying to find a strength inside. 'When we had Adaira, I couldn't sleep for the first year. I kept waking up, watching her breathe.'

'I never blamed you. Never.' His mouth came to hers in a kiss that offered absolution.

'Everything will be all right with this child, Laren. I'll take care of you.'

She turned around, resting her palms upon his chest. 'I want to believe it.'

'Lie down,' he urged. 'Rest, and I'll watch over you.'

Laren obeyed and as she lay upon her side, he rubbed her back and shoulders. She felt herself slipping beneath the spell of his hands, the weariness dragging her under. Though she knew she shouldn't close her eyes, shouldn't succumb to the intense relaxation of his hands, she couldn't resist for a few moments.

The heaviness of her need swept her down until she fell asleep at last.

When she awoke, it was dark outside. Alex had covered her up with a blanket, and she didn't know where he'd got it from. Likely he'd returned to the fortress to fetch it for her, along with the foods he'd brought.

It was a strange array and when she sat up, there was only the light of the furnace to illuminate the room.

'How long did I sleep?' she asked.

'A few hours. I suppose you needed it.' He reached out

for the platter of food and brought it to her. 'Would you like some bread?'

Laren blinked for a moment, but took the slice from him. When she saw the food he'd brought, she realised he'd brought nothing with a strong odour, no foods to turn her stomach. Only a selection of cheese, bread, oat cakes and dried cherries.

'You remembered.' She took the cherries with a smile and another surge of unexpected emotions passed through her at his thoughtfulness. She'd eaten their entire store of dried cherries when she'd been pregnant with Adaira, for it was a craving she couldn't seem to satisfy.

'I've already eaten,' he added. 'I know you don't like meat during this time.'

The piece of bread whetted her appetite and after her stomach grew settled, she tried more of the food.

'Are you feeling better?'

She was, and once she began eating, it seemed that she couldn't get enough. The cherries were the perfect blend of tart and sweet, and she found herself devouring them by the handful.

When she had sated her hunger, she drew her knees up beneath her skirts and looked up at Alex. There was amusement in his eyes and she raised an eyebrow. 'What?'

'I was almost afraid to put my hand near the food for fear you'd eat it, too.'

She flashed a smile. 'Never come between a pregnant woman and her food.'

He sat beside her, dropping his hand around her back. The warmth of his arm was comforting and she found herself leaning against him. 'I remember how we went walking around the loch when you were pregnant with David. You brought bits of food to eat along the way.'

The knife of memory sliced through her, but she understood what he was trying to do. The pain of losing David would never go away. But there were a few good memories left to hold on to.

'You laughed at me,' she said. 'You've never known that sort of hunger before. It consumes you.'

She reached out and laced her hand with his. His palm was warm, his fingers touching hers with gentleness. 'He was a handsome bairn, wasn't he?'

'I always wondered if he would have had your eyes or mine. All our children had blue eyes when they were born.'

He wiped a tear away from her cheek and she struggled to find a smile. 'He'll always have a piece of my heart. Even in Heaven.'

'He took a piece of mine as well,' Alex admitted. He brought her fingers to his chest where she could feel his heart beating. His mood grew dim and he admitted, 'We're leaving in the morning to find the MacLachors. Bram will come with me, but Callum, Ross and the rest of the men will stay behind to guard Glen Arrin. Now that the walls are finished, you should be safe enough.'

'What if they attack?' Her fears gathered up into a tight ball within her stomach.

'If anything happens, send Callum to us. We'll come back as fast as we can ride.'

She held on to him, wishing he wouldn't leave. 'I need you to come back to me.' Especially if the pregnancy went badly. 'If the worst happens…I don't think I can go through it again.'

Alex rested his hand upon her hip. 'You're stronger than you think, Laren. But I pray this child will be safe.' His hand moved over to her stomach again, as if he could command it to be so.

Chapter Thirteen

'I don't want to go,' Mairin wept, her arms around Laren's neck.

She gripped the young girl as though she could hold on to the last remnants of her daughter's childhood. Though Mairin would visit from time to time, it broke her heart to see her leave. She would be so far away.

'You'll be on an adventure,' Laren said, smiling through her tears.

'Mama, did you go off for fostering?'

Laren shook her head. 'My father couldn't send me. We were too poor and had no family that would take us. But think of what it will be like. You'll see the places where the Norse raiders came. And you'll have everything you need.' They had given the Sinclairs cattle and sheep, as well as a horse for Mairin.

Laren reached into a fold of her cloak and pulled out a flat disc of white-and-yellow glass that she'd shaped into a flower. 'I made this for you.' She kissed her daughter again, adding, 'We'll see you in the summertime.'

The wagon slowly rolled away and Laren raised her hand in farewell as Mairin left. The tears were cold on her cheeks, but Alex gave her hand a squeeze. 'She'll be well cared for, Laren.'

'I know it.' She wouldn't have let her go if she weren't convinced Mairin would be safer in the north. But worse, she would lose her husband today as well. He'd promised to bid Mairin farewell before he departed with Bram.

'I need to check our supplies before we go,' he told her.

She nodded, but though she wanted to wait by the horses, Grizel approached and said, 'Alex, I want a word with your wife.'

Laren said nothing, flinching at Grizel's tone. But she allowed the woman to lead her back into the keep. She smelled the aroma of meat from yesterday and fought back her unsteady stomach as she followed Grizel inside. The older woman brought her to a chair and ordered, 'Sit down.'

'Is something wrong?'

Grizel caught the attention of a servant and gave her hushed instructions. Then she pulled a chair over and sat across from Laren. Her piercing gaze made it difficult to look her in the eye.

'It's not easy to let your child go off for fostering,' Grizel began. 'But it must be done. Especially if you want Mairin to have the status you lacked as a child.'

Laren coloured, wondering when she would be able to escape the older woman's criticism. She made no reply, not wanting to engage in an argument.

When the serving girl returned, Grizel took a steaming mug of tea and gave it to her. 'Drink this.'

Laren sniffed the tea and caught a strong herbal aroma. 'What's in it?'

'Chamomile, mint and some other herbs to make this pregnancy easier.'

She sent a sharp look towards Grizel, who folded her arms across her chest. 'I know when a woman is breeding. And I know it hasn't been an easy pregnancy. You've been sick a lot, haven't you? I imagine you're afraid of losing it.'

Stung, Laren forced herself to drink a sip of the brew to avoid speaking. Why would Grizel say such a thing? Aye, it weighed upon her thoughts, the fear that this child wasn't well. But she hadn't lost it yet.

'You haven't denied it,' the matron remarked with triumph. 'But if you drink this tea each morn, you'll find it easier. It will ease your sickness and help to steady the bairn in your womb. I'll bring you the herbs.'

Laren took another sip, wondering what Grizel meant by it. Never once had the older woman spoken a kind word or done anything to make her feel accepted as Alex's wife.

Grizel stood and pointed to a table on the far end of the Hall. 'I suppose you might want your mother or sister with you when this babe comes.'

Laren's fingers curled over the cup, too startled to speak. She hadn't seen her mother Rós or her sister Suisan since they'd left for St Anne's. 'I do miss them,' she admitted.

'I'll send for them at summer's end.' The older woman stood, gave a grim nod and strode away. Laren finished the tea, realising it was as close as Grizel would ever come to an apology.

'I don't like leaving our clan alone,' Alex admitted to Bram, when they'd set off on their journey. The last raid weighed heavily upon him, for he didn't know whether or not to believe the claim that there was a bounty on his head.

By going to meet with the MacLachor chief, he might be walking into a trap of his own making.

But he needed information. If Harkirk was recruiting the other clans to rise up against the MacKinlochs, Alex had to be ready. The MacLachors were his best hope in finding out exactly what the English Baron was planning.

He cast another look back at the stone walls surrounding Glen Arrin, his mood heavy. Laren's hair gleamed red against the wintry stillness as she watched from the gate. In a few months more, her belly would be swollen with child. He'd always loved the way her body softened in those months, her breasts full and lush while the child grew inside of her.

'Things are better between you and Laren?' Bram prompted, when they crossed over the hill.

'Aye.' He recalled the way he'd made love to her in the cavern the other night. Just thinking of it made him want to ride back to her, touching her until she grew breathless. Though he'd kissed her goodbye, it wasn't enough. He felt as if he'd left a part of himself behind.

'We're expecting another bairn,' he told Bram.

His brother gave a nod, but there was something else beneath his perfunctory smile and his murmured good wishes.

'And Nairna?'

'I don't know,' Bram admitted. 'She won't tell me if she is or not. It's something she wants badly.'

'I hope all goes well for the both of you.' Bram only grunted, and Alex added, 'It's never easy, even when the child isn't born yet.'

The more he thought of Laren, the more he worried. Though she had admitted that she wasn't feeling quite herself, ever since the night they'd spent together, she'd grown quieter.

'It will be all right,' she tried to reassure him. 'I promise, I'll take no risks with this bairn.'

She'd appeared paler than usual, but when he'd questioned it, she'd simply embraced him, saying, 'I'll miss you, that's all.'

Every part of him wanted to stay with her, though it wasn't possible. He could only pray that they would remain safe from harm.

They travelled west for most of the day, and when night fell, they reached the outer boundaries of Moristerry, the MacLachors' stronghold. 'Remain hidden,' he said to Bram, drawing their horses away from the open land and more towards the tree line edging the mountains. He wanted to gather more information about them before they approached in the morning.

Bram drew his horse to a stop. 'We should climb to higher ground and make our camp. Then we can watch them and see what's happening.'

Alex followed Bram into the trees, until they reached a flattened section of the hill where a tiny waterfall streamed downhill, offering a place for the horses to drink. As they set up their camp for the night, Alex reached into a fold of his cloak, intending to strike flint for a fire. His hand came into contact with tiny teardrops of glass.

The hard bits of glass were emerald, ruby and sapphire in colour, along with a few clear droplets. Laren must have put them there when she'd said goodbye. They were the same pieces of glass he'd given her, years ago.

The physical reminder of his wife caught him without

warning. He squeezed the hard pieces, as if he could hold on to her.

And he knew then that she was thinking of him, just as he held her image in his mind.

Finian stared at the young girl in the afternoon light. She reminded him of his own daughter, with her sunny smile and innocence. His fists clenched as he remembered Iliana and the way she used to run into his arms as he scooped her up. He remembered her laughter when he tossed her into the air and how she'd clutched his neck when she came down again.

His throat closed up and he wondered what ills she had suffered at Harkirk's hands. Was she alive? Had they harmed her?

It had been too long. Now that the MacKinloch chief and his elder brother had left, his opportunity was at hand. He needed to act now, for his daughter's life depended on it.

Finian smiled at the child and offered his hand. She stared a moment, unsure of what to do. When he pulled a handful of dried cherries from a fold of his cloak, she took a step closer.

'That's right, wee one,' he coaxed. 'Come and have a taste.'

God forgive me for what I must do.

'Where is Adaira?' Laren demanded.

Vanora sent her a questioning look. 'I thought she was playing with Grizel by the loch. Isn't she?'

'Grizel hasn't seen her in the last hour.'

Laren's skin grew icy. From deep inside, she sensed something was wrong. She started running towards the loch, but there was no sign of her daughter. Her heart pounded faster as she searched, agonising over the thought of any harm coming to Adaira.

I should have stayed with her. Her side ached as she kept running, praying she would find her unharmed.

She stumbled inside the cavern and her heart froze with fear. A foreign piece of parchment lay atop her glass with writing she couldn't read. And resting upon the paper was a lock of Adaira's hair.

Laren gripped the lock of hair and a rage erupted inside her. Someone had taken her daughter. But where? And why?

Whoever had taken her daughter hostage was a dead man.

She seized the parchment and ran back to Glen Arrin, her anger brewing hotter until it boiled over. 'I need someone who can read,' she demanded when she saw Dougal. Anyone to interpret the writing and discover what it meant.

'What's happened?'

The lad looked confused and Laren answered, 'Someone has taken Adaira. I need to find out who.' She held up the parchment and repeated, 'Help me.'

Startled gazes eyed her and Laren realised that she'd been shouting. Her hand clenched the lock of her daughter's hair and she wished to God that Alex were here. If he were, he'd be tracking the man even now.

She took a deep breath, trying to find the inner strength she needed to keep from falling into hysteria. Adaira was her baby, her sweet girl who kept crawling into her bed when she was supposed to be sleeping with her sister.

Dougal was already off and running, but before he could get far, she spied a horse and rider approaching. Dressed in a priest's robes, the man continued on until he reached the gates. He dismounted and walked towards them, a parcel in his hands. When he greeted them, introducing himself as Father Ossian from Inveriston, Laren couldn't gather her thoughts together. She didn't want to hear about the new kirk or answer questions about why the glass panels weren't finished. Right now, every thought was with Adaira.

Calm yourself, she ordered. *This priest can read the markings, the same as any other.*

'Can you tell me what it says on this parchment?' Laren asked quietly, her pulse racing.

'It's the MacLachor crest,' he answered. 'They want your chief and his brothers to meet them at Lord Harkirk's fortress.'

Laren's mouth tightened into a line and her hands started shaking. Though she managed to thank the priest, she focused her thoughts on how to get Adaira back. Alex had left to meet with the MacLachor chief only a day ago. Would he find Adaira there? Or had they already taken her to Lord Harkirk's stronghold?

'I've come to speak with your glass artist—' Father Ossian was saying.

'Father Stephen already inspected the windows not long ago,' Laren interrupted. Her mind was scattered, not wanting to think of the glass when her daughter had been taken captive.

The priest sent her a curious look. 'Father Stephen?'

'Aye, one of your brethren.' She stared at him, not understanding why he wouldn't know Stephen. There were fewer than twenty men at the abbey. 'You sent him with the measurements and instructions for the kirk windows.'

'We have no priest of that name,' Father Ossian replied. 'And the plans you speak of were stolen, nearly a month ago. The priest we sent was robbed of his horse and belongings after he tried to help a wounded man. He returned to us and we had to redraw everything.'

The breath in her lungs seized up at the realisation that Father Stephen was not who he'd claimed to be. *Sweet Mother of God.*

Laren let out a curse, for she knew, without any doubt, that the so-called priest had slipped past their boundaries and taken her daughter.

Alex awoke the next morning to find men surrounding them. He unsheathed his claymore and stood with his brother, slowly moving until he was back to back with Bram.

'We came to talk with your chief about Harkirk,' he said. 'I want to know more about the bounty he placed on my head.'

A tall blond man moved forwards, a shield and sword in his hands. 'I am Brochain MacLachor, the *tánaiste* of our clan.' With a glance to his men, they spread out their forces. 'And the bounty was on the heads of you and your brothers.'

'We didn't come to fight,' Alex said quietly. 'But if you strike the first blow, we'll defend ourselves. And I don't think you want to lose any more men.'

Brochain's face tensed, but neither he, nor his men, moved.

'Harkirk is trying to stir up trouble among the clans,' Alex continued. 'He wants us to turn on one another, because dividing the clans will weaken us.' With his weapon held steady, he never took his eyes off Brochain. 'The chief's daughter may not even be alive,' he pointed out. 'Why would you attack us instead of asking for help?'

'We lost a dozen men trying to break into his fortress,' the man admitted. 'Even with your forces, we aren't strong enough.'

'Where is your chief now?' Alex asked. He'd never met Finian MacLachor, though he'd heard of the man.

'He left us a few days ago to go after Iliana on his own.' But there were doubts upon the man's face as though he viewed it as a hopeless endeavor.

'Our younger brother Callum was Harkirk's prisoner,' Bram interjected. 'He knows the interior of the fortress like no one else. We got him out alive. There's no reason we couldn't do the same for your chief's daughter.'

'And why would you help us? Especially after we attacked you.' Emptiness settled over the man's expression, as if he had little hope left.

'Because we've a greater need for allies than enemies. You have information about Harkirk; between us, we can put a stop to his threats against the clans.'

'How do we know you'll keep your word?' Brochain asked.

'You don't,' Bram replied. 'But if you kill us here, what chance do you stand of getting your chief back alive?'

Brochain seemed to consider it and after a long moment, he sheathed his weapon. One by one, the others drew back. 'Come with us back to Moristerry and we'll talk.'

From the look the *tánaiste* sent to his men, Alex trusted him even less. He kept his hand poised upon his weapon as he followed them down the hill towards the MacLachor stronghold.

Laren mounted her horse, with Dougal and Callum at her side. Though they'd spent hours searching the surrounding areas for Adaira, there was no sign of her daughter. A dull sick feeling had settled within her stomach at the thought of anything happening to her baby. There was no choice but to confront the MacLachors and take Adaira back.

'Gather the clansmen together,' she ordered Nairna. 'I want to speak with them.'

Although her old fears swam in her stomach, she couldn't hide behind her shyness. She needed the remaining men to help her; without them, her daughter might suffer.

'I'm sorry about Adaira,' Nairna said, her face pale. 'I can't even imagine the pain you must be suffering.'

'I'm going to find her and bring her home,' Laren insisted. 'No matter how long it takes.'

Though she still suffered from the exhaustion of her pregnancy, the nausea had at last subsided. Only Alex and Grizel knew of it and now she was grateful she'd kept silent. No one would allow her to leave Glen Arrin if she'd admitted her condition.

She hardly slept any more. How could she, when her baby was gone? While Nairna gathered the others, Laren paced, going over the words in her mind. She'd never before addressed the people and it terrified her. Ever since Alex had revealed her glassmaking, they'd grown even more distant, behaving as though she were engaged in sorcery instead of glass.

One by one they assembled and Laren studied them. *They have children, too,* she reminded herself. If they understood even half of the fear that burned through her, they might be willing to help.

'The MacLachors have taken Adaira,' she began. When a slight shifting alerted her that her voice wasn't loud enough, she forced herself to add more volume. She couldn't hide the trembling tone, but the men and women didn't seem to blame her for it. 'I need your help in bringing her home.'

'Have they demanded a ransom?' Ross asked. In his wrinkled face, she saw sympathy and the silent offer of help. During the few months she'd stayed with him and Vanora, he'd come to think of the girls as his grandchildren.

'No.' She held up the parchment with the mark of the MacLachors and the lock of her daughter's hair. 'This is all I have as proof.'

There were murmurings among the men, as though they doubted whether the MacLachors were truly responsible.

'I'm going to find Alex,' she told them. 'But I'm asking for a few of you to join me, in case we have to fight for her.'

Callum stepped forwards, holding his bow and quiver of black-feathered arrows. Laren started to protest, for they needed his skill at Glen Arrin. But when she tried to speak, he reached over and touched his finger to her lips, silencing her.

He stared at the remaining men, as if daring them to protest.

'I'll go with you,' Ramsay offered. He sent her a hopeful look, but he was far too young to face such danger.

'I need you to tend my furnaces,' she said. 'I'm relying on you and Monroe to continue the glassmaking.'

Though he looked disappointed, his offer had an effect upon the others, as if shaming them into agreeing. Two more men joined Callum and Laren turned to Ross. 'Defend Glen Arrin while we're gone,' she ordered. The older man inclined his head.

Laren exhaled a breath and studied the people. It hadn't been as difficult as she'd imagined, speaking before them.

There hadn't been judgement or criticism in their eyes—only understanding.

'I'm going to find my daughter,' she finished, not caring that her cheeks were wet with tears. To her surprise, she saw Grizel approach.

The matron squeezed her hand. 'Aye, you will. And God help any man who tries to stop a mother from saving her child.'

Chapter Fourteen

Finian MacLachor held the sleeping child in his arms. The young girl had cried for most of the afternoon until she'd fallen into an exhausted stupor. He drew his cloak over her for warmth and stared at the fortress that lay ahead. More than anything, he wished he could turn back. But his time had already run out and he was afraid of what had happened to Iliana.

He walked forwards through the gates, still carrying Adaira in his arms with the cloak wrapped around her. The soldiers watched him as he entered, their weapons held in readiness, though there was no need. Two soldiers crossed in front of him. Finian eyed the men. 'I've brought Lord Harkirk a hostage in exchange for my daughter.'

There was doubt upon their faces, but they led him toward the main tower. Inside the fortress, he saw men dressed in rags, laying stones atop one another to form walls to reinforce the keep. One sent him a grim expression, silently damning Finian for what he was about to do. Aye, this girl was an innocent. And though he hated himself for handing her over to the enemy, he could see no other choice. He hadn't enough men to save Iliana. He could only hope that Harkirk would trade one daughter for another.

The soldiers led him into a room where Harkirk was speaking with a group of men. The Baron wore chainmail armour and a conical helm, as though he'd recently come from a battle. When he saw Finian, his gaze turned interested. 'What have you brought me?'

'The MacKinloch chief's youngest daughter. In return, I want Iliana back.'

The man gave a thin smile. 'So, you think to bargain for her. Why would you believe I kept her alive after all this time?'

'Because you want the MacKinlochs dead. And they will fight for this child. They will come to you…all of them.'

The Baron sent him an amused smile. To one of the soldiers, he said, 'Take her.'

Out of instinct, Finian's hands tightened around Adaira. The motion awakened the child and, when the soldier seized her, she started wailing again. Harkirk gestured to the man and the soldier disappeared with the baby. The young girl's cries would haunt him, for he'd now done the unthinkable—handing over an innocent to the devil himself.

'The child could belong to anyone,' Harkirk said. 'You've no proof that she's a MacKinloch.'

'She is. I swear it.' His courage ran cold, for he now realised he'd made a fatal mistake. He'd believed that Harkirk would accept the hostage exchange and that he'd get Iliana back. Now, it was clear that Harkirk had no intention of honouring such a bargain.

'Put him with the others,' Harkirk ordered. 'And we'll see if anyone comes for the child.'

Four men seized him, the cold metal of their armour biting into his arms. Finian struggled to free himself, but his strength was no match for the others. 'What about my daughter?' he shouted as the men started to drag him away.

'She's already dead.'

'Harkirk's men attacked us a sennight after they burned Glen Arrin,' Brochain said. 'They took Finian's daughter Iliana and, in return, they wanted your heads.'

Alex tossed a peat brick upon the fire, understanding what the Baron had intended. 'If Harkirk hired you to kill us, then he'd keep his hands clean.'

'Aye.' Brochain's gaze tightened. 'He's nearly annihilated our clan. We've hardly any men left at all.' Bitterness lined his tone when he added, 'My brother took a group of the others, planning to attack Harkirk's forces and rescue his daughter. He was the only survivor.'

Alex took a sip of ale from the drinking horn he'd brought with him and passed it to Brochain. The *tánaiste* hesitated a moment—drinking from it would signify an alliance between them. But eventually he drank, passing it on to each of his men.

'Do the other clans know about the bounty?'

Brochain shrugged. 'I don't know. And now I may not see my brother alive again.' He nodded at the others, who numbered fewer than a dozen. 'We can't attempt another rescue. It would be suicide.'

Alex settled back to think. 'Have you spoken to the other clans?'

'They refused to help us.' Brochain rested his wrist upon his knee, staring into the fire. 'I fear our only chance of surviving this is to let Finian go.' His hand clenched into a fist. 'But he's my brother.'

'We'll help you get them back,' Bram spoke up. He eyed Alex and said, 'I swore I'd free Harkirk's remaining prisoners.' He raised his wrists, showing Brochain the scars that remained from the chains he'd worn for seven years. 'But we won't attack them directly. We'll have to get inside another way.'

Alex read his brother's mind. 'You want the MacLachors to take us in as their prisoners?'

'No. We'll get help from Nairna's father.' The chief of the MacPhersons had formed a fragile truce with Harkirk, but it was wearing thin.

Alex began outlining his idea, drawing in the sand. Brochain added his own information that Finian had gathered from his two encounters with Harkirk. They spent hours discussing their plans, and when it was done, Alex felt a sense of satisfaction. If they freed Harkirk's prisoners, it would diminish his power. Not only that, but when those men returned to their own clans, it would help them to solidify stronger alliances.

After they finished an evening meal prepared by Brochain's sister, they heard the sounds of horses approaching. Alex stood, reaching for his shield and weapons as he left the shelter. Outside, the sun was sinking below the horizon and he saw Callum, Laren and two other MacKinloch men approaching.

From the distraught look upon his wife's face, he knew something terrible had happened.

'What are you doing here?' he demanded.

Her cheeks were ghostly pale and her lips trembled as she spoke. 'Adaira was taken hostage by the MacLachors. She's gone.'

* * *

Laren stared in shock as Alex grabbed one of the MacLachors by his tunic, choking off the man's air. 'You said nothing about seizing my daughter, Brochain.'

Her husband had tightened his grip, hardly caring that his enemy couldn't answer. Laren dismounted and ran to his side. 'Alex. We need answers from him.'

At last he let go and Brochain's face went from blue to red. He coughed heavily, bending over as he struggled to breathe. 'Finian,' was all he could say.

The fury on Alex's face didn't diminish and Laren wrapped her arms around his waist. She held on for a moment as if she could steady the rage.

He took the man by his arm and forced him up. 'Did you know about this?'

MacLachor shook his head. 'No. But…when we attacked Glen Arrin, Finian wanted a hostage. It didn't work then, but he must have returned.' He sat down, reaching for a cup of ale to clear his throat. 'I suppose he thought to trade one daughter for another.'

Laren gripped Alex's arm for support. A hostage? Her baby? The tenuous thread she had on her own anger was ready to snap. The Baron of Harkirk was heartless, an Englishman who kept Scots as slaves and worshipped silver. To even imagine her own daughter in the same vicinity as such a monster…it made her feel sick to her stomach.

Callum was standing next to Bram and a ruthless air of fury emanated from him. He knew, full well, what Adaira would face in Harkirk's stronghold. Though his outer scars were healing, no one knew what horrors Callum had witnessed. Though he'd helped the others with the rebuilding, Laren could see the hollowness that haunted him.

'We'll get her back,' Brochain said. 'Finian wasn't thinking clearly.' He eyed Alex, rubbing his throat. 'We'll leave at dawn.'

Alex took Laren into one of the abandoned homes and started a fire in the hearth. Laren's fingers were trembling, her face filled with worry. Alex stood beside her and rested his arm around her. 'I'll find Adaira. I swear it.'

'*We* will find her,' she corrected. 'I'll not be left behind while my daughter is in the hands of that monster.'

Alex took her hand. 'If you think I'll allow you to endanger yourself, bringing you into Harkirk's fortress, you're mistaken.' He brought his hand to her swelling womb. 'Or have you forgotten that there's another child that must be kept safe?'

'I won't go back without her,' she insisted. Her eyes filled up with tears. 'What kind of a man would take a baby and hand her over to the enemy?'

'One whose daughter was already taken,' he answered. He kept his voice emotionless and it seemed to set off her temper.

'How can you be so calm about this?'

He ignored the question, for he couldn't let himself think of anything happening to Adaira. Right now, he needed to focus on what needed to be done, keeping his personal feelings locked away. 'Tomorrow, I'm sending you home with your escorts. Callum will stay with us.'

She lowered her head, her fingers clenching her side. 'I don't understand you. You act as if you're going off to battle. As if nothing's wrong.'

He stared at the fire, but it did nothing to warm the coldness inside of him. 'I *am* going off to battle, Laren.'

'Don't you care at all? This is our *daughter*.'

'I know well enough what's at stake, Laren.' He didn't need her to remind him that their baby's life lay in his hands. If he made a mistake, Adaira could die because of it.

Laren shook her head, backing away from him. 'You were like this when David died. It was as if his life didn't matter.'

'It mattered to me.' The words were emotionless, but beneath them, he felt the shadow of loss. The more she dwelled upon the past, the more it dug into him like a dull blade. 'Right now, I have to think of how we're going to get inside Harkirk's fortress. And how we'll free her.' He used a heavy staff to poke at the fire, sending up a shower of sparks.

'You never mourned for David, did you?' she murmured. 'You visited his grave…but that was all.'

The accusation sliced through the shell surrounding his heart. He caught her wrists and held them in front of her. 'Don't you *ever* accuse me of not loving our son. I mourned for him, aye.'

He was holding her too harshly and released her, feeling the frustration rising higher. 'But I'm the chief of this clan. I can't let anyone see what's inside of me. Not them. And not you.'

Every word she spoke was grinding against him. Couldn't she see that he felt pain as deeply as she, even if he could never show it?

'I'm your wife, Alex,' she whispered, her eyes filled with tears. 'If you don't confide in me, who else is there?'

When her hands moved up to his face, he gripped her hard, lowering his face to her hair. 'We won't lose another child. I swear it to you.'

Despite his efforts to block the memory of his daughter, he saw Adaira's face in his mind. He remembered the sweetness of her smile and the way she would skip and gallop instead of walk. He'd surrender every last drop of his blood for her.

Just as he would for his wife. In her eyes, he saw the disappointment. He didn't know what she wanted from him. Dwelling on the past wouldn't change it.

But perhaps…by holding back his thoughts, he was hurting her more.

'When we lost our son, there was nothing I could do to comfort you,' he said at last. 'Nothing I could say to take away your pain.'

'I was afraid to reach out to you,' she admitted. 'You never spoke of it.'

'It was the worst moment of my life. I'd wanted a son so badly…and then to lose him so soon—' The only thing worse than losing David was losing his wife.

She reached up to take his face in her hands. 'We'll have another son one day. And he'll grow up to be as strong as his father.'

He kissed her. 'One day, perhaps.'

Laren reached for his hand and brought it to rest upon her womb. She remained still and he moved his fingers in a circular motion. 'Have you felt the bairn move within you yet?'

She shook her head. 'But I'm feeling a little better. Not as tired or sick.'

For a time, he rested his hand there, as if willing their unborn child to be safe. 'I won't fail you, Laren,' he vowed. 'I'll bring Adaira home.'

She drew him to lie down beside her, but he remained protective of her body. He smoothed her hair back from her temple and she twined her legs with his. The future was too uncertain right now. He didn't know what threats awaited them or what had already happened to their daughter.

Laren was staring at him, her blue eyes filled with unspoken emotions. He cradled her face, as if he could hold the image in his mind for ever. God above, he loved her.

He kissed her mouth, drifting lower to her throat. Though the layer of her gown separated him from her bare skin, he kissed her ribs, the swell of her hip, then he laid his mouth upon their unborn baby.

'You're going to live,' he whispered to the child, 'and grow strong. I promise you.'

No matter what happens to me.

His wife reached down to him and guided him back up to look at her. 'You speak as if you're not coming back.'

He couldn't lie to her about this. Instead, he caressed her cheek, looking steadily into her eyes. 'I will do anything to send her back to you.'

'Don't make me choose,' she ordered. 'Don't ever make me choose between your life or Adaira's.' Her voice was trembling and she closed her eyes, pressing her mouth to his palm.

'It won't come to that.' Especially if there was no choice to be made. Any father would willingly sacrifice himself for his child. Just as Tavin had surrendered his own life for Bram.

When he was a boy, he hadn't understood it. He'd been the one to find his mother raging over her husband's body. He'd looked into his father's sightless eyes, unable to understand why Tavin had taken the sword that was meant for his brother.

Now he did. And though he planned to do everything possible to survive this, he understood the risk.

'Do you think she's alive?' The torment upon Laren's face carved itself into his heart. He held her close, not wanting to see her anguish.

'She's alive. Harkirk will use her to get to us.' But he didn't doubt that Harkirk would relish the opportunity to kill Adaira in front of him. The thought numbed his heart and he felt Laren's tears dampening his tunic.

'Be careful.' Her words were below a whisper, hardly there at all. Then she was kissing him with desperation.

He tasted the salt of her tears, trying to be the strength she needed right now. She touched his tongue with hers, seeking him, her hands moving beneath his clothing.

As she drew back the layers that separated them, he helped her until they both lay skin to skin. He felt the transformation in her body, the lushness and beauty of her. Though her waist held only a slight bump, her breasts were fuller.

Her arms wound around his neck, and he rubbed his hands down her spine, to her lower back. 'You give me a reason to come back, *a ghràidh*.'

And when she pulled him down to love her, he savored every touch, every moment. Knowing it might be their last night together.

Laren's eyes were dry as Alex rode away. There was nothing worse than trying to go through each day, when her heart was with her husband and daughter. She wished now that she'd sent Adaira with Mairin to be fostered—at least then her baby would be safe. Her desire to have a little more time with Adaira had resulted in a terrible nightmare.

She couldn't even work with her glass any more. Though it had once been an escape, she'd lost her desire to create. Laren spent the first day inside the keep, going through the motions of her duties. When she sat at the wooden trestle table, blue and gold lights shone upon her hands. She looked up and saw that Ross had arranged for one of her windows to be mounted within the keep. The image of the Madonna and Child rested high above them, the sunlight spilling through the colours. The emptiness was sinking deeper, the despair shadowing every aspect of her life.

Nairna came to spend time with her later that morning, and from the happiness on her face, Laren guessed what the woman was going to say. It made her more determined not to upset her by revealing where Bram and Alex were. Better to let Nairna think they were still negotiating with the MacLachors.

'It's been nearly two months,' Nairna said, her voice holding excitement. She rested a hand over her middle, the fervent hope giving her smile a warm glow. 'But I haven't been sick at all. Do you think I could be wrong?'

'Some women aren't ill,' Laren said. 'You may be one of the fortunate ones.' She rested her hand upon her own swelling womb, understanding Nairna's joy. 'But I think, yes, you'll be holding a bairn in your arms, come the winter.'

Nairna burst into tears and hugged her. Laren moved over on the bench, unable to stand up to return the embrace. 'It's all right. I know you've wanted this for a long time.'

'I can't seem to stop crying,' Nairna wailed. 'And I know I should be happy.'

'It doesn't take much to make a pregnant woman cry.' Her own eyes dimmed with tears, the worry rising up. She wanted to be with Alex right now, despite the danger. Though he had men of his own and the MacLachors, it wasn't enough. He'd known it when he'd spent their last night together.

Something snapped inside of her. Why was she sitting here, waiting for them to die? She'd always hung back, letting others make decisions for her. And if she did nothing, they weren't going to come back.

A sudden fire pushed through her. She didn't have to stay here. They did have other allies. And though she didn't know the other clans that well, she had silver pieces left over from the window she'd sold.

She could hire men to help Alex and the others. A surge of energy pushed through her and she rose to her feet. She would start by travelling to speak with Kameron MacKinnon, Lord of Locharr. He'd been a friend and ally in the past. Surely he could grant her a dozen men to help Alex.

'What's wrong?' Nairna asked. 'Are you feeling all right?

Laren ventured a smile. 'Aye.' She had a purpose now, to secure defences for the men and help them. All she had to do was assume her true role as Lady of Glen Arrin, lifting her courage to do what had to be done.

'I need to speak with Grizel.' The older matron had a special friendship with Kameron MacKinnon. It was likely that she would go with Laren to speak with the Baron.

Nairna sent her a worried look. 'If you're wanting to speak with Grizel, then clearly you're not feeling well at all.'

Laren only smiled.

Four days later

The Baron of Harkirk had added to his holdings, but the fortress was still constructed primarily of wood. With a high tower house and several outbuildings surrounded by a wooden palisade, it would be difficult to infiltrate.

They had made their camp at the top of a large hill, allowing them to look down inside the fortress. Groups of soldiers trained within the walls while smoke rose from outdoor fires.

Bram had gone to recruit help from Nairna's father, Hamish MacPherson, while Callum stared at the walls, his thoughts unreadable.

'Did they cut out his tongue?' Brochain MacLachor asked. 'Can't he tell us anything about their defences?'

Callum said nothing, but his fingers curled over his bow. Alex made no demands, but he knew his brother understood their words. He put up a hand, shaking his head at the others as he approached his brother. Callum had turned his back and Alex walked up beside him. 'How many soldiers did Harkirk have, when you were a captive? Two dozen?'

Callum held up four fingers. Nearly fifty, then.

'How many dozens of slaves?'

His brother held up only one finger, then signalled a little more.

Alex rested his hand on Callum's shoulder, in silent thanks for the information. Callum sat down, adjusting some of his arrows. The black-feathered tips were distinctive and he checked to be sure that his weapons were ready.

But was it reasonable to ask his brother to return to the fortress where he'd been held prisoner? He didn't believe it was a good idea at all.

'I want you to stay behind with your bow,' he said. Callum stiffened, his face transforming with anger. 'Not because I don't think you're capable of fighting,' he amended.

'But I don't trust Harkirk. If we're taken captive, we need someone on the outside to get us out again.'

When Callum shook his head in refusal, Alex continued, 'You need that distance for your arrows.'

In reply, Callum reached out and seized Alex's sword, unsheathing it. Though his arms were thin, there was a tight strength there. Alex saw the ruthless determination, the blood vengeance on his brother's face.

'If I were in your place, I'd feel the same,' Alex said. He held out his palm for his sword hilt. Callum held the weapon a moment longer before returning it. 'But unless you can speak to us, you can't come.'

A furious resentment lined Callum's face, his eyes filled with rage, but still he didn't speak.

'If you were in trouble, you couldn't call out to us,' Alex pointed out. 'And you can't tell me what I need to know about the fortress and its defences.'

Callum pointed in the direction where Bram had travelled, to the MacPherson holdings. And he understood what his brother meant. Nairna's father would know about Harkirk's weaknesses, well enough.

His brother turned his attention back to his arrows, refusal evident from his posture. There wasn't any argument Alex could make that would convince Callum to remain behind. With no other choice, he returned to their camp and sat down.

Brochain came close and sat across from him. 'When do you want to confront Harkirk?'

'When it's dark, we'll go below into the valley and spread out around the fortress. We need to know if Adaira and Finian are there.'

'What about Iliana?' Brochain pointed out.

'If she's alive, we'll do what we can to get her out,' Alex

said. 'But if your chief tries to sacrifice my daughter for his, rest assured, I will find him. And he won't come back alive.'

Alex adjusted the conical helm and gripped his spear as he entered Harkirk's fortress. Brochain MacLachor's men had killed an English soldier who had spied them and Alex had stripped the dead man of his armour. The disguise would allow him to infiltrate the fortress without being recognised, as long as he kept his head down and behaved like one of the others.

Bram had returned with a few of the MacPherson men and they formed a perimeter around Harkirk's fortress, searching for Adaira. Alex moved inside, his eyes adjusting to the light from the torches.

It was nearing midnight, he guessed, from the moon's position in the sky. There were about a dozen men patrolling the walls, while inside he saw a large tower that likely housed Harkirk's quarters. Had the MacLachor chief brought Adaira here? Or had he turned back?

Alex silently walked through the grounds, keeping to the shadows as best he could. Often he joined other soldiers, obeying orders when they sent him to patrol another section of the wall.

When he reached the interior portion of the fortress, he heard a man gasping for air. In the shadowed corner, he saw a bound prisoner, bleeding upon the stones. His back was raw with lash marks and he was shivering from the winter cold.

It was the chief, Finian MacLachor. Alex recognised the man who had disguised himself as Father Stephen and his first instinct was to leave the man there to bleed. He deserved death for what he'd done, but he was his best hope for answers. With reluctance, Alex came closer and dropped down on one knee. 'MacLachor.'

The man raised his head and recognition dawned in his eyes, before he started to lose consciousness. 'She's dead.'

Alex's hand tightened on MacLachor's throat, a rush of fear and fury filling up inside. 'Adaira?'

'No. My daughter, Iliana. Harkirk has your child,' the chief said.

Alex didn't know whether to be thankful Adaira was still alive or furious that she was now Harkirk's prisoner. 'Where is she?'

Finian's eyes raised up to the tower, where a lone window overlooked the fortress. 'Lady Harkirk has her.' Alex hadn't known that Harkirk had brought a woman here. It meant that the English intended to settle in Scotland, not as an outpost, but as a permanent location.

The window was shuttered tight and Alex could see no parapets or battlements nearby to reach the tower. The only way was through the keep…or by climbing up. He dismissed the latter idea, for it would only make him an easy, visible target.

Alex walked past MacLachor, leaving him there. When he reached the tower, he listened hard, but there came no sound. He knew the other clansmen had surrounded the fortress, but he didn't dare go inside the tower. Not unless an opportunity presented itself.

He spent the next few hours patrolling the fortress with the other soldiers, listening and hoping to catch a glimpse of Adaira. It occurred to him that, without seeing her for himself, he didn't know if she was truly here. The chief might have been lying, trying to lure him into staying. But then, if it was true he would have alerted Harkirk's men to Alex's presence. Instead, he'd held his silence.

Alex stared back at the man and, in Finian's broken posture, he saw the mirrored grief he'd felt at David's death. The chief looked as though he had no desire to live, nor did he care any more.

Although he was going to regret this, Alex crossed the fortress and unsheathed his knife. 'You may want to die, but I'll not grant that wish yet. You're going to help me get Adaira back.' He sawed at MacLachor's ropes, but the man didn't move, his head hanging down.

'You took an innocent child away from her family and it was all for nothing.' Alex gripped the man's wrist, dragging him up. 'Your daughter may be dead, but mine isn't. Honour her memory by righting the wrong you committed.'

Finian's gaze was empty. 'There's nothing I can do.'

'Find her. And bring her back to me,' Alex ordered.

The chief stared up at the tower, as if trying to form a decision. 'There's one staircase. You'd have a better chance of getting inside than me, with your armour.'

Before Alex could say another word, one of the captains in the distance barked out a command. 'Get away from the prisoner and attend your duties!'

With his face averted, Alex obeyed. MacLachor had fallen to his knees, pretending to still be bound. It was too soon to make a move, not until he'd learned more about his surroundings and the layout of the fortress. But the longer he waited, the greater his chance of being caught.

Laren retreated into the forest, hardly able to see at all. The moon cast a faint glow, but the clouds veiled it from time to time. She'd ordered Lord Locharr's men to remain behind until she learned what Alex's plans were. Using her glass and the silver pieces as payment, she'd hired over three dozen soldiers to help them. She took a single escort with her, Sion MacKinnon, one of Lord Locharr's most trusted men.

Laren lowered her hood, for her red hair might help Alex's men recognise her from a distance. They used no torch as they climbed up the hillside.

'How do you know where we'll find them?' she'd asked Sion.

He nodded toward the top of the hill. 'They'll be using the high ground to scout out Harkirk's defences.'

They climbed in silence and, as the incline grew steeper, Laren struggled. Though she was only a few months' pregnant, the physical walk was starting to hurt. Sion helped her, and when they reached the clearing, an arrow struck the ground at her feet.

Sion pulled her back, reaching for the arrow. 'That was a warning.' When he studied it, Laren saw the familiar black feathers.

'Callum?' she called out.

Within seconds, the young man emerged from the trees, his bow gripped in his palm. Laren crossed the space, embracing him. He appeared startled by her appearance and pointed to Sion, a question in his eyes.

'We brought reinforcements,' she told him. 'Lord Locharr has several of his men, and I've recruited more fighters.' She introduced him to Sion and asked, 'Where is Alex?'

Callum pointed to the fortress below and her nerves tightened. 'And the others?'

He spread out his hands, gesturing that they had surrounded the fortress.

'Will you lead the other soldiers to join with Alex?' she whispered. 'He'll need them.'

Callum hesitated, reaching out and pointing to her.

'I'll be all right,' she whispered. 'It's dark and no one will see me here. I'll stay out of the way.'

He brought her to sit down and built a low fire behind a small pile of stones. Her heart softened at his kindness. When the flames offered a warmth, she removed her gloves and held out her hands before the heat.

Callum set his hand upon her shoulder and motioned that he would take Sion and the others below. Then he pointed to himself and to her.

'You don't have to return for me,' she said. 'I know you want to join them.'

His expression grew tight and he shook his head. It was then that she noticed something gripped in his other hand. Laren reached out and gently opened his palm. Inside, she saw a blue silken ribbon.

'This was Lady Marguerite's, wasn't it?' she asked.

He gave a single nod, curling his fingers around it once more. The stony resignation on his face was of a man who knew he could never have the woman he wanted. As the third son, he had nothing to call his own. Never could he marry the daughter of a Duke, no matter what his heart wanted.

Laren's throat ached, for she knew exactly how he felt. She'd believed herself beneath Alex for so long, that being with him seemed an impossibility. Their worlds were so far apart…and yet he had never cared about her family's poverty, not the way she had.

As she stared at Harkirk's stronghold, she thought of how hard Alex had worked for Glen Arrin. He believed it was worth rebuilding. He'd seen beyond the ruins, knowing that it could be something beautiful beneath the desolate exterior.

The way he'd seen beneath her family's circumstances, fighting for her.

He loves me, she realised. And she'd hidden herself from the people, never believing she was worthy of his love.

But I am worthy, she thought. A strong resolution flooded through her, for she wasn't going to let Alex die. Not while she breathed.

A new truth had surfaced, while she'd gone to visit the clans. Being Lady of Glen Arrin wasn't about giving orders to the people or putting on a false confidence. It was about taking care of her loved ones. It was something she'd always known how to do. Something that had always been inside of her.

The clan needed Alex, just as she did. And she wouldn't hesitate to fight for the man she loved.

She reached out to Callum and curled his fingers over the ribbon once more. 'Marguerite cares for you,' she told him. 'Find her, when this is over. Tell her what's in your heart.'

A look of regret crossed his face and he shook his head. With one finger, he touched his lips, reminding her that he'd lost the ability to speak.

'That doesn't matter to her and you know it.' She reached out and took his hand in hers. 'You're hurting by being apart from Marguerite, aren't you?' She offered him a tentative smile. 'Surely she would find it romantic if you were to steal her away, taking her back with you.'

Callum sent her a look of disbelief, before drawing a line across his throat.

'Aye, her father might kill you.' She sent him a wide smile. 'But you'd die a happy man.'

A guttural laugh broke forth from Callum. The unexpected sound took her aback and he touched his throat as though he couldn't believe it had come out.

'You'll speak again,' Laren predicted. 'And I think you'll have a stronger reason to, if you find her.'

Callum met her gaze. In his eyes, she saw the mirror of the person she had been before. Someone who didn't believe it was possible to be loved.

He took her hand and pressed the ribbon into it. A moment later, he disappeared into the darkness, with Sion at his side.

Chapter Fifteen

Laren jerked to her feet when she heard footsteps approaching. Though she couldn't see who was there, it wasn't Alex or one of the others. She hid herself within the trees, crouching low behind a bush. Within seconds, she heard the sound of dirt poured upon her fire. Darkness blinded her and her pulse tightened.

'I know you're there,' came a whispered voice. 'But you shouldn't have lit a fire. They'll see it from the fortress.'

Laren didn't speak, not knowing if it was a trap of some sort. Her fingers curled around a tree and it took several moments for her eyes to adjust. The scent of ashes cloaked the atmosphere, a cloying odour that heightened her fear.

When a hand touched her shoulder, she let out a shriek. A boy stood in front of her, older than Mairin, but not yet an adolescent. His hair was ragged against his neck and he wore warm clothing against the cold. 'You have to come with me. She wouldn't want you here alone.'

'She?'

'Lady Harkirk.'

Laren didn't trust any Harkirk, Lady or not. But what was a child doing alone in the hills?

'Is she your mother?'

'No. Come.' He took Laren by the hand. 'They can see your fire from the fortress. I'll bring you to another shelter where you'll be safe.'

'I have to wait here,' Laren argued. She pulled her hand free. Although it was growing colder without a fire, she could huddle among the fallen leaves if she had to. Then another alarming thought occurred to her. 'Does Lady Harkirk know that I am here?'

The boy shook his head. 'I came on my own. I wanted to see what the fire was.'

'Who are you?' Laren asked. 'You're not English. Are you one of Harkirk's prisoners?'

The child shrugged. 'Not any more. She helped me to hide.'

Given the boy's age, Laren was glad of it. No young child should be forced to labour alongside adults. 'Where do you live, then? Where are your parents?'

The boy didn't answer and Laren suspected they were dead. When the child started to disappear into the trees, she called out, 'Wait. Don't go, yet.'

'I have to leave. If you come with me, I promise you'll be safe. But the soldiers are coming. They saw your fire.'

Laren didn't know what to do. Although she'd believed that the fire Callum had built would not be visible from behind the stones, clearly the boy had seen it. If he'd found her, the soldiers could, too.

'Where are you going?' she asked, following the boy into the trees.

'Come with me and I'll show you.'

Another thought occurred to her, one that deepened

her fear. 'Did you…see any other children at Harkirk's fortress? A young girl, almost two years of age?'

The boy nodded. 'Lady Harkirk has her. She's taking care of her.'

All the blood seemed to rush to her head and Laren leaned up against a tree. Thank God. Adaira was alive. Hot tears rushed to her eyes, and she admitted, 'The child is my daughter. I need to bring her back. Is she inside the fortress?'

'She is.' The boy offered his hand to her. 'If you come with me, I'll take you to my shelter. Lady Harkirk will come in the morning and you can ask her about your daughter.' There was a slight note of regret in the boy's voice, as if he were thinking of his own family.

Laren hesitated, torn between obeying Alex and learning more about Adaira. The night air was growing colder and she knew the dangers of sleeping without a fire to keep warm. The lack of shelter would make it a painful night.

'I'll go with you,' she agreed at last. If there was any chance of learning about Adaira, she had to take it. 'But I'll need to return before morning.' She didn't know if Alex would return, but she wanted to be there if he did.

The boy held out his hand and she followed him down the hillside.

'You,' ordered a voice. 'Take your spear and join the others.' The captain gestured towards a group of a half-dozen men who were leaving the fortress.

Alex waited for further information and the English soldier added, 'One of the men saw a fire on the hillside. Find out who was trespassing.'

He bowed his head, letting nothing betray his features. Would Callum have been foolish enough to light a fire?

Aye, it was freezing outside, but he couldn't think of any reason why his brother would do such a thing. Unless it was meant as a signal of some sort.

Inwardly, he cursed, reaching for a torch. Since he was dressed in chainmail, Callum wouldn't know it was him in the darkness. His brother might unleash a storm of arrows before they ever reached the hillside.

'You won't be needing that,' one of the others said, seizing the torch from his grasp.

Alex thought about arguing, but then reconsidered. He needed to maintain the disguise for now. Better to drop back and disappear into the trees as soon as he had the chance.

The men travelled in pairs and Alex made certain he was in the last group. When he started to move away, the soldier on his right followed. 'Where are you going?'

'I thought I heard a noise coming from this side,' Alex said. 'I'll go and have a look.'

'We stay together,' the man argued. 'It's safer.'

But when Callum's arrow struck the first soldier, Alex tore off his helmet and ran out of his brother's range. The wind was bitter, ripping through his skin with the cold. He dived for cover and hurriedly stripped off the chainmail armour, wearing only his trews and a light tunic.

It was freezing outside, but he bit back the discomfort and kept to the trees as the soldiers charged forwards.

'Callum, hold your arrows!' he shouted in Gaelic, letting his brother hear his voice. The arrows stopped abruptly, and Alex suddenly realised that his brother was nowhere near the camp where he'd left him.

The remaining two soldiers retreated back to the fortress, and it wouldn't take long before they gathered more men. He needed to get his brother out of there, before anyone found him.

Callum appeared through the trees, another clansman at his side.

'Who is that?' Alex demanded.

'I am Sion MacKinnon,' the clansman answered. 'Your wife recruited us to fight after talking to Lord Locharr. There are others from the surrounding clans as well. About three dozen.' He gestured towards the trees, and Alex spied a few of them, spread out on both sides.

His wife? Alex stared blankly, not understanding. Laren had gone to seek help for them?

'She paid them in silver and gave Lord Locharr one of her glass windows, in exchange for our service,' MacKinnon continued.

He couldn't even think of what to say, he was so stunned that she would venture out of Glen Arrin, much less speak to the clan chiefs. 'Are they all here?'

'No. Some are waiting a mile from here. We wanted to attack with several groups on all sides.'

'Where is Laren now?' Alex demanded, hoping to God the man would say that she'd remained at Glen Arrin.

But his brother Callum turned and pointed to the hillside, where the fire had been burning earlier.

'You left her there alone?' Fury poured through Alex and he reached for his brother, wanting to choke him for letting her stay. Callum unsheathed his dirk and held it out with a warning look. He held a finger to his lips. Then he pointed towards the fortress, reminding Alex that the soldiers were going to return.

'Help me find her,' Alex commanded, and Callum sheathed the knife again. To Sion, he ordered, 'Go back and tell your men to join with ours, around the perimeter of the fortress.' He gave instructions and the MacKinnon disappeared to obey.

Alex climbed up the hillside, searching for his wife. Callum led him to where he'd left Laren, but the fire was now cold. It was too dark to track her footprints and he called out to her in a harsh whisper, but there was no reply.

As he searched through the woods, with every moment that passed, his fear sharpened. He should have listened to his doubts, for now he might lose both Laren and their daughter.

And he couldn't live with himself if that happened.

Laren couldn't sleep, despite the straw pallet the boy had offered her. The wind blew through the crevices in the crude shelter. Made of stone and wood, it seemed that the boy had built it himself.

'How long have you been here?' she asked, when she saw that he wasn't sleeping either.

'I don't remember.' He huddled beneath an old woollen blanket, gathering the edges to keep warm.

'You shouldn't stay here,' Laren said. 'It's not any safer for you than it is for me.'

'And where would I go? Everyone's dead,' he said, drawing up his knees. His voice held a quaver, as though he were holding back tears.

'You could come back with me,' Laren offered. 'Tell me how I can get Adaira back and I'll make sure you have a place to live.'

The boy lowered his head to his knees and, after a few minutes, Laren realised he was crying. She came up beside him and touched his ragged hair. 'It will be all right. You'll see.' She whispered words of comfort to him, and in time, the child laid down on the pallet. She covered him with the rough blanket and noticed that his features were softer than she'd originally noticed. He was so young, possibly only a few years older than Mairin. She wished she'd remembered to ask his name.

Laren closed her eyes for a moment and a shudder of dizziness swept through her. She'd forgotten to eat anything tonight and was ravenous. Her back ached and the terror that lay dormant suddenly roared to life.

I shouldn't have left Glen Arrin, she thought to herself. *Alex will be so angry when he finds out.* But she'd believed that it was safe with so many clansmen to defend her. Now, she wasn't so certain. She lay down beside the boy and, in time, her physical exhaustion overcame the fear.

When she awakened in the morning, she saw an English noblewoman staring down at her.

'Who are you?' the woman demanded in heavily accented Gaelic. Laren sat up slowly, but she didn't leave the boy's side. The woman was dressed in a burgundy samite gown trimmed with fur. Her gloved hands were slender and her brown hair was bound up in a golden barbette trimmed with rubies.

'I am Laren MacKinloch,' she answered. 'I suppose you must be Lady Harkirk.'

The woman nodded, but there was a shadow of unhappiness in her eyes. 'You shouldn't have come here. It isn't safe.'

'Lord Harkirk has my daughter prisoner. Where is she?'

'If you're asking about the young baby, I left her with my maid,' Lady Harkirk answered. 'She has red hair, like yours. Blue eyes?'

'Adaira is her name.'

Lady Harkirk lowered her head and nodded. 'My

husband is using her to lure the MacKinlochs here. After what happened a few months ago, he wants vengeance.'

'I don't know if you have children of your own,' Laren said, 'but my daughter is an innocent. And I will do whatever I have to, to get her back.'

'It won't be easy.' Lady Harkirk risked a glance back at the fortress, then shivered.

The young boy yawned and stretched upon the straw pallet. Lady Harkirk pulled back her cloak and revealed a bag she'd brought with her. There was a small amount of food inside and Laren wanted to cry at the sight of it, she was so hungry. But the child needed the food and she said nothing, letting him take what he needed.

The boy devoured the meat, but he tore off a bit of a bread crust, handing it to Laren. 'Here,' he offered.

She savoured the small crust, though it did little to take the edge off her hunger. It reminded her of the nights when she'd gone hungry with her sisters. Since she'd married Alex, food was never something they'd lacked.

Laren rose to her feet, but as soon as she stood, her legs buckled. The boy caught her before she hit the ground and she let out a curse, lowering her head between her knees.

'You look pale,' the Lady said. 'If I had more food, I'd—'

'No. I need to find my husband.' Laren fought to remain conscious, angry with herself for the weakness of her pregnancy. She took slow, deep breaths, and then managed to face Lady Harkirk. 'They're going to attack your fortress.' Laren stared at the woman, praying there was compassion within her. 'If you can help me to get my daughter out, I can stop them from fighting.'

Lady Harkirk's expression grew bitter. 'If my husband dies in battle, it would only be a blessing.' She returned to the entrance of the shelter. 'I'll do what I can to help you, but I can't bring your daughter out of the fortress. I've already risked too much, coming here alone.'

'Bring her near the entrance, at nightfall,' Laren said. 'We'll find a way to get her out.'

Lady Harkirk stared at her, then lowered her head. 'No. I don't think I can. Not without him suspecting something.'

'If my daughter dies—'

'She won't,' the lady assured her. 'I protected this one from harm.' She pointed towards the young boy, before she shivered and wrapped her cloak around her for more warmth. 'I can't say how I'll manage it, but be ready to claim her at nightfall.'

Laren stood up and faced the Lady, eye to eye. 'She's just a baby. And I won't lose her.'

Lady Harkirk took her hand. 'I'll keep her safe.'

Alex's eyes were dry and raw from lack of sleep. He'd searched every last inch of the forest, but there was no sign of Laren anywhere.

Had she been taken when Callum had left her alone? If anything happened to her, he blamed himself. The thought of her falling into Harkirk's hands infuriated him.

'If she's in that fortress, we'll find her.' Bram had returned early this morn, with the promise of aid from Nairna's father. He gripped Alex's arm in silent support. 'We may as well assume she's there.'

Alex's grasp upon reason was slipping away. The very thought of Harkirk touching Laren, hurting her... It made him understand why Bram had lost control in the battle several months ago when Nairna was threatened.

The thought of Laren's gentle face, her fiery red hair falling over her shoulders, made his heart twist. He remembered how he'd slept with her in his arms, their unborn child resting beneath his hand. And the thought of losing them sent his temper roaring.

He crossed towards Callum, shoving his younger brother against the back of a tree. 'Why did you leave her? She could be dead right now, because you left her alone!'

Bram and Brochain dragged him back, but Alex's lungs were tight, his rage unchecked. And seeing the emptiness in his brother's eyes only provoked him more.

Callum didn't know what it meant to love a woman. He didn't understand. Losing Laren would be like ripping his heart out of his chest. There would be nothing left but an emptiness that would never be filled.

'If we're going to find them, you need to get control of yourself,' Bram insisted. 'If you strike out at one of us, you're not helping Laren.'

He knew it. But damn it, the need to lash out was all consuming.

'While you were inside last night, we found a possible way to break into their stronghold,' Bram interrupted.

He nodded towards Brochain MacLachor, who offered, 'There is one part of the fortress that has suffered from water damage. The wood is rotting, almost crumbling in places.'

'Go on.' Alex eyed the man, not knowing what he was suggesting.

'I broke away sections of the wood. The beams behind it aren't stable. If we set them on fire, the walls will crumble.'

Alex nodded. 'Good. We'll split our forces and distract Harkirk's men with a direct attack while you take down the other part of the fortress.'

'And what of my brother?' Brochain asked. 'Did you find him last night?'

'He's hurt, but alive.' Alex gave no further information, for he hadn't forgiven the MacLachor chief for putting Adaira in danger.

'And what of his daughter?'

'She's gone.'

Brochain's mood grew sombre. 'We have to get Finian out.' He rested his hand upon his sword. 'And your daughter.'

'We'll free them,' Alex said, 'and all the other slaves who were left behind with no clan to help them.' His gaze drifted over to Callum, who gripped the handle of his bow in silent agreement.

'I spoke with Hamish MacPherson last night,' Bram continued. 'He promised a dozen men of his own to provide a distraction while we bring down Harkirk's fortress.'

'What kind of a distraction?'

Bram only shook his head and shrugged. 'He didn't say.'

Alex didn't like all the unknown factors that would impact their attack and an unsettled feeling permeated his mood. 'Harkirk will be waiting for us,' he said. 'He sent the soldiers last night to find out about the fire they saw. Since the men never returned, he'll know we're here.'

'That may be,' Bram acknowledged, 'but there's no other alternative. Unless you have another idea?'

'I do,' came a female voice from the trees.

When he spun around, he saw Laren standing there. As he crushed her into his arms, he didn't even care what anyone else thought.

Chapter Sixteen

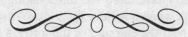

'Where were you? And why did you leave Glen Arrin?' he demanded, holding her so tightly, that Laren could hardly breathe. The worry on his face, along with the sleepless shadowing under his eyes, made her cling to him.

'You needed help.' She touched his hair, dragging his mouth to hers for a soft kiss. 'I couldn't let you face Harkirk's soldiers with so few men.' The strain upon her husband's face made it seem that he'd aged fifteen years at the thought of losing her. She tried to soothe away his dark mood, though she was secretly glad he'd been so worried.

'It was too dangerous to stay here with the fire Callum built,' she went on. 'A boy came to warn me,' she answered. 'He led me to a shelter where I spent last night.'

'Who was he? And where was this shelter?'

Laren shook her head. 'I don't know his name. But he wasn't English.' She described the location of the shelter to him, then raised her hands to rest upon his shoulders.

'Alex, he knew where Adaira was.' She would have followed anyone with information leading to her daughter. It didn't matter that she didn't know the boy's name. 'Lady Harkirk is taking care of her. She came to us early this morning and has promised to help us.'

Alex stiffened at the mention of the Lady. 'Why would she venture beyond the fortress, unless it was at her husband's bidding?'

She predicted the direction of his thoughts and shook her head. 'No. She was angry with Harkirk. She said she'd be glad if he were killed in battle.'

'Or she might have lured you into trusting her.'

Laren didn't want to believe it. 'She promised to bring our daughter near the entrance of the fortress at sunset.'

'Where Lord Harkirk will be waiting with soldiers to cut us down.'

'I don't believe that,' Laren argued. 'She helped save the life of that boy—she's kept him in hiding.'

Her husband shook his head. 'You're too trusting, Laren.'

It was clear that he didn't believe Lady Harkirk at all. And it might be that the woman wasn't telling the truth. But Laren had seen regret in her face, as though Lady Harkirk wanted nothing to do with her husband's deeds.

'Does she know about the attack?' he asked.

'She knows we're here. But she doesn't know how many of us there are.'

Alex's face turned grim and he exchanged a glance with Bram. His brother said, 'The MacPhersons will be here soon. We need to get our men into position.'

'Go, then,' Alex ordered. 'I'll join you in a moment.'

Bram obeyed, taking Brochain with him. Callum picked up his bow, but Alex motioned him back. 'You're staying with Laren. And, so help me God, you'd better not leave her.' His brother gave a nod, his fist curling around his weapon.

Before Laren could voice a protest, Alex cut off her words. 'Trust me on this, Laren. Trust me to get Adaira back.'

In his eyes, she saw his frustration and worry. He drew close to her, his hand moving down to the swelling at her waist. 'When I thought I'd lost you, you can't know what that felt like. I worried that you were Harkirk's prisoner, that he'd hurt you somehow.'

He lightly stroked the unborn bairn. 'I won't let that happen. Even if I die this day, at least I'll die knowing that you're safe. That this child will live.'

In his eyes, she could see the intrinsic need for her to remain out of harm's way. 'All right,' she acceded. 'I'll stay behind with Callum.'

He touched his forehead to hers. 'Good. Go to the top of the hillside and wait behind the rocks. Hide yourself.'

She moved into his arms, holding him tightly. He stroked her hair back from her face, ordering, 'No matter what happens to the rest of us, promise me you won't interfere.'

'If your life is threatened—'

'It's a risk I'm prepared to face. But not your life.' He lowered his mouth to hers. 'Swear it.'

Her eyes were bright with unshed tears, but she lowered her head in a silent promise.

Alex waited with Bram at his side. In the distance, he saw Hamish MacPherson's men approaching, led by the chief himself. Hamish wore elaborate clothing trimmed with gold thread, along with jewelled rings upon his fingers. Alex walked up to the chief and Hamish sent him a faint smile. He seemed extremely uncomfortable about the visit.

'Harkirk knows of your intentions,' Hamish said without prelude. 'His men are positioned at every part of the fortress. If you ride in with us, you won't come out alive.'

Alex met the man's gaze with his own resolution. 'We have reinforcements ready. And if I can get Adaira out, that's all that matters.'

Hamish nodded to one of his retainers, who dismounted and offered his horse to Alex. 'So be it.' He glanced around and asked, 'Is Bram with you? Nairna won't be at all pleased with me if I get her husband killed.'

'This isn't Bram's fight.'

Hamish grunted. 'It is, if you're is involved. I know him too well for that.' The older man shifted his weight in the saddle and Alex brought his horse alongside the chief. With a heavy sigh, Hamish admitted, 'I don't know if there is enough silver in Scotland to pacify Harkirk's greed. Or to save your throat.' His expression grim, the chief asked, 'Are you sure you want to do this?'

'I'm going to bring back Adaira, whatever the cost may be.' Alex nudged the horse forwards, leaving Hamish with no choice but to follow. They rode up the path toward the gates and the archers tightened their bowstrings. If he didn't have Hamish at his side, Alex didn't doubt that the soldiers would murder him where he stood. They held their arrows in check, only because they honoured the tentative truce between the MacPhersons and their own men.

When they reached the first wall, more soldiers stood. They closed the path behind them, cutting off any escape. Alex stared at the spears, wondering if he would feel the cold thrust of the metal tip within his ribs before his men attacked. Or would his death come with a blade to slit his throat?

He let the morbid thoughts run through him, deadening any emotions he felt. He would accept his fate, as long as he saved Adaira.

Lord Harkirk awaited him at the top of the stairs that led into the tower. The man wore chain mail, his bearded face flushed with satisfaction. Beside him stood Lady Harkirk, and in her arms was Adaira.

'Da!' his daughter shrieked, stretching out her arms. She started crying and Alex felt his control slipping away. He saw her baby-fine red hair, tinted with gold. Her hands reached for him, and in his mind, he thought of David.

I won't let you go, he swore silently to his daughter. *I won't let him hurt you.* She was his flesh, born from his spirit just as much as Laren's. One day she would grow into a beautiful woman, like her mother. Even if he wasn't there to see it.

'I understand you wanted my head, Harkirk,' Alex called out. 'I've brought it to you. But first, you're going to return my daughter into the care of Hamish MacPherson.'

'Am I?' The Baron walked slowly down the stairs, as if savouring the moment. 'And what if I refuse?'

'You would harm an innocent child?' Hamish demanded. 'Because of your bloodlust?'

'She carries MacKinloch blood in her. As far as I'm concerned, the fewer MacKinlochs, the better.'

Lady Harkirk looked alarmed when her husband reached for the child. She never took her eyes off Harkirk, and when he held Adaira above the stairs, he said, 'Come here, if you want her.'

Alex hesitated, knowing that as soon as he left the safety of the MacPherson soldiers, he risked his life. But neither could he let Harkirk harm his daughter.

'If I drop her, she'll break her neck,' Harkirk taunted. 'Is that what you want?'

Alex moved forwards, but was startled when Hamish's men accompanied him, covering his back. He hadn't expected them to guard his life with their own. With a grateful look towards Hamish, he moved to the bottom of the stairs.

'Take her, then.' With that, the English Baron tossed Adaira down the stairs and Alex dived forwards, catching his daughter before she could strike her head. His heart was racing at the thought of her near encounter with death and he held her tight as she cried in his arms.

Lady Harkirk sent a frigid look towards her husband before she disappeared into the tower. The Baron didn't seem to notice.

'Give her over to Hamish MacPherson,' Harkirk ordered, 'or my archers will kill both of you.' His soldiers moved in closer, several archers poised at the ready.

Alex held tight to Adaira, whispering in her ear, 'I love you, *a nighean.*' *Be safe,* he prayed.

He gave Adaira over to Hamish, murmuring, 'Signal the others to attack.' It was harder than he'd thought it would be, for he was afraid it was the last time he'd see his daughter. But at least she would live. He'd kept his promise to Laren, regardless of what happened now.

Numbness settled across him as the soldiers took him into custody, binding his wrists behind his back. And when they struck him, he sank to his knees, tasting the blood in his mouth.

Lady Harkirk didn't care that she was betraying her husband and countrymen. When Robert had thrown that child down the stairs, any fragment of loyalty she'd ever felt had disappeared.

Now that the baby was with Hamish MacPherson, she hoped the child would be safe, but she had to make certain.

She went to the far corner of the main room and walked down the spiral stairs leading to the storage chambers. Robert had built a passageway to escape the fortress, in the event of a siege. Right now, she wanted nothing more than to walk away from this place.

The sound of chains rattling caught her attention. She peered into the darkness and saw the prisoner her husband had ordered beaten. He'd been brought below last night and it occurred to her that he might prove useful, though he was weak.

The man was shivering violently while his breath clouded the frigid air. If she left him here, he would die. Already he was suffering from exposure, his body half-frozen with cold.

This is a mistake, she thought, as she reached for the keys to unlock his shackles. The man was larger than Robert, his body heavily muscled despite his weakness.

'If I release you, will you promise not to harm me?' she asked quietly. His face jerked upwards, as though he hadn't been aware of her presence. He blinked, and she wondered if he could see her.

'Who are you?'

'Alys Fitzroy. Lady of Harkirk.' She shivered in the cold, reaching for his manacled wrist. 'Don't even think of using me as a hostage. I want to leave this place, just as you do.'

The man stared up at her and she saw something flicker on his face, almost like a sense of regret.

'What is your name?' she asked, as she released the second manacle.

'Finian,' he answered. 'I'm the MacLachor chief. Or…I was, before this.' His face grew weary, as if he no longer cared about anything any more.

Alys folded her hands in her skirts and retreated. 'If you follow me, I'll show you a way outside the fortress. That's all I can do for you. You'll have to make your own escape.'

'Why would you offer me help?' the chief asked. He struggled to his feet, wincing at the pain as he took one step, then another. 'Surely Harkirk would be furious.'

'I've been his prisoner for four years now. I don't need anyone else to endure what I have.' She swallowed hard. 'If I could free the others, I would. But he keeps them locked away, nearer to his soldiers. I don't know why he put you here.'

'Because they caught me trying to escape last night. He intends to make an example of me.' Finian rested his hand upon the wall and Alys saw another shiver rack his body. She removed her cloak and set it around his shoulders.

He stared at her and she couldn't say why she'd done it. What had begun as pity had suddenly transformed into necessity. There was something about this man that reached inside her, almost as if she needed to save him.

'I can't accept this,' he said, holding out her cloak.

'You need it more than I do.' And with that, she fled. Before she could reach the exit, he caught up to her.

'Why me?' he asked, his voice dark. 'I'm the last person who deserves this.'

She didn't speak, nor would she look at him. He was frightening her with the tone of his voice.

The chief's hand curled against the wall. 'It's my fault. This battle...the loss of men's lives.' He shoved the cloak at her, as though it were on fire. 'If the MacKinloch's daughter dies, it'll be on my soul.'

Alys started to speak, but held her tongue. Though she

wanted to condemn him, she saw the desperation and the fierce guilt in his eyes.

'Then make amends for what you did.' She pushed gently against his chest, gaining distance. 'Or go, if that's your wish.'

'I deserve to die,' he admitted.

Alys held out the cloak again. 'That's not for me to decide.' Her heart trembled as he took it, huddling beneath the wool. More than anything, she struggled to hold back the words she wanted to speak to him. But what he needed now wasn't comfort; he needed redemption. And sometimes redemption wasn't kind.

'If you're truly sorry for what you did, you could help them.' She led him up the stairs and showed him where her husband's weapons were stored. 'Will you atone for what you did? Or will you turn your back on those who are suffering?'

Laren huddled behind the rocks and when she spied motion below, she crept from her hiding place. Hamish MacPherson rode out and she could hear Adaira weeping.

Her eyes swelled up with tears, but she couldn't stop herself from crying. She wanted to leave the forest, to go running after her child. Yet she'd made a promise to Alex. She'd given her word that she wouldn't leave the trees.

When she saw Hamish riding away with Adaira, she started climbing higher, ignoring the pains in her side as she struggled uphill. Callum started to follow and she said, 'You don't have to come with me. I'll just go to the top of the hill. To watch over them.'

When she reached the highest point, she saw the small group of travellers leaving. From her vantage point, she saw that Alex was not among them. And she knew that he'd given himself up, to save their daughter.

The pain burned through her, like a ball of molten glass. Was he already dead? She sank down, her knees giving out. Though she'd known the risk, this was something she had prayed wouldn't happen.

Images flashed through her mind, of the times they'd walked through the woods together, making love near the stone circle. Of the glass droplets he'd given her, spilling the pieces over her naked flesh like gem stones.

She remembered the afternoon he'd brought her dried cherries to satisfy her cravings. Laren rested her hand upon her womb, letting the tears flow freely.

And then, beneath her fingertips, she felt a flutter of movement. Like a tiny hand reaching out to touch hers.

Alex had given her the gift of this child. And though she'd promised him she wouldn't leave the forest, she couldn't simply sit back and let him go.

I need to know, she thought. *Even if the worst has already happened, I need to know.*

Callum stood nearby with his longbow drawn. When Laren reached him, she said, 'I need you to find out what's happened to Alex. I saw them bring Adaira out…but I don't know if my husband is still alive.'

Taking her hand, Callum led her back downhill. When they reached the forest edge, he pointed to the fortress. He sniffed at the air and she understood what was happening. Though she could see no sign of Bram or the others, she could smell the smoke.

'They're burning it down, aren't they?' she asked. Just as their own fortress had been lost to Harkirk's fire, the men were enacting the same vengeance upon him.

'But what about the others? The reinforcements I sent?'

Callum gestured for her to wait. She supposed that meant they were waiting for a signal of some sort. The fire was gaining strength, rippling from the back of the fortress as if aided by oil or another fuel.

He checked his quiver for arrows, running his fingers along the black-feathered tips. He would go after his brothers, she knew. And although Laren wanted to have faith that all would be well, she couldn't let go of her anxiety.

As if in answer to her fears, she saw a dozen soldiers leaving the fortress, riding after Hamish's men. 'Callum,' she breathed, pointing towards them.

In horror she watched as they attacked the MacPherson men. And she couldn't stop the cry that broke forth when she heard her daughter scream.

Chapter Seventeen

Alex was prepared for the worst. Harkirk's men had bound him to a wooden post and he knew that they were going to kill him once his brothers arrived.

The fire raged along the outer wall, while Bram and the other men fought their way through. Already a group of soldiers had left the fortress, likely to search the perimeter for the invaders.

He wasn't about to remain their captive. Not without fighting to stay alive. The only reason Harkirk hadn't killed him yet was to use him as leverage, baiting his brothers.

Alex fumbled with the tight knots, his hands freezing in the cold air. He was bound with both hands raised above his head and they were numb from the lack of blood to his limbs. A spear tip rested against his throat and he'd been stripped of his cloak and tunic.

'If you manage to free yourself, I've orders to drive this blade into your throat,' the guard said. 'Don't waste the effort.'

'What kind of prisoner would I be, if I didn't make the effort?' Alex responded with a wry smile. Nodding to the outer wall, he added, 'The fire is getting closer.'

The guard shrugged. 'Then you'll burn to death.'

Dark smoke rose into the air and Alex shifted his wrists, watching for a sign of Callum. He stared out at the forest and a slight movement caught his attention. There, standing amid the trees on the hillside, he saw Laren. She didn't move forwards, but watched from her position, her long red hair blowing past her face in the wind.

God above, but he loved her. Beautiful and talented, with a soft heart, he wanted to spend the rest of his days at her side. Their marriage was a gift, one he'd neglected for too long.

The vision of her renewed his determination to free himself. Alex's gaze fell upon the soldier's spear and he tightened his grip upon the ropes above his head.

Lifting his feet off the ground, he struck out at the soldier, kicking him in the face. The man stumbled and Alex lashed out again, knocking the man unconscious. The fallen spear lay on the ground and Alex seized it with his feet. Though it was awkward, he managed to raise the blade higher, slicing at his ropes.

Once he'd freed the first hand, he untied the remaining ropes and grasped the spear with both hands. Pain radiated through his arms from the lack of circulation, but he pushed it aside, using the spear to take down one soldier and seize the man's sword and shield.

'Alex!' came Bram's shout.

He spun and blocked a sword blow. Diving to the ground, he kicked the man's legs out from beneath him, sliding his sword deep into the man's gut. His vision seemed to blur with the motion of battle, but he was conscious of the men moving closer, starting to surround them. He raised his shield to deflect their arrows, all the while searching for a way out.

Lord Harkirk had his own weapon drawn, and from the way he slashed a path through the men, it was clear the Englishman was well trained.

'There are too many of us, MacKinloch,' Harkirk taunted. 'And when this is finished, the other clans will know that I won't tolerate any uprising against our garrison. Your heads will be displayed outside the fortress.'

'You'll have to take it first,' Alex answered, rushing towards him with his sword. It struck Harkirk's shield, but other soldiers joined in the fight, forcing Alex to defend himself on all sides.

Bram came forwards, and they fought back to back while the flames moved towards the slave quarters. 'Nairna's going to be furious if I get myself killed,' he said, holding his claymore with both hands. 'I never told her I was planning to fight Harkirk.'

'You'd better not die, then,' Alex said, lifting his shield. As he blocked a sword blow, he kept the image of Laren fixed in his mind. He fought with every last bit of strength, willing himself to survive the battle. And then he reached Harkirk.

The bastard had threatened his family more than once. Scotland would be safer without him and he didn't care what the consequences might be. Alex fixed his gaze upon the man, waiting for the chance to strike a killing blow. The glint of chain mail flashed before his eyes when he raised his sword.

But when he heard his daughter call out to him, he jerked out of instinct. There was no sign of Hamish MacPherson or any of the others. No one to protect Adaira.

Blood swam before his eyes, a primal cry tearing from his throat when he saw the soldier holding his daughter with a blade to her throat.

'Don't,' came a woman's voice. Laren turned and saw Lady Harkirk standing just behind her, within the forest. 'I know you want to go inside the fortress. But the moment you do, my husband will use your life against your husband. He'd be glad to kill both of you.'

'I won't let anyone threaten my daughter,' Laren insisted.

'You can't help her if you're already dead.' Lady Harkirk took her by the hand. 'If you want to see what's happening, I'll take you into another guard tower. It's empty right now because Robert ordered the men into the keep. Follow me.'

She led Laren around the outside of the fortress, bringing her to a small overlook. But before Laren could take another step, a hand clamped down on her shoulder. She jerked with surprise and saw Callum.

He stared at Lady Harkirk, an open threat in his eyes. She glanced at his bow and arrows, as if making a decision. Then she beckoned to him. He gestured for her to lead the way and when they passed through the entrance, Callum shot a soldier who happened to see them. He dropped to the ground, thankfully unnoticed by the others.

As Lady Harkirk had predicted, the guard tower was empty, giving them a clear vantage point.

A subtle motion caught Laren's attention and she saw the imposter priest, Father Stephen, lurking against the far wall. He was shadowed, wearing a dark cloak, but Laren recognised his features when he drew closer to the men.

Callum drew his bow in readiness, waiting for the right moment to strike.

'Wait,' Lady Harkirk pleaded. 'Finian MacLachor may be of use.'

Laren wasn't certain, for the man was unarmed. She didn't know his intentions, but if he were discovered, it would provide a distraction for Harkirk's men.

Below, Alex was clearly torn between Adaira and the English Baron. He kept his shield raised, but his attention was focused on their daughter. Laren's nails dug into her palms, as she uttered silent prayers for Adaira's safety.

'Did you believe I would let her go?' Harkirk said coolly. 'She still has use to me.'

'She's naught but a bairn,' Alex gritted out, 'and you'll rot in hell if you harm her.'

'It's interesting, what a father will do for his daughter.' Harkirk lifted his sword, poised at Alex's throat. 'He'll commit murder. Steal. Turn against his own allies.' With a twisted smile, Harkirk asked, 'What would you do for yours?'

With a signal, the Baron's men moved in on Bram. Laren saw the anguish on her husband's face and Harkirk demanded, 'Whose life has more value? Your brother's? Or your daughter's?'

Alex turned on Harkirk, unleashing his rage as his sword struck the Baron. His movements forced Harkirk backwards, allowing him to keep Adaira in his sight.

He abandoned himself to the fight, not caring what happened to him. If he died, so be it. But he'd strike down the Baron with his last breath.

'Kill her!' Harkirk ordered and Alex shoved the man backwards into the group of soldiers.

At that moment, he saw Finian MacLachor running forwards with a dirk in his hands. The man raised the weapon towards Adaira and Alex's heart stopped. He couldn't reach her in time. The thought of watching her die was unthinkable.

But instead of killing her, Finian embedded the blade in the back of the soldier's throat, pulling the child away. He held his blade in readiness, to defend her.

Alex breathed easier and his reinforcements invaded the fortress, until they slowly regained control of the battle. Turning back, he saw that Harkirk had disappeared. The coward. He couldn't stop to search for him now, but his sword bit through flesh and bone as they drove back the soldiers. And when Alex reached his daughter's side at last, Finian MacLachor stood near the child, his dirk still in hand.

'You saved her,' Alex said, grateful beyond words.

'Were it not for me, she'd never have been in danger. I'm sorry for it.' Finian moved aside so Alex could reach for his daughter.

He picked her up in his arms and Adaira clung to him. Though she wasn't safe yet, it meant everything to hold his child again. 'It's all right, sweet one.' He pressed a kiss against her hair, embracing her tightly.

To the MacLachor chief, Alex added, 'Harkirk's fled. I think you should find him.'

Finian's face tightened and he went in pursuit of the English lord. Alex started to move toward the gates, where he saw Hamish MacPherson approaching. Blood streamed from a cut on the man's face, but he seemed to breathe easier when he spied Adaira. 'I'm sorry, Alex. They killed three of my men. I rode as quickly as I could.'

'She's all right,' Alex said. His hand moved to Adaira's head, protecting her as they retreated from the remaining soldiers.

'Mama!' Adaira suddenly shrieked. Alex turned and saw Laren running towards them. He caught her in his arms, holding her so tightly, it was as if he needed to absorb her into his skin. His wife gripped him hard, then took Adaira into her arms, smiling even as she wept over both of them. Alex held them, his throat constricted with emotion.

But he didn't feel safe yet. Not until they'd found Harkirk.

'Search for the Baron,' he ordered his men. 'I want him found.'

'He's here,' came the voice of Finian MacLachor. The chief stood at the top of the stairs leading to the fortress tower and at his feet was the body of Lord Harkirk.

A black-feathered arrow lay embedded in the Baron's throat.

Lady Harkirk stood outside the fortress with the others, her face colourless. The Scottish prisoners had been freed and they'd set the rest of the fortress on fire, driving the remaining soldiers out. Lord Harkirk's body had been left to burn.

Laren stood beside the Lady, uncertain of what to say.

'I'm glad he's dead,' Lady Harkirk whispered. 'I just… don't know where to go now.'

She rubbed her shoulders from the cold and Laren touched her shoulder. 'Do you have family you could return to, perhaps in England? We could arrange an escort.'

The woman shook her head. 'I have no one.'

Before long, Laren spied a young boy watching from within the tree line. It was the same child whom Lady Harkirk had hidden in the forest. His expression held fear as he stood, watching the fire spread.

The sight of the boy seemed to urge Lady Harkirk into motion. She hurried towards the trees, signalling for the boy to come forwards.

The boy took a few hesitant steps, but when he spied the MacLachor chief, he took off running. Throwing himself against the man, the child burst into tears. It was then that Laren realised the young boy who had brought her to his shelter that night was not a boy at all, but a girl whose hair had been cut short.

The MacLachor chief's face broke into an incredulous smile as he gripped the girl hard. 'Iliana, you're alive?'

'Yes, Da. She rescued me.' The girl hugged him tightly and he smoothed his hand across her shorn hair.

'I bribed one of the soldiers to help me get her out,' Lady Harkirk explained. 'I disguised her as a boy and let my husband believe she was dead.' With an apologetic smile she added, 'I didn't know she was yours.'

Finian kept his arm around his daughter, but he reached out and took Lady Harkirk's hand. 'There are no words to say how grateful I am.'

Laren didn't miss the fierce blush upon the woman's face. Perhaps it was unnecessary meddling, but she said, 'Lady Harkirk will need a place to live, now that the fortress is gone. Will you provide her with an escort?'

'Anywhere she wishes to go.'

Alex approached with Adaira's hand in his. Laren lifted her daughter into her arms, kissing her soft cheek. 'Shall I escort you home as well, Lady?'

Laren's answer was a smile.

Over the next few months, it became impossible for Laren to blow any more glass, for her pregnancy had made it too difficult to balance the pipes. With Ramsay and Monroe's help, she'd finished the windows. Alex had delivered the completed panels to the abbot a sennight ago.

She was thankful beyond words to be done with the work, for she could no longer stand up for any length of time. It seemed that her stomach had swollen to enormous proportions and she'd had to work in bare feet, for her shoes would no longer fit. She hardly slept any more and her back ached all the time.

Though Alex tried to help her, there was nothing he could do. Nairna was the only one who fully sympathised with her, for her own pregnancy was progressing as well. And though they were only a few months apart, Laren's girth far surpassed Nairna's.

'Are you certain it will be at least two more moons before this bairn is born?' Nairna asked, as they walked along the shores of the loch. The summer wind blew across the water and Laren was grateful for the breeze.

'I've no doubt this child will be born in autumn, not the summer.' Laren sent her a faltering smile, adding, 'Somehow, I'll manage.'

In the distance, the sunlight illuminated the castle keep, that was nearly completed in stone. Since they'd defeated Lord Harkirk, the MacKinlochs had gained more support from the neighbouring clans. The MacLachors had merged their clan with the MacKinlochs and the added men had made it easier to rebuild.

Laren had started working inside the castle keep to be with Alex more often. He'd built a stone table for her, and she spent her hours cutting the glass and piecing it together with lead lines while Ramsay and Monroe had taken over the glassmaking. She smiled to herself, remembering how her husband would often find an excuse to come inside, just to steal a kiss or to visit her.

The cream-coloured gown she wore was strained across her belly, and she walked within the cool water, letting it soothe her swollen ankles. A sudden pain rippled across her spine, radiating in a tight contraction.

Laren stopped walking, pressing a hand to her back. It hurt, but she didn't want to alarm Nairna. It wasn't at all unusual to feel pain during the last few months. When Nairna paled, she reassured her, 'It's just harder to walk. The child is positioned so low, I have to stop along the way. If you want to go on ahead, I'll be fine.'

'I'm not in a hurry.' Nairna waited beside her and Laren took a deep breath. Each step was excruciating, but she kept reminding herself that soon she would be back at home. She could lie down, put her feet up and rest.

Spots swam before her eyes and she gripped Nairna's hand a little harder than she'd meant to.

'You're in pain, aren't you?' Nairna said. 'Don't lie to me about this. You need help.'

Laren took another step and felt a light pop. Then a warm wetness ran down her legs. *No. Not this.* It was far too soon for this child to be born.

Please, God, no.

'Laren?' Nairna whispered in a small voice. 'We need to get Alex. Your gown—'

'My birth waters broke, that's all.' She steadied herself, not wanting to frighten Nairna. But she knew that once the waters were gone, there was no stopping the child from coming.

Nairna took her hand. 'It's not the birth waters that worry me, Laren. It's the...the blood.'

Chapter Eighteen

'You're not supposed to be here when she's giving birth,' Grizel ordered.

'She's my wife.' Alex tried to push his way past his mother, but she blocked the chamber door.

'This child will be born too soon,' his mother said quietly. 'The chances of it being able to breathe on its own aren't good. Laren knows it.' She touched his shoulder, her face weary. 'I am sorry that it had to happen to both of you again.'

The anguish of losing another child wasn't something Alex wanted to face at all, but neither would he leave Laren's side if it happened again.

He pushed his mother aside and opened the door. Laren was lying naked upon the bed, holding her stomach with both hands. She was trembling with pain, her eyes closed tightly. A coverlet lay discarded beside her.

From the worry on Nairna and Vanora's faces, he knew it wasn't going well. Nairna was holding a rosary, silently praying, while Vanora wiped Laren's forehead with a damp cloth.

'I'm here, *a ghràidh*.' He moved to sit beside his wife and Laren's eyes opened.

'I want to talk with Alex alone,' she said to the other women. With a weak smile, she added, 'It will be hours yet. I'll call out if I need you.'

Vanora and Nairna obeyed, closing the door behind them. Grizel didn't look pleased about being dismissed, but she left after a sharp look from Alex.

'I'm afraid,' Laren said. 'It's too soon, and...I'm bleeding.' She started crying and the sight of her tears augmented his silent fear.

Alex touched her face. 'Whatever happens, I'm here for you. I won't leave.'

'I can't bear it.' Her hands moved to cover his and she struggled to sit up. 'I don't want to lose another bairn. Not like David.'

He helped her to lean against him and held her in his arms. 'Don't give up hope.'

'It's too soon,' she protested. 'And I can't stop the labour pains. Not now.'

He touched his lips to her forehead. From a pouch at his waist, he pulled out tiny droplets of coloured glass. 'Do you remember when I gave these to you?'

She nodded, touching the stones. 'You wanted to give me jewels.'

'Some day I might.' He placed a few of them on her distended stomach, and they caught the firelight, gleaming. 'But you're the greatest treasure I have.' He stroked her hair back.

'Stay with me,' she whispered.

'I'll not leave you. Not during this. No matter what happens.' He raised up the coverlet to her body, moving to support her.

Laren's labour continued through the night and into the next morning. Alex couldn't sleep at all, and when the sunlight pressed its rays through the crevices of the window, Vanora and Grizel interrupted. 'Laren, there's someone here to see you.'

A young woman with hair as red as his wife's entered the room. Despite the vicious pain, there was a startled joy upon Laren's face. 'Suisan? Is it you?'

Her sister came forwards and took her hand. 'I received a missive from Grizel. She tried to send for our mother, but Rós couldn't come. She's too weak, but she sent you this.'

Suisan pressed a small wooden cross into Laren's hands. His wife braved a smile. 'She's happy at St Anne's, then?'

'She took her vows years ago. And she is content to live there, as is Gara.' Suisan sent her a teasing smile. 'I was the black sheep of the convent and got married two years ago. I live on the Isle of Skye now, with my husband.'

Alex sent his mother Grizel a questioning look and the old woman muttered, 'I thought she would want her family here. But it took a long time to find them.'

He said nothing, but went to his mother and gave her a slight hug. 'You have our thanks.'

Grizel frowned. 'Be off with you. A birthing chamber is no place for a man.'

'I'm not leaving.' Even if the worst happened, if the child didn't live, he'd not abandon Laren now. Not when she needed him.

'Nairna, you should go,' Vanora ordered. 'Fetch hot water for us.'

When Bram's wife hesitated, Grizel clamped down on her wrist and none too gently shoved her out.

'Why would you send Nairna away?' Alex asked.

'There's no need to frighten her, not when she's expecting her own bairn in the winter,' Vanora explained.

Suisan took her sister's hand, murmuring prayers. In the next few minutes, his wife's labour grew worse and she cried out in pain. Grizel and Vanora examined her, proclaiming it was time to push.

Alex moved to her side, supporting her as she eased into a squatting position. She took a deep breath, straining to give birth. He held on to her, trying to lend her his strength.

Over the next quarter of an hour, Laren endured the pain, pushing as best she could. Suisan retreated into the corner, murmuring more prayers.

Soon, the head appeared and Grizel helped to deliver the tiny infant. Alex heard the miraculous newborn cry of life and saw that he had another daughter. Vanora cut the cord and wrapped the child in a soft blanket, handing the infant to him. While Laren worked to deliver the afterbirth, he marvelled at how small his newest daughter was. Blue-grey eyes stared at him, and her hand was the size of his thumb.

Let her live, he prayed. *Let her grow strong.*

'Keep pushing, Laren,' he heard Vanora urge. To his shock, he heard the cry of another child. Alex watched as a tiny baby boy emerged from Laren and he, too, gave a mewling cry.

'Two of them?' he asked Laren, feeling as though he'd

taken a blow to the stomach. He sat down on the edge of the bed and handed their daughter to Laren, while he took the precious bundle of their son. A fist seemed to grip his heart and he couldn't say a single word, seeing the miracle in his hands.

'They're alive?' his wife whispered, unable to tear her gaze from the babies.

'Aye. And breathing.' He held his son close, vowing that he would do everything to protect him. 'They're going to live. Both of them.'

He laid the children in her arms and embraced the three of them, feeling as though they'd been given a second chance.

Laren sent him an exhausted smile. 'Neither of us will sleep much over the next few months.'

'But we'll manage,' he said. 'Together.'

Epilogue

Three years later

'I feel guilty, leaving the children,' Laren admitted. She held her husband's hand as they walked together to the circle within the forest. The afternoon sun speared through the tree branches, casting shadows across the standing stones.

'Do you want me to take you back to them?' Alex asked, drawing her back against the cool limestone.

'Not yet.' She drew his mouth down to hers, kissing him deeply. 'I want this time with you.'

In the privacy of the forest, Alex undressed her. The sun was warm and Laren lay down upon the cloak he'd spread upon the ground. Her husband discarded his own clothing and lay beside her, drawing her on to her side.

'Your men will wonder where you are,' she said, moving her hand over his broad chest. 'Weren't you supposed to be training them?'

'If they knew I was with a beautiful naked woman, rest assured, any man alive would understand my absence.'

She smiled against his mouth and his hands moved over her skin in reverence. With his mouth and tongue he tasted her flesh and she felt him growing thick and hard against her feminine core.

'I love you, Laren,' he murmured, his mouth caressing her stomach and outer hip. He parted her legs, then kissed her erect nipple, teasing it while her flesh grew wet beneath his stroking fingers.

'Touch me everywhere,' she commanded.

Alex's expression grew sinful. With a single finger, he touched her eyebrow. 'There?'

Laren shook her head, smiling at his playful change in mood.

'Or did you mean here?' His hand moved to her elbow, where he began caressing the tip.

'I could touch you here,' she teased, stroking his chin.

'Or did you mean here?' he whispered, sliding two fingers into her wetness.

The unexpected invasion made her ache with longing and she returned the caress by taking his erection in her palm. With each time she stroked him, he rewarded her by using his fingers to coax a stronger response.

'Or here?' he whispered, using his wet fingers to arouse her breasts. A moan escaped her and she shuddered as he provoked a staggering response that echoed deep in her womb.

'Kiss me again,' she murmured.

But instead of moving to her mouth, he drew his kiss to her breasts, licking her skin until he took the nipple with a gentle suction. He kissed her ribs, the swell of her hip, then he laid his mouth above the core of her womanhood. Gently, he licked her, arousing her hooded flesh.

His tongue stimulated her, moving sideways in a rhythm that took her breath away.

She shivered with delight as he worked her flesh faster, begging him not to stop with words that were hardly coherent. She arched against him, her fingers digging into the ground as he found the place that made her shatter apart. Dark waves of ecstasy broke over her, mindless physical fulfilment that pulled her body over the edge.

'I want you,' she pleaded, and with one thrust he was within her wetness. She felt molten inside, her body receiving him with aching shivers.

He never ceased his lovemaking, but penetrated her over and over, until cries escaped her. Another release crashed through her and she didn't think she could take any more. But he kept going, thrusting hard, until he emitted a ragged groan and took his own pleasure.

Alex rested against her, the sweat of their bodies mingling. Then he rolled her on to her side, bringing her leg over his hip. She was still shivering with aftershocks, and he covered them both with the cloak, holding her close.

'Did that please you?' he asked against her cheek, before sending her a feral smile.

She kissed him softly. 'Very much.'

He brought her head beneath his chin, cuddling her close. 'If I had my way, I'd stay with you here and never go back.'

'We'll have to rescue Mairin…' she sighed '…sooner or later.'

Her husband sent her a wicked smile. 'Later sounds better to me.'

When they returned at twilight, they found visitors waiting. Mairin stood at the entrance to the keep, looking relieved at their return. 'Eve and Kerr are trying to kill each other.'

'Where are they now?' Laren asked.

'Adaira and Ramsay are playing with them.' Mairin rolled her eyes and led them inside. Laren gave her a light hug, touching her daughter's hair. Both she and Adaira were visiting from fostering and it tugged at Laren's heart to see them growing up so fast.

Their three-year-old twins, Kerr and Eve, were playing inside the keep, running in circles until Ramsay picked them up, one under each arm. He strode forwards, his adolescent face red with embarrassment, while at the far end of the Hall, Laren spied visitors from the abbey. She caught one of the women and ordered food and ale for them.

As soon as he saw them, Kerr wiggled free and raced over to Alex, grabbing his leg. Laren smiled as her husband lifted their son into his arms and she took Eve from Ramsay. 'Thank you for watching over them,' she told the young man. He gave a nod, looking eager to return to his glassmaking. His father had died two years ago and Alex had invited Ramsay to live with them inside the keep. Though he was far more comfortable with the furnaces than with people, she was glad to give her apprentice a true home.

Laren approached the priests, with Alex at her side. After he offered them a greeting, she asked, 'Are you enjoying the windows for the kirk?'

The abbot's face revealed his discomfort at having to speak with her. Even after he'd learned that she was the artist responsible for the glass, he'd felt uneasy about it. 'Many pilgrims have stopped to adore the Holy Cross,' he admitted. 'And the glass has attracted more visitors every year.'

The abbot nodded to one of the priests, who withdrew a scroll of parchment. 'Bishop William de Lamberton has asked me to commission another window for the cathedral at St Andrews, on his behalf. I have brought the plans for you to consider.'

Laren took the scroll and inclined her head. 'I will look over the plans. But Nairna will negotiate the terms.'

There was nothing Nairna loved so much as to haggle over prices and Laren was happy to indulge the young woman. She had recently given birth to her second child and would welcome the distraction of bargaining.

Laren invited the priests to enjoy a light evening meal; after they blessed the food, she set the twins down to eat beside Mairin and Adaira. Once they were settled, she took the plans over to the stone table and unrolled the parchment to study them.

Alex came up beside her and she asked, 'What do you think?'

'It's your decision. If you wish to make the glass, I've no objection.'

She noted that these windows would be larger than any others she'd made before. It was a challenge that would push her beyond whatever skills she had now. 'I want to try.'

Kerr moved away from the table and toddled over to them. He started to whine and Laren picked him up. He wrapped his arms around her. 'Kiss, Mama.'

She pecked his small lips and after she set him down, Alex sent her a teasing smile. 'Kiss.'

Alex drew her into a darkened corner, out of view from everyone else. Then he seized a kiss that held the promise of desires they would share later. Firm and evocative, he continued kissing her until Kerr gave him a light shove.

The young lad glared at his father. 'That's my Laren. Not yours.'

Laren couldn't stop her laugh at her son's possessive nature and his sudden desire to call her by her first name. 'I'm your mother, not your Laren,' she corrected.

Alex drew his hand around her waist as they returned to the others. 'You're wrong, son. She's my Laren.'

The words warmed her heart and he leaned down to kiss her temple. 'I love you.'

'As I love you.' She rested her hands upon his shoulders, and in his eyes she saw the steadfast love and faith. With her hand in his, she walked by his side towards all the blessings that awaited them.

* * * * *

COMING NEXT MONTH FROM

HARLEQUIN®
HISTORICAL

Available August 30, 2011

- **GOLD RUSH GROOM**
  by **Jenna Kernan**
  (Western)

- **VICAR'S DAUGHTER TO VISCOUNT'S LADY**
  by **Louise Allen**
  (Regency)
  Second in *The Transformation of the Shelley Sisters* trilogy

- **VALIANT SOLDIER, BEAUTIFUL ENEMY**
  by **Diane Gaston**
  (Regency)
  Third in *Three Soldiers* miniseries

- **SECRET LIFE OF A SCANDALOUS DEBUTANTE**
  by **Bronwyn Scott**
  (1830s)

You can find more information on upcoming
Harlequin® titles, free excerpts and more at
www.HarlequinInsideRomance.com.

HHCNM0811

REQUEST YOUR FREE BOOKS!

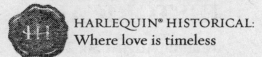

HARLEQUIN® HISTORICAL:
Where love is timeless

2 FREE NOVELS PLUS 2 **FREE GIFTS!**

YES! Please send me 2 FREE Harlequin® Historical novels and my 2 FREE gifts (gifts are worth about $10). After receiving them, if I don't wish to receive any more books, I can return the shipping statement marked "cancel." If I don't cancel, I will receive 6 brand-new novels every month and be billed just $5.19 per book in the U.S. or $5.74 per book in Canada. That's a savings of at least 17% off the cover price! It's quite a bargain! Shipping and handling is just 50¢ per book in the U.S. and 75¢ per book in Canada.* I understand that accepting the 2 free books and gifts places me under no obligation to buy anything. I can always return a shipment and cancel at any time. Even if I never buy another book, the two free books and gifts are mine to keep forever.

246/349 HDN FEQQ

Name _____ (PLEASE PRINT)

Address _____ Apt. #

City _____ State/Prov. _____ Zip/Postal Code

Signature (if under 18, a parent or guardian must sign)

Mail to the **Reader Service:**
IN U.S.A.: P.O. Box 1867, Buffalo, NY 14240-1867
IN CANADA: P.O. Box 609, Fort Erie, Ontario L2A 5X3

Not valid for current subscribers to Harlequin Historical books.

Want to try two free books from another line?
Call 1-800-873-8635 or visit www.ReaderService.com.

* Terms and prices subject to change without notice. Prices do not include applicable taxes. Sales tax applicable in N.Y. Canadian residents will be charged applicable taxes. Offer not valid in Quebec. This offer is limited to one order per household. All orders subject to credit approval. Credit or debit balances in a customer's account(s) may be offset by any other outstanding balance owed by or to the customer. Please allow 4 to 6 weeks for delivery. Offer available while quantities last.

Your Privacy—The Reader Service is committed to protecting your privacy. Our Privacy Policy is available online at www.ReaderService.com or upon request from the Reader Service.

We make a portion of our mailing list available to reputable third parties that offer products we believe may interest you. If you prefer that we not exchange your name with third parties, or if you wish to clarify or modify your communication preferences, please visit us at www.ReaderService.com/consumerschoice or write to us at Reader Service Preference Service, P.O. Box 9062, Buffalo, NY 14269. Include your complete name and address.

New York Times *and* USA TODAY *bestselling author*
Maya Banks presents a brand-new miniseries

PREGNANCY & PASSION

When four irresistible tycoons face
the consequences of temptation.

Book 1—*ENTICED BY HIS FORGOTTEN LOVER*

Available September 2011 from Harlequin® Desire®!

Rafael de Luca had been in bad situations before. A crowded
ballroom could never make him sweat.

These people would never know that he had no memory
of any of them.

He surveyed the party with grim tolerance, searching for
the source of his unease.

At first his gaze flickered past her, but he yanked his attention back to a woman across the room. Her stare bored
holes through him. Unflinching and steady, even when his
eyes locked with hers.

Petite, even in heels, she had a creamy olive complexion.
A wealth of inky-black curls cascaded over her shoulders
and her eyes were equally dark.

She looked at him as if she'd already judged him and
found him lacking. He'd never seen her before in his life.
Or had he?

He cursed the gaping hole in his memory. He'd been
diagnosed with selective amnesia after his accident four
months ago. Which seemed like complete and utter bull.
No one got amnesia except hysterical women in bad soap
operas.

With a smile, he disengaged himself from the group

around him and made his way to the mystery woman.

She wasn't coy. She stared straight at him as he approached, her chin thrust upward in defiance.

"Excuse me, but have we met?" he asked in his smoothest voice.

His gaze moved over the generous swell of her breasts pushed up by the empire waist of her black cocktail dress.

When he glanced back up at her face, he saw fury in her eyes.

"Have we *met?*" Her voice was barely a whisper, but he felt each word like the crack of a whip.

Before he could process her response, she nailed him with a right hook. He stumbled back, holding his nose.

One of his guards stepped between Rafe and the woman, accidentally sending her to one knee. Her hand flew to the folds of her dress.

It was then, as she cupped her belly, that the realization hit him. She was pregnant.

Her eyes flashing, she turned and ran down the marble hallway.

Rafael ran after her. He burst from the hotel lobby, and saw two shoes sparkling in the moonlight, twinkling at him.

He blew out his breath in frustration and then shoved the pair of sparkly, ultrafeminine heels at his head of security.

"Find the woman who wore these shoes."

Will Rafael find his mystery woman?
Find out in Maya Banks's passionate new novel
ENTICED BY HIS FORGOTTEN LOVER
Available September 2011 from Harlequin® Desire®!

HDEXP0911